E.D. HACKETT

Mending Broken Threads

First edition

ISBN: 978-1-7374679-8-4

Editing by Granite Editorial
Cover art by Sara Shelby Haraldsen

This book was professionally typeset on Reedsy.
Find out more at reedsy.com

This novel is dedicated to Margaret "Peggy" O'Halloran Marine and Maureen "Mo" Durkin Hackett.

May your stories, secrets, and experiences continue to live within us.

Chapter 1

Lynette walked through the old bookstore, running her fingers up and down the spines of the aged, brittle books. She squinted her eyes at the faded and missing text, intrigued by the illegibility of such fine works. Yanking an old Shakespeare from the shelf, she raised the book to her nose and inhaled the scent of all the people who had held that book before her. Her heart lifted, thinking about the stories within the pages, but also the stories of those who had escaped through the symphony of words, just like she did.

"Lynette."

The familiar voice of her best friend, Martha, drew her away from the antique books, and she turned with a smile. "Hi, Martha. How have you been?"

The small round woman with thick glasses and short, curly hair, smiled a wide grin. "Great, thanks. How's your day going?"

Lynette looked past Martha at the rows and rows of books, scanning the aisle for a hidden prize. "Good. I'm on my way to the cemetery, and wanted to stop in."

"In this weather?" Martha gazed out the large windows overlooking the busy main strip.

"Yeah, it's the first Monday of the month. I've been going for over a year now."

Martha chuckled. "Have you hit up every grave yet?"

"Not yet, but I'm getting close. It makes me feel good knowing they're getting some extra attention." Lynette's mind wandered to the flowers in her car, and she peered out the window. "I have to go soon, but I'm teaching my literature class on British classics later. Do you have any original Dickens or Brontë sisters?"

Martha hurried through the tall aisles like she was navigating a labyrinth, and Lynette followed. Lynette knew this layout like the back of her hand. She had worked here with Martha twenty-five years ago as a poor newlywed and graduate student who struggled to afford her rent. When the owner passed, Martha scooped up the store and had been running it ever since. Lynette found the store to be her safe harbor when life got rocky. Her love for books never faded, and the untold stories of the yellowed pages, uneven edges, and embossed covers captivated her.

"Right here," Martha said. "We've been going through the stacks, discounting the copies that are in worse wear than the others."

"Ah, no wonder I couldn't find them." Lynette thanked her old friend and continued to peruse the hardbacks.

Martha returned to the counter and resumed marking the consigned books.

Lynette handled a copy of *Middlemarch* and *Tess of the D'Urbervilles*, analyzing the copyright, spine and page quality. At her large home outside of Chicago, she had an entire wall dedicated to antique books. These would fit perfectly on the top shelf with her treasured finds of Dickens and Austen.

"I'll take these," Lynette said, placing the two books on the crowded table beside the register. Martha rang the books, wrapped them, and placed them in a bag.

"Be careful for rain," Martha said, jerking her head toward the window. "I think a storm is coming."

"I won't be there long," Lynette said. "Just dropping some comfort to those without friends or family." Lynette paid for her belongings, waved goodbye and drove in silence through the neighboring suburbs of Chicago.

A sweeping cemetery appeared on the right, and Lynette's car crawled down the paved road to the center. She had found this place about a year ago after a colleague had passed away. Unable to pull herself out of bed to attend the funeral, her guilt had dragged her to the cemetery weeks later.

She grabbed the dozen roses sitting on her passenger seat and walked up and down the rows. The wind howled and the trees along the perimeter of the grassy labyrinth waved over her. She visited the retired professor's tombstone and dropped a rose on the cold granite.

On her first visit, an ominous feeling prickled her skin when she noticed the headstones in various disarray. It was evident some had received more love than others, so Lynette walked around and dropped roses from her grocery store bouquet onto the most neglected stones. Even though they were dead, she wanted to brighten their day. By doing such a thoughtful deed, her spirits lifted, as well. Soon, she looked forward to her monthly delivery of kindness and compassion.

These visits reminded her that life could be worse. She could be dead. Surrounding herself around the departed reminded her to keep living. She tried to acknowledge and respect all the tombstones she passed, but neglect pulled her toward certain graves as she examined the attention and care. The overgrown brush around the stone and the lack of personal touches surrounding the base made her heart ache. Even though Lynette didn't believe in ghosts, she hoped this little act of kindness brought them peace.

A heaviness grew in Lynette's heart as she tried to forget the pain from the past three years. Sometimes, in the quiet of the night, she wondered if she had neglected the people she loved or had they neglected her? Would her gravestone be dirty, dreary, and unloved, like so many that called for Lynette's attention?

As she placed the last flower on a nondescript stone, her heart tugged at the short lifespan of this young woman. Just twenty-three years old, she was practically still a girl, and Lynette couldn't help but wonder what wonderful things she could have done if she'd had more time. Her breath caught, reminding her that her own daughter could be dead and she would never know. A single tear escaped her eye, and Lynette quickly wiped it away. Her throat tightened, and she prayed for Ruby's safety, desperate for a miracle.

She kissed her fingers and placed them against the stone, talking in her mind to the mystery woman below her feet.

"She's okay, you know."

Startled, Lynette turned and peered at a woman dressed in black holding a red rose directly in front of her long, shimmery skirt. "Excuse me?"

"Eleanora Claren," the woman said, dropping the flower next to the rose Lynette had left. She nodded her head down and Lynette recognized the name behind decades of dust and grime. "She's okay. She's resting. You've given her comfort."

Lynette shivered and pulled her arms around her torso. "Do you know her?" She had passed away in 1942.

The woman smiled. "I know them all, when they want to talk to me. You have something special."

Lynette struggled to break her gaze from the woman's dark eyes. Her stomach squeezed, and the cemetery around them tilted. She grabbed the woman's arm to steady herself and a zap traveled to her shoulder.

A wind blew down the aisle, breaking their trance, and Lynette stumbled back. "I have to go. It looks like rain." Her long legs carried her back to her car, where she sat until her heart stopped pounding. She slowly pulled out of the driveway and looked back at Eleanora's grave. The woman was gone.

4

Lynette's chest tightened as she drove out of the cemetery to her home. She couldn't get that woman out of her mind, with her eyes as dark and drab as coal, frail frame, and strange words. Eleanora's grave and that unexpected zing pushed at Lynette's mind like a yo-yo.

After she pulled into her garage, she sat in the car trying to make sense of the last hour. Filling her lungs with air, she grabbed her purse and entered the colonial revival home that she and her ex-husband had built together. When he left for another woman, it had become a constant reminder of Lynette's failure as a wife.

She dropped her keys on the side table in the living room. A single framed photograph of her daughter's high school graduation stared back at her. Anger billowed under Lynette's skin, but she refused to expel her negative energy for a child who cared so little about her. She gripped the edge of the table and stared at her daughter's memory. The daughter she no longer had.

Ruby's long blonde hair framed her smooth, bright face, and her smile lit up the photo with rosy cheeks and crinkled eyes. Lynette's heart tugged at what could have been, and her anger transitioned to sadness and regret. She stroked the glass, wiping a layer of dust off the top.

Five years ago, life had been easy. She had a beautiful daughter, and was happily married to Anthony, her college sweetheart, until the truth smacked her in the face. A blindside like no other caused Lynette's world to crumble, and every relationship that had held her above water sank. She used to be happy, but now she lived on autopilot finding comfort in her routine. She prayed before bed each night that the people she loved were also safe and happy, but fear of rejection prevented her from reaching out.

Lynnette picked up the photograph of Ruby and recalled the memories of that day, that year, that lifetime. She missed her, but Ruby had left her. When and if Ruby ever came home, it had to be because she wanted to, not because Lynnette guilted her into returning.

Dropping onto the dainty loveseat, Lynette kicked up her feet and stretched her tired muscles across the antique hassock. She pulled out the books from Martha's shop, hoping they would calm her nerves. Built-in bookcases lined the study, creating an environment Lynette had dreamed about as a child. Old yet graceful. Historical yet pristine.

A thin laptop sat closed on the cushion beside her, hiding the hours upon hours of work that she needed to complete. She spent the night highlighting and commenting in the margins of her students' first theses.

When midnight arrived, Lynette climbed into her perfectly made king-sized bed and stretched out her legs like a pair of scissors. The cool material rubbed against her bare legs, welcoming her to sleep.

When Anthony left her the house, she threw away every piece of furniture that held broken memories. The bed frame and mattress were the first to go. Brimming with superhero strength, she had hauled the mattress outside and made it clear to the neighborhood that her marriage was over. She promised herself she would never let a man hurt her again.

Now she lay alone in a bed she had picked out just for her. No compromise needed. Since Anthony, there hadn't been anyone else, and Lynette enjoyed her independence. Most of the time. Some of her colleagues, friends, and acquaintances thought a man and a rocking night of sex would solve her problems, but she knew better, and she was perfectly fine alone. Without Anthony and without Ruby, she often wondered if the life she loved had been intended for someone else. Someone more romantic who believed in happily ever after.

Lynette knew fairy tale endings didn't exist for anyone and when push came to shove, everyone was alone. That was why she escaped from reality and dove headfirst into her books. Perhaps the old stories could teach her a thing or two about life without her having to experience the pain associated with living it.

The next morning, Lynette's alarm sounded at six. Her first class was at eight, and she finished her day at two. She had created her schedule to get in and out early, in case she wanted to get her nails done or try out a new restaurant. Her divorce had destroyed her, but at least now she was in charge of her destiny. She handpicked her outfit, flipping through a series of black pants, white blouses, and black blazers. Her hair rested in a secure ponytail at the base of her neck, and a heavy coat of makeup covered the irreversible evidence of age. Staring at her reflection, years of worry, sadness, and stress disappeared with her wrinkles. She knew a fifty-three-year-old woman didn't need a made-up face for a ninety-minute class on British Literature, but she felt exposed and unseen without it. Forgettable at worst, and homely at best.

Like clockwork, she pulled into her parking spot, walked into her classroom, and stood in front of her half-sleeping class. Looking around the room, her regular stragglers meandered their way in. Mustering up her enthusiasm for Thomas Hardy, she engaged the class in a lecture on the social and industrial influences of Britain.

Before driving home from work, she listened to her voicemail, and jotted down appointment reminders for the upcoming week. A cryptic message from her sister, Loretta, nestled between her messages from her arthritis doctor and her hair salon. Lynette scrunched her eyes and placed her phone in the passenger seat. She hadn't heard from her sister in almost a year. A wave of heat coasted through her body and the sound of the cars around her dwarfed the message as she listened again. A throbbing emerged in the center of her forehead and she dug through her bag for two Tylenol.

She'd call her back later. Or maybe never. Lynette hardened her mouth and slit her eyes as she maneuvered out of the parking lot and onto the freeway.

Despite being at the bookstore yesterday, Lynette couldn't get that woman from the cemetery out of her mind. She pulled into the parking lot and stopped at the coffee shop before visiting Martha for a quick chat. The feel of old paper, scent of candles, and soothing music wrapped her in a warm cocoon. Lynette justified her book-obsession against other common activities people indulged in to escape from their lives...at least books never hurt her.

Martha stood behind the counter, ringing up a customer.

"Coffee?" Lynette asked, showing Martha the cup she'd purchased for her.

"Yes, please. You read my mind." She sipped the hot drink and closed her eyes before swallowing. "So good."

The two friends walked around the shop, while Martha pretended to work. She scanned the stacks, and led Lynette to a small table in the back corner.

"I have to tell you," Martha began. "Please don't get mad at me." She hesitated while reaching into her pocket, sighed, and pulled out her phone. Tapping her fingers on the table, and taking short, quick sips from her travel mug, Martha's eyes darted around the room.

Lynette narrowed her eyes and tilted her head. "Uh, okay." This was not like Martha. Usually, when Martha had a story to tell, she blurted it out in one fell swoop.

"I found Ruby."

Lynette clasped her hands behind her head and she struggled to fill her lungs with air. "What?"

"I was bored the other day, so I started googling people I know. Like old boyfriends, high school best friends, old teachers, that kind of stuff. I really had to do some digging. I googled Ruby Franklin, and a magazine article popped up. This must have been when she first got out there. There was a little Instagram logo at the bottom, and when

I clicked on it, it brought me to Ruby Southby's profile. Wasn't that a family name of yours?"

"Yeah, on my mom's side. It was my mom's maiden name."

"It was her Lynette." Martha grabbed Lynette's arms and squeezed. "It was her."

The air in the room escaped through the cracks in the wood plank floor, and Lynette's body turned to gelatin. She dropped into a chair and everything stopped. The people shuffling around, the coffee cup burning her fingers, even Martha's voice didn't register. She felt the blood drain from her face, and she stared at the wall, unable to face her friend.

"Lynette? Lynette..." Martha's voice sounded under water.

Lynette hadn't heard from her daughter in three years. At the end of her sophomore year, Ruby had dropped out of college, packed her bags, and left. Lynette had sacrificed her and Anthony's hard-earned money for Ruby's education, but Ruby threw it away for the promises of stardom in L.A.

She couldn't believe Ruby had been so careless, throwing her education away like that. Anthony's attitude was, 'Let her grow her own wings and fly,' but Lynette couldn't do that. Ruby had thrown away her college education and exchanged her Advertising and Marketing degree for a life of chaos. A life of uncertainty. Didn't she know beauty doesn't last forever? Lynette couldn't accept Ruby's selfishness, even if it was for a pipe dream.

Now that Lynette had years to dwell on her departure, could she blame her for leaving? She had been young once, too, but she thought Ruby would have learned from her mistakes. A small voice crept behind her ear. *But you never told her.*

Lynette blinked and rubbed the worn corduroy on the arm of the chair. "Oh, yeah?" Her voice cracked, and she cleared her throat.

"She's doing something with her life, Lynette. She did it. She's modeling. You should check out her Instagram page. That girl is absolutely stunning." Martha pushed her phone in front of Lynette, but Lynette couldn't focus. She glanced at the screen and swatted the phone away.

She had tried finding her once, but she failed at that too. It was after the divorce when she could barely get out of bed, let alone be a semi-functioning human. She had wanted to scream at Ruby, and blame her for her ruined marriage. In Lynette's tunnel vision memory, that was how it had happened. Anthony hadn't seemed to mind when Ruby threw her education away and then had the audacity to offer financial help in California. Of course, Lynette had refused. If Ruby made dumb choices, she'd have to suffer the consequences.

It had become a wedge between them that developed into a fissure. When she saw the undisclosed wire transfers from their bank account to hers, it was the beginning of the end.

"You know I don't do social media. I'm a magnet for bad news. I'd rather stay in my hobbit hole and escape in books than dive into the internet."

"So you caught your husband being shady. Don't you think it was a blessing in disguise? He wasn't right for you, anyway."

Then the other women had appeared. A burning erupted at the base of Lynette's belly, just as it had when she took his phone to RSVP to his thirty-year high school reunion. Notifications from his social media popped up from his high school sweetheart, Candy. Like a vulture searching for prey, Lynette had read the string of texts and her heart shattered into a million pieces. He had planned on meeting her for dinner.

Filled with rage, but no proof of anything, she had marched into their bedroom demanding answers. That was the middle of the end.

Everyone she gave her life to had turned on her. Everyone except Martha.

"You weren't happy," Martha said.

Lynette scoffed. "Like I am now?"

"It's been two years since your divorce. He's moved on, and so has Ruby. Don't stay stagnant. If you refuse to move forward with the times, you're going to get left behind."

"I don't want to know if she isn't okay. When I see her in my heart, she's five years old, still needing her mother," Lynette said. "I see her snuggled next to me on the couch when I was her favorite person. When I could protect her. When she cared about me. If she isn't okay—if she's homeless or addicted to drugs—I will never forgive myself."

"Really, Lynette. Maybe it's time you let bygones be bygones. She's your only daughter."

A steely cage rose around Lynette, trapping her from reaching out. "Yeah, maybe tomorrow."

Martha held out her phone. "Here, just look. I would never lie to you. She's okay."

Stepping closer, Lynette peered over her friend's shoulder. Tears erupted from her eyes and streamed down her face. Her baby. Her beautiful baby posed in photo after photo. That radiant grin matched the photos decorating her walls. As her racing heart slowed, she took the phone and scrolled through each photo. Familiarity, love, and regret mingled inside her.

Her shaking fingers struggled to zoom in. "She looks beautiful. And happy."

A gentle arm fell over her shoulders. "She does. Here's the message button if you want to reach out," Martha said.

Tension grew as stubbornness overpowered compassion. "Maybe later. I need to think about what I want to say."

Martha gave her a sad smile. "When you're ready, I'll be there for you."

The steely cage around her heart fractured, and she fought to keep

11

her resentment close. Afraid of admitting she was wrong, she needed more time. "Thank you," she whispered, "but I'm not ready yet."

Chapter 2

Ruby brushed her long, golden locks, pulled at her bangs, and readjusted her bag before sliding her chunky sunglasses over her eyes.

"Where're you headed?" her roommate Shayla asked.

Two years prior, the women had met at an audition for a new makeup company. The agents selected both women with their long, slender legs, tanned shoulders, and gentle makeup. It wasn't their idea to live together, but the gigs paid little and they understood the dreams and desires protected within their hearts. A year later, the company dried up and Ruby and Shayla were back at square one.

"Modeling class. I'll be home at seven." The door closed and Ruby hustled to her car, considering the mounting afternoon traffic. The stop and go jerkiness was typical for two p.m. on a Wednesday, so Ruby cranked her pop music and bopped her head with the beat. She purposefully booked the four-hour evening session to avoid the extraneous time in the car during the evening commute.

Like all classes, she strutted, posed, and emoted into the camera. Practically a dinosaur at twenty-three, she gave herself a deadline of twenty-five before she would throw in the towel and bury her dreams of becoming the number one model in the industry. Single and childless, this was her time to be selfish, focus on her goal, and prove her mother wrong.

"Bravo!" Maurice clapped as he waltzed around her. She froze like a statue. "Nice lines. Nice posture. Your thigh, a little in. You don't want to create a shadow there."

Ruby contorted her body uncomfortably, but reminded herself it was for the best. *No pain, no gain. Those who suffer reap rewards. You're living your best life.* The mantras ran through her head in a loop. While twisting her body, she smiled and pouted and smirked at the camera. She threw her arms and legs askew and matched her face to evoke whatever emotion Maurice requested.

By the end of the night, her legs ached and her stomach rumbled. Swinging by McDonalds, she indulged in a large order of fries and soda. The salty decadence lingered on her lips, and her stomach quieted at the first bite of food all day.

When she arrived home, she plopped onto the sofa and slurped her soda. Shayla huddled in the couch's corner with a blanket over her legs. Julia Roberts pranced across the screen with Richard Gere, and Shayla took notes in her little black notebook.

"Do you have a test?" Ruby asked. She tilted the McDonald's bag at her friend. "Want some? They're kind of cold, but still good."

Shayla shook her head. "I'm watching the evolution of Julia Roberts. I'm looking at facial expressions, movement, and tone of voice. She's a natural."

"Is this homework?"

"Yeah, I have to work on my eyes."

Pleased she hadn't been assigned this task, Ruby leaned back and enjoyed the film. They sat together in silence, entranced in the romance until the credits ran.

"I'm beat. G'night." Ruby tossed her trash in the overflowing garbage can and checked her socials on the short walk to her bedroom. Three hundred hearts on the photo shoot from the beach. Tossing the phone on her nightstand, she dreamed of stardom and notoriety.

The next morning, Ruby woke to a quiet house. Shayla had left for her nine-to-five at the dentist's office, where she scheduled and billed patients. Modeling paid little, so both women juggled their dreams with reality. With the help of Ruby's grandmother, Mema, she had graduated from college with an advertising degree. The largest movie theater franchise in America gave Ruby her first actual job, but when COVID hit, there were no more movies or customers. Suddenly, everyone was streaming, and the theater couldn't transition quick enough. Layoffs occurred in rapid fire, and Ruby, being the newest agent, was the first to go.

By this time, Ruby and Shayla had found each other and moved into a small apartment in Culver City. Los Angeles was a dog-eat-dog world, and without a steady income, she was in trouble. She accepted the first job that still allowed her to focus on modeling. Old Books and Café needed her twenty hours a week, which was just enough to pay her grocery bill. Surrounded by hipsters and starving artists walking the streets looking for the next best thing, Ruby had found the perfect balance.

A year before, she had stumbled on Jolie Belle, a fashion company new to the California scene. She aced her audition and worked her way up to lead influencer. Now she juggled both jobs, but her heart remained in the fashion industry.

Ruby's closet overflowed with free clothes from the shoots, which was her favorite perk of the job. She loved the rack of clothes taking over her room, and sometimes she bear hugged the garments to feel success against her skin.

Jolie Belle wanted her to wear their products daily, and Ruby took their request seriously. She incorporated one item into her wardrobe each day, posting daily photos to all her socials. When someone purchased an item through her affiliate link, she made a small commission, which helped pay for her gas.

Posing in the fashion magazines and appearing on billboards and buses around L.A., people noticed her. At least she thought they did. The paparazzi had just started to pay attention to her, and as much as she craved attention, she needed to be cautious. So far, it seemed her photos hadn't reached her mother. With the support of her family and away from the judgmental eye of her mom, Ruby was proving to herself and all those who doubted her she could and would make something out of her life.

Before leaving for work, Ruby dropped a birthday card on Shayla's bed. She stepped outside her apartment into the hot, dry air and walked the city block to Old Books. Waving to Clara behind the counter, she dropped her purse under the register and busied herself with the to-do list Clara had written.

"Morning Ruby. The shop opens in ten minutes. Are you ready?"

Clara always asked if Ruby was ready, like Ruby was in charge of a NASA space shuttle or something of equal importance. Ruby worked there because she loved to escape in books. "Ready." She reached into her bag and touched her phone, a nervous habit she had picked up during the long wait for auditions.

"Great, I'll see you at four."

Ruby watched Clara walk out of the store, leaving her alone to wait for customers. She took a few selfies, changing the background and adjusting the lighting before posting to every social media platform online. *Done.*

Today was slower than normal, and Ruby fell into a steamy romance full of scenes that made her blush from head to toe. She devoured them, unconcerned if someone saw the half-naked man on the cover. If anything, Ruby liked to watch people's reactions, knowing they wanted to read it too. She couldn't turn the pages fast enough, and loved to pretend she was living their love story. Swoon-worthy, for sure.

When Clara returned for the night, Ruby stopped at the grocery store and picked up a bottle of wine and a skinny cheesecake sampler.

The fully lit apartment poured pop songs through the Bluetooth speakers and out the open windows. Throwing her hips from side to side, she pushed open the front door and raised the bag over her head. "Shayla, I'm home."

The tall brunette pranced out of her bedroom wearing a pair of sleep shorts and a loose-fitting tank top. Already holding a glass of wine, Shayla hugged Ruby and a few drops sloshed on the floor.

"Aw, for me?" Shayla hopped over and removed the wine and cheesecake from Ruby's arms.

"Happy birthday!" Ruby said.

Shayla danced to the kitchen and emptied the bag. "You remembered my favorites." She immediately pulled two cups out of the cabinet and filled them to the brim with white wine.

Ruby placed pre-cut slices of cheesecake on two napkins and passed one to Shayla. "It's original, and that one over there is strawberry."

Shayla's plump lips puckered as she took a bite. "I love them both."

Ruby lifted her cup. "Happy birthday, roomie."

"You're the best roommate ever," she said.

The best friends drank the night away, talking about their dreams of becoming the next big Hollywood thing. This life may not have been what Ruby's parents wanted, but it was the best life for her.

Chapter 3

Lynette needed security and stability. When activities and events sprung on her, she immediately refused, letting the facts around the activity marinate until her mind was like a wobbly Jello mold. When people asked her to do something new, like water skiing or hiking up an unfamiliar trail, she often declined, but occasionally surprised herself with a hesitant yes.

That's what made her relationships so difficult to maintain. She could never be vulnerable with her actions or emotions, and when people she met or loved didn't feel supported by her, they pulled away. Colleagues, her sister, her mom, her daughter...she kept all her relationships an arm's length away. Besides Martha, she couldn't think of one person she could call in the middle of the night when things went to shit. Actually, she had tried to lean on Mom and Loretta when Ruby left without a trace, but they made excuses for Ruby, completely ignoring Lynette's feelings. It was then that Lynette realized no one would understand her journey because her shoes didn't fit their narrative.

When Lynette was a child, her sister Loretta was her closest friend, but as they turned from children to adults, the relationship became more of an acquaintanceship. Now, Loretta lived in Florida, playing Bingo, Cribbage, and Bridge during her free time, and Lynette had lost touch.

Growing up, Loretta wasn't afraid to say no to their parents, and

Lynette watched in awe at her tenacity to fight for what she wanted. Actually, Loretta and Ruby's impulsivity flowed against Lynette's structure, forever leaving her to stand on the outside.

She frowned at her lukewarm coffee, contemplating if she wanted to warm it in the microwave. Too tired to care, Lynette sipped her cool coffee, and scrolled through the news, noticing the number of terrible stories that claimed real estate on the homepage. War, mass shootings, robberies...it was like the world had gone mad. In the bottom corner, Lynette spied a black box with bright, bold text overpowering her screen.

"Illinois Post," Lynette read. "Send us your happiest photo from life in Illinois, and we will put the top ten winners in a lottery for a trip for two to L.A." Lynette slid the paper down. *Huh. That was where Ruby lived.*

She imagined herself and her daughter driving in a convertible to California beaches, dining at fancy restaurants, and shopping on Rodeo Drive. Her limbs became heavy with her growing heartache. This sudden longing confused Lynette, and she toyed with the macaroni necklace Ruby had given her on her fortieth birthday. This necklace stayed with her, whether it was on her neck, in her pocket, or in her purse. Just a touch away to remind her of how life could have been. *Why was she was suddenly missing her?* It had been years. *Shouldn't time make hope disappear?*

She sighed and scrolled through her camera app, finding a beautiful waterfall captured at Starved Rock State Park. In the photo, Ruby stood at the base of the waterfall, water up to her knees. The sun created a prism across the cascading water, and Ruby threw her hands up to catch it. Despite the gorgeous backdrop, Lynette's eyes fixated on her daughter's bright smile and joyful eyes.

Nostalgia embraced her as she remembered that day. She, Anthony, and Ruby had driven almost two hours to have a picnic. It had been

Ruby's idea, and Anthony said yes before Lynette could say no. An all-day trip for a quick bite to eat? It sounded frivolous. She had argued that the weekends were the only time she could clean the house, go grocery shopping, and relax before the busy work week.

"Come on, Mommy," her ten-year-old said. Ruby only called her 'mommy' when she wanted something. "Please? Daddy said yes." Ruby had learned early on that if she rounded her bright eyes and clasped her hands under her chin, she mostly got what she wanted.

Lynette hated when Anthony said yes before discussing it with her. It always painted her as the bad guy, or the 'killer of fun', as Ruby once said. Excuses to stay home poured from her mouth. "You have school tomorrow."

"So?"

"It's going to rain."

"Daddy said not until tonight."

"It's a long drive."

"But Mommy, you love nature drives."

That was true.

Somehow, Anthony had disappeared from the room, leaving her with an obstinate pre-teen.

"Fine." She leaned over the kitchen counter and stewed in silence. This was not how she wanted to spend her weekend, but she could be a team player. It could be fun.

As Lynette gazed at the picture, she smiled at the memory. It had been fun. The three of them settled a blanket on a rock beside the waterfall and ate sandwiches and potato chips. Rhythmic water had hypnotized Lynette, and the spray misted her face until moisture saturated her hairline. By the time they left, the constant mist-filled breeze had soaked her hair and heightened her senses with gratitude.

Without thinking, she opened her email and copied and pasted the email address to enter the contest. Attaching the photo image, she wrote a quick note, explaining how the location had been one of her happiest memories, and with one push of a button, she submitted it. Maybe she could send some beauty into the world, and perhaps this could be her reason to reconnect with her daughter.

That night, Lynette slept soundly until her phone rang, startling her out of a dreamless state.

Quickly turning on the light, she grabbed her phone and saw Loretta's name fill the screen. Goosebumps erupted on her arms. "Hello?"

"Lynette. Sorry to wake you. Why didn't you call me back?" Her sister's husky voice was unmistakable from too many cigarettes throughout her life.

"Sorry, what's up? Is everything okay?" She rubbed her eyes, avoiding the light.

"Not really," Loretta said. "Mom's dead."

Sitting up in bed, Lynette stared across the room into the bathroom doorway. "What?"

"Dead. Mom's dead." Loretta's voice shook and Lynette heard a sniffle through the phone.

Wide awake, Lynette swallowed loudly. "How?"

"Not sure yet. I guess she fell and wasn't wearing her lifeline. You know, that thing we got her for Christmas last year when she refused to go to the nursing home? Well, she wasn't wearing it, the stubborn woman. She fell yesterday. I tried to call you. Her neighbor Kate found her unconscious, but when she got to the hospital she had already died."

"She fell? Why didn't you call me?" Lynette's voice hardened.

"I did. And I texted you."

Lynette slouched her shoulders, hearing the voicemail in her head and seeing the notification she had never opened. "But you didn't tell me it was an emergency."

"I'm your sister. Why should I have to? I didn't find out until after the fact. Kate got a hold of me after the ambulance came. With Mom in Maine, and all of us gone, it's not like we could have gone to the hospital with her. I'm her healthcare proxy and the executor of the estate. I've been on the phone with the hospital all night. Mom was a DNR. Did you know that?"

Lynette shook her head.

"Lynette? You there?"

"Yes. Here. I can't believe this." This was not something Lynette had expected. She imagined when her mother died, she would have an opportunity to say goodbye. Not that she said hello very often, but she always imagined they'd fix their fragile and complicated relationship one day.

"Yeah, I know. Can you get a flight to Portland? I need help with the arrangements."

"Of course. I'll be there tomorrow."

Lynette had a busy day between teaching and grading, but work would understand. She had a week for bereavement, and if she had to take the rest of the semester off, she would. Lynette knew Loretta wasn't equipped to handle this. Often flighty and impulsive, Loretta wasn't organized or good with money. She'd need Lynette to step in and take over the estate, the will, and the organization of the services. Her older sister needed her, and she would be there to pick up the pieces.

Lynette welcomed the sense of need. Finally, someone needed her. Her eyes welled with tears, and she wasn't sure if it was sadness for her mom or recognition that she was finally wanted.

A sudden shock rolled through her as Ruby's beautiful face appeared in front of her. *Ruby.* She had to tell Ruby...or maybe Ruby already knew? When Ruby was a child, she held a special bond with her Mema, often visiting her for entire summers. Looking back, it may have been a way to get away from Lynette, or maybe she sensed their marriage crumbling. Anthony's face interrupted Lynette's thoughts. *Anthony.* She hadn't reached out to him since his second wedding, but she'd have to call him.

Jolted awake with adrenaline pumping through her veins, she pulled out a piece of paper and pencil. Jotting down everything she needed to do in the morning, she wrote **Ruby** in big bold letters.

Martha would have to help track down her only daughter for a reunion neither one of them expected.

Chapter 4

The California sun melted Ruby's skin as she sat in traffic, heading toward Burton Chace Park. Whenever she needed to escape the hustle and bustle of the city, she ran to the deep blue water, where the sunning sea lions and active marina made the world turn a little slower. Just like books, the beautiful scenery took her out of her chaotic world and into another.

The air conditioner in her second-hand car had crapped out a few months ago, and she hadn't scraped up enough money to fix it yet. Rent in Culver City cost more than her parents' mortgage back in Chicago, and most of her paycheck went to Shayla.

Ruby rolled the window slightly up as her thick hair blew across her face. She needed a new car, and it would be her first purchase when she had some extra cash saved. She turned the radio knob, hoping that day came sooner than expected.

Alone in her car, she didn't even mind the chaos surrounding her on the freeway. Truck fumes, horns beeping, and music blaring from the surrounding cars wafted over her. Los Angeles didn't feel like home in her heart, but it was her current home, and she did her best to embrace it. This was where she'd make something of herself and prove to her family that her sacrifice was necessary.

Her phone rang and Auntie Lori's number popped up. "Hi, Auntie Lori," Ruby said.

"Hi, honey." Auntie Lori's throaty voice covered Ruby like a warm blanket. "Have you talked to your mom?"

Ruby scowled at the mention of Mom. "What do you think?" Ruby asked matter-of-factly.

"Okay, okay. Listen, your Mema passed away last night."

Ruby focused on the brake lights ahead and she turned down the music, sure she'd misheard. "What?"

"Mema, honey. She's gone."

The last image Ruby had of her grandmother was of her standing on the rocky Maine beaches with her beautiful face, bright blue eyes, and curly white hair searching for sea glass. It had been spring break of sophomore year. Instead of going to Florida like all her sorority sisters, she flew to cold Maine to visit Mema.

Crushed by an invisible boulder, Ruby's chest heaved, begging for oxygen. "What happened?"

"She fell and by the time Kate found her, she was nearly gone."

"Poor Kate," Ruby said.

"She had a head injury, which led to cardiac arrest, and Mema had a DNR in place. She shouldn't have been living alone, sweetie."

Auntie Lori's voice calmed Ruby as her car crawled to the next exit.

The lump in her throat stopped the words, but her inner voice asked, *What about Mom? Is she okay?* She wanted to know, but didn't ask. "When are the services?" she asked instead.

Auntie Lori sighed. "Not sure, honey. Your mom and I are flying up today to complete the arrangements, so probably within the week. Do you think you can come home?"

"Of course." Mema was one of the most important people to Ruby, and to know she was gone broke her in half. It wasn't fair. Why did she have to be so far away? Why hadn't she visited more often? "I'll be there." The words were out of her mouth before she rationalized the consequences of returning. "I talked to Mema last week, and she sounded fine."

"Mentally, she was with it, but physically her body kept crapping out on her. Her knees were no good, and she needed a hip replacement. She's fallen quite a few times over the past year."

"She wanted me to visit over the summer, but I said no. I shouldn't have done that. I should have gone." Her voice cracked. "I never got to say goodbye."

"Oh, honey. She knew how much you loved her. The two of you had a special relationship."

Ruby struggled to breathe, and a thrumming emerged in her ears. She needed to pull over.

"And Ruby?"

Ruby knew what Auntie Lori was going to say. She said it every time they talked, and every time Ruby politely declined. "Yeah?"

"You really should call your mom."

Instead of responding, Ruby bit back the tears, unsure if they were for her lost grandmother or her lost mother. "Will Dad be there?" He was another broken thread in her life, too busy to check in on her with his new wife and new life.

"Yes, I assume so. Your parents were married for twenty years. Despite what happened between them, he and your grandparents had a solid relationship. I think he'd make a point of showing up, and if he can't because of work, I'm sure he'll send flowers or something."

"I haven't seen him since before his wedding," she said. She gripped the steering wheel as she maneuvered through the busy streets, and her knuckles whitened.

"I guess we'll all meet his new wife then."

"You think she'll be there too?"

"I don't know. I would think so, but your dad has surprised me before."

Ruby considered her dad and whether he would show. Just thinking about him standing between his new wife, only a few years older than Ruby, and his estranged wife and daughter for the first time made the heat rise in her chest and her heartbeat thud in her ears. Maybe it would be best if their first contact occurred publicly, like at a funeral. It would keep their words in check, forcing the tough conversations to be had another day. "Okay, Auntie. Please keep me posted. I'll be there."

Stopping at an In-N-Out parking lot, the long journey to Burton Chace Park seemed unimportant right now. She needed to clear her head, but doing so in bumper-to-bumper traffic wasn't the best idea. Instead, she sat in the parking lot for two hours, jotting down her favorite memories of her grandmother. Baking cookies, shopping, cooking fresh Maine Lobster...every memory filled Ruby with a sadness that she could no longer compartmentalize. They traveled from her heart to her gut to her head.

After she placed her notebook on the passenger seat, she looked up to find a small red cardinal hopping across her hood. Ruby watched the bird march its way to the windshield. Ruby stared, never having seen a bird so close. She couldn't recall ever seeing a cardinal in California. The tears welled behind her eyes as she stared at this beautiful bird, tilting its head from side to side, looking at her with curiosity.

"I'm sorry, Mema," she whispered to the bird. "I should have done better."

The bird lifted its wings and flew away, leaving Ruby alone in her car with just her notebook of memories.

Chapter 5

L ynette neatly rolled her clothes, placed them in her luggage, and zipped the overflowing bag. Unsure of when she'd return, she overpacked, preparing for all scenarios. Martha had agreed to check her mailbox and send her mail to Maine if Lynette stayed longer than a week.

Lynette had just vacuumed her home, emptied the dishwasher, and placed all the folded towels and washcloths in the linen closet. Recognizing the fridge full of food, she grimaced at the mess that would materialize if she extended her trip. She knew she'd be gone at least a week, and didn't want spoiled milk or left over broccoli stinking up her house, so she quickly swiped the items from inside the fridge and into the trash. All the containers and bottles sank to the bottom. It was only half full, but heavier than she'd expected, so she mustered up her strength and yanked. The steady achiness of an osteoarthritis flare radiated from her knees and ankles. Pulling the bag up and out, she stretched on her toes while the stiffness in her knees halted her. Fighting through the pain, she dragged the bag outside, pulling the bin to the front.

All that money and all that food, gone. She'd have to ask Martha to move the empty trash bins tomorrow.

Popping an Advil to clear the aches and pains, Lynette scanned the house and praised her efforts. It looked good. Good enough for her to

CHAPTER 5

leave for a while.

She had called Anthony the night before, first talking to his new wife, Kai. Kai had been the end of the end for Lynette and Anthony's marriage.

Lynette "hmm'd" and "uh-huh'd," fully disengaged from Kai's pleasant voice until Anthony's baritone boomed through the phone. "Hey Linnie."

"Please don't call me that." Her voice held steady.

"What's up?"

"My mom died unexpectedly and I have to go to Maine. We don't know when the services are and I know you are busy, but I wanted to let you know. I'm not expecting you to come."

"Oh, Lynette, I'm sorry. Are you okay?" His voice warmed and Lynette felt her armor rise.

Funny. No one had asked her that before. *Yes, I'm fine. Empty, but fine.* "I'm okay."

"Of course. Please keep us informed."

A burning sensation erupted in the pit of Lynette's belly. The idea of Anthony being with a woman young enough to be their daughter irked her, and her skin prickled at the thought of Kai standing beside her at the services. What she wanted to say was, "Kai isn't invited," but she knew that was childish, so she bit her tongue. "Yes. Um, I need to get in touch with Ruby. Do you know where she is?" Lynette leaned over the counter and rubbed her forehead. So many wrinkles had formed recently, and she couldn't fathom the amount of aging her body had experienced since Anthony left. To ease her racing heart, she swallowed a gulp of wine. She knew she could send a message through her social media, but a death in the family deserved a phone call.

"Last I knew, she was in an apartment in Encino, but her birthday card got returned to me. I'll find out."

With shaking legs and jumbled thoughts, Lynette let the tears roll

29

down her cheeks, but steadied her voice. "So, you had an address for her?"

"I did, yeah, but she must have moved."

"Martha found her Instagram profile. I'll send her a message to call one of us. Please let me know if you get in contact. It's important that she knows. She loved my mom, and I'd never forgive myself if she misses it."

Anthony's tender voice flowed through the phone. "Of course, Linnie. I'll try to find her. Please keep me posted on the details."

Lynette disengaged the call and cried heavy tears, with no one except herself to wipe them away.

She texted Martha and asked her to send Ruby a message. Although she worked in academia, and interacted with all the tech-wizards of the younger generation, technology had never been important to her. Beyond her email, the occasional searches, and streaming, she barely used the internet. Lynette had tried social media after Anthony left, but she was afraid of what she'd find. Too many women lurked in the shadows, and she couldn't handle another heartbreak.

Now, she stood in the kitchen with her luggage, holding a one-way ticket to Portland, a place she'd long forgotten. A jumbled mix of emotions seeped through her, and her stomach dropped as she imagined herself walking back into her childhood home.

The door clicked behind her and Lynette picked up her head, marching toward the taxi waiting in her driveway.

"To the airport," she said to the driver.

As the car drove away, she stared out her window.

She wasn't ready to face her family or her past, but it was now or never.

Chapter 6

With six uninterrupted hours ahead to process what the next few days may look like, Ruby boarded the crowded airplane and focused on her breathing. Just thinking about seeing Mom and Dad made her chest tighten. She didn't plan on staying long, but Auntie Lori had transferred some money into her bank account, making sure she had enough to pay her rent next week. Ruby hated taking money, but this flight across the country cost more than her monthly grocery bill.

Shayla had rubbed her back as she cried on the couch, supplying emotional support and comfort foods, like frozen yogurt and chardonnay. With each bite, her memories replayed in her mind. Guilt, sadness, and regret mixed in with her tears as she told herself she needed to be brave.

She hadn't heard from Mom, but knew she'd be at Mema's house, ready to attack Ruby for not keeping in touch. Her stomach tumbled and rocked at the thought of seeing her mother after their falling out three years before.

The monotonous airplane engine soothed Ruby and helped her fall asleep for most of the flight. Her earbuds rested in her ears, and her head leaned against the small, oval window. With a layover in New York, her total travel time was close to half a day.

Excited to get out of the hustle and bustle of L.A. and into a place where weight and height didn't define you, Ruby pleasantly recalled the evergreen background and rocky shore. Although she didn't have any winter clothes, she knew the October temperatures in Portland were about thirty-degrees colder than the temperatures in Southern California. She needed a warm fall jacket and a pair of waterproof boots for her stay. Maybe it was excessive for such a quick trip, but she was returning to a different world.

Auntie Lori encouraged Ruby to stay in the old house. Mema had two extra bedrooms, and Auntie Lori was certain there would be room. Ruby didn't want to stay there, especially if Mom was there, but she didn't have the financial flexibility to get a hotel room. Hesitating at first, she had agreed.

By the time the second flight touched down, Ruby's wide eyes and jittery hands had woken up, alert to the unknown. Following the crowd to baggage claim, her steps slowed and her fingers chilled.

Standing at the luggage carousel, Ruby saw Auntie Lori, with her long, wavy hair and full-length peacoat. Her bright smile spread from ear to ear and her face lit up like sparklers.

Comforted by her familiar smile, Ruby's steps quickened and she wrapped her arms around Auntie's neck. "Auntie Lori!" The last time Ruby saw her was after her high school graduation, five years before.

"Look at you!" Auntie Lori grabbed Ruby's hand and Ruby spun in a circle. "You look so beautiful, and so tan!"

Ruby's face dropped. "Oh, thank you. I'm sorry about Mema."

Auntie Lori's face fell too, and her gaze dropped to her feet. "It's okay, sweetie. It's life, right? The only thing we can't escape is death. You never know when your number is up, so you have to live a life that's true to you."

Ruby nodded and bit her lip, feeling a tear well up. "Yes. Well, I haven't been able to stop thinking about you."

A loud beeping rang, and the baggage belt jerked forward. Ruby turned her attention to the array of luggage making its way to its rightful owners.

They made small talk as Ruby grabbed her small suitcase off the belt.

"That's it?" Auntie Lori asked. "When are you going home? Tomorrow?"

Chuckling, Ruby said, "No, I'm here for eight days. I couldn't take any more time off. All my clothes are tiny. I'm in warm weather, remember?"

"Same here, but did you pack jeans? Or a sweatshirt?" Ruby's tank top hugged her torso and Auntie handed her a winter hat.

Ruby pulled it over her head, and checked her reflection in the mirrored column. "Eh, let's just say I have to go shopping." Ruby raised her suitcase to remind Auntie of how little she had brought.

"We'll do it tomorrow."

As Ruby followed Auntie to the car, she needed to ask about Mom, but couldn't quite form the words. She knew she'd find out Mom's travel plans eventually, and she considered if knowing or not knowing would be better for her mental state.

The car zipped out of the airport and into Mema's suburban neighborhood, about a mile from the ocean. The three-bedroom Cape Codder sat on a hill, and if Ruby squinted from the top floor, she could make out the ocean. Everything looked just as Ruby had remembered. Flooded by summer memories, she noticed the tree she used to climb as a kid had nearly doubled in size. The image of Mema pushing her on the tire swing hanging from the almost naked branch settled on Ruby's unsettled stomach.

She turned toward Auntie Lori. "Who's here?"

Auntie Lori slid the shifter into park before placing her hand on Ruby's. "Your mom, and probably the neighbors." Her phone vibrated, and she raised it to her cheek. "Hello, this is Loretta....uh, yes, that would be great, thank you." She placed the phone back in her bag and smiled. "You ready?"

Ruby slid her head back against the headrest. "Oooo-kay." Her stomach somersaulted, and her legs stiffened.

"Sorry, sweetie. Your mom doesn't know you're coming, and she doesn't know we kept in touch over the years. When we walk in together, expect an explosion. Or maybe a river of tears. I'm not sure how she'll react."

Ruby's blood raced through her veins, and her head throbbed. "Great. Thanks for the heads up."

Chapter 7

While waiting for her sister, the eerily quiet house haunted Lynette. Mom's absence had left a void that she hadn't expected to feel. To pass the time and ignore her unease, she politely spoke with Kate, who had invited herself in an hour earlier.

Lynette imagined a heavy responsibility sitting on Kate, but all she wanted was for Kate to stop talking about the weather, plants, and the lobster festival. It had been so long since she'd been in this house, she wanted to examine every nook and cranny for happy memories that may be hidden under the dust bunnies in the most neglected corners of her mind.

Lynette remembered visiting one year for Easter and pots of transplanted roots sat in tiny buckets filled with soil on her mother's front porch. Gifts from Kate equaled work for Lynette and Anthony. Now, with snow in the air, Lynette wondered if those plants still thrived or if they had died.

Kate assembled a casserole dish and tossed it into the oven. "This will be ready in thirty minutes. Chicken broccoli and rice. I used to make it for your mom when she was sick with a cold."

Lynette eyed the casserole, swimming in cream of chicken soup, and disguised her disgust by turning toward the window. She couldn't recall eating this hodge-podge as a child or imagine Mom indulging in this high cholesterol comfort food. "Thank you," she said civilly.

A few other neighbors had popped in and out of the old home, dropping flowers, cards, and random baked goods. Lynette accepted them all with gratitude, but she knew most of it would go uneaten and into the garbage.

The door swung open and a gust of chilly air traveled through the kitchen. Lynette shivered and tightened her cardigan, crossing her arms and standing on guard.

"Hi," Loretta said, dropping her keys on the counter.

Lynette draped her arms over her older sister's shoulders and pulled her close. "Hey, sis, you look great."

"Thanks. I found a hitchhiker."

Always the jokester, Lynette mustered a smile. Maybe it was Anthony. Hopefully without his wife. Lynette's politeness around the neighbors sucked up any extra energy she had in her reserves for Kai.

In the other room, the coat closet door opened and closed, and shoes kicked off, clattering against the dusty hardwood floor. Whoever it was knew their way around the house. "The more the merrier," Lynette said.

A long shadow entered the kitchen first, and Lynette watched Loretta's face fight into a grin. Lynette's eyes traveled from the head of the shadow to the feet, and up the lanky body. Tanned legs and a tight tank top, more suitable attire for the beach, not a funeral, emerged and Lynette's heart stopped beating, knowing who was wearing such ridiculous clothing for New England weather.

Her breath caught, and she stared at the figure before her. Long blonde hair hung below a knit hat that matched the blue of her eyes. Lynette would know that beautiful face from anywhere and her heart lurched out of her chest. Holding onto the fridge for support, she picked her mouth up off the floor and smiled through the uncomfortable moment, like Mom had always taught.

"Hi, Mom." Ruby shifted her weight from one hip to the other. Her

36

arms hung stiff at her sides, and she looked equally nervous with her fleeting eye gaze and stuttered movements.

"Hi." Lynette looked around the room from Loretta to Kate and stumbled through the introduction. "Kate, this is my daughter, Ruby. I don't know if you remember her."

"I do," Kate said, and pulled Ruby in for a hug, which Ruby reciprocated. Lynette leaned against the counter and forced a smile.

Ruby leaned into Lynette, who tapped between her shoulder blades a few times. Ruby returned to the side of Loretta and asked, "Is there anything I can do? To help?"

"No, all set." Lynette's voice clipped each word as she preoccupied herself with the oven light. She needed to calm her racing heart, but the questions surrounding her daughter's whereabouts and how she ended up in this house rolled past her. "Loretta, can I speak to you a moment?"

The tension in the room intensified, and Kate grabbed her coat. "Lori, I'll be back tomorrow to help with the arrangements."

"Bye, Kate," Loretta said.

Lynette led Loretta into the den, and away from Ruby. Glancing around the perimeter for lurking eyes and ears, Lynette hushed her voice. "What the hell is going on?" Lynette pinched her lips and gave her sister a cold, intense stare. A sharp pain in her chest lapped against her like ocean waves. "Did you bring her here?"

Loretta widened her stance and crossed her arms. "I did. Her grandmother died. She should know."

Lynette tossed her hands up in the air. "Of course she should know." Her volume doubled and then dropped to a whisper. "How did you find her? I tried, but she ignored me."

"I called her. She reached out to me when she first landed in California."

"Three years ago?"

"Yeah, about that."

"How'd you get her number?"

"She texted me after she got settled."

Stunned by the news that her daughter had caused worry and sleepless nights, when her own sister knew she was safe, boiled Lynette's blood. Lori's frankness caused her face to grow hot.

She remembered how many times she had lied for her sister when they were teenagers. How many times had she stepped in or took the blame to save her sister when she stayed out all night, disappeared for a weekend, or got caught smoking pot? She would do anything for her sister, and somehow that relationship disappeared like a worn-out piece of sand glass. Loretta had done the unthinkable. Hiding her daughter, during the hardest years of her life. "I have nothing to say to you," Lynette murmured.

"She wasn't ready to talk to you, and I promised her I was a safe person to confide in. I couldn't break her trust." Loretta spoke with such practicality; Lynette was at a loss.

"How dare you." She spun on her heel and stormed into the kitchen, where her estranged daughter sat. Ruby's fingers intertwined and her thumb tapped the table.

"Hi, Mom." Ruby swallowed and Lynette watched her leg bounce under the table. "How've you been?"

It wasn't much, but at least it was a question of concern. It was more concern than Ruby had shown her over the past few years, since Loretta was there to alleviate her guilt for running away.

In a trance, and ready to crumble into a puddle, Lynette sat down with her arms tightly crossed against her chest. She examined her daughter before responding. Radiant skin, precise eyebrows, and a sun-kissed face made her appear healthy and well. "Well, not great." Lynette wanted to add more, but she couldn't reveal her agonizing mental state that had nearly destroyed her over the past three years.

"Do you want to talk? It's been a while."

Lynette swallowed, unsure how much to say. "Well, it's been about three years."

"I'm sorry about that." Ruby looked down and her shoulders slumped forward. Lynette's heart reached out to her, but her brain reminded her she needed to be strong.

"I saw your profile on Instagram, so I knew you were still alive."

Ruby leaned forward, her blue eyes inviting Lynette to say more. "I didn't know you were on social media," she said.

"I'm not," Lynette scowled. "Martha found you and we both sent you messages."

Ruby's head bobbed up and down like a buoy trying to stay afloat in the ocean. "Sorry. I get a lot of spam with my modeling. Companies preying on me, creepy men, and bots. If I don't recognize the name, I don't even open them."

"Of course. You can't imagine how surprised I was when Martha pulled up your face and I realized you were actually living the life you told me you'd live." Lynette held Ruby's gaze, daring her to either confirm or deny her success.

Ruby's eyes dropped. "Yeah, it's been quite a wild ride. I'm the spokesperson for Jolie Belle. Have you heard of them? In all my Instagram posts, I'm wearing their products. And I wear something every day. Like this." She held out her wrist and two gold bangles clanged.

"Pretty."

"Jolie Belle is a new designer based in L.A.. It's for hip, young women, and they selected me from my modeling portfolio."

Lynette heard her, but the words traveled over her shoulders and swirled above her head. "Great." She hadn't intended sarcasm, but the word had been out before she could stop it.

Ruby's head pulled like she'd been hit by a slingshot.

"I'm sorry, it's just that I didn't expect to see you here. A phone call would have been nice."

"I was happy in L.A., Mom. I didn't want to complicate it by—"

Lynette's eyes shot up. "What. Contacting me? Do you know how many days and nights I worried about you? Did you have enough money? Were you living on the streets? Did you have a job? Were you alive? You left, and I never heard from you again."

Ruby's shoulders hunched down, and she mumbled, "People knew. I thought they'd tell you."

Glaring at her only daughter, Lynette fumbled for the words. "I don't even want to talk about that right now. What about your parents, huh? What about me? Your father? Did you even know the divorce was finalized? Did you know your dad remarried? Do you even care?"

Ruby's voice dropped to her chest. "I knew. Auntie Lori told me and Dad sent me an invite."

Without thinking, Lynette's anguish and frustration erupted. "I sacrificed over twenty years to give you a good life, and you trampled over me, throwing me out like a bag of trash. I haven't heard from you in three years. I deserve more from you. I deserve respect."

Ruby's eyes widened and tears splashed against her bronzed cheeks.

"Stop. Right now. You have no right to cry," Lynette scolded. "You left on your own free will."

Loretta barged into the kitchen wearing a thin grimace. "Lynette. Enough. Ruby, go upstairs, take a shower, get unpacked, relax. You're in your mother's old bedroom at the front of the house."

Shoulders shaking, Ruby moved upstairs.

Afraid she'd just pushed her daughter away for good, Lynette whipped her head toward her sister's voice. Her muscles quivered, and she stepped directly in front of Loretta, standing nose to nose. "Don't. Talk to me." Her hand flew up and her pointer finger jabbed Loretta's shoulder. "Stay out of this."

Shaking, Lynette ran to Mom and Dad's old room and locked the bedroom door. She flopped on the bed and cried into her mother's pillow. *First Ruby, then Anthony, and then Mom.* Everyone she loved had left her. Everything Lynette touched turned to dust, leaving her to manage life alone. It wasn't fair.

"Mom," Lynette sobbed, inhaling the scent of lavender on her pillowcase. "Please, Mom. Please help me save my relationship with Ruby. I can't bear to lose her again."

When Lynette removed the pillowcase from her face, she saw a shadow move in the corner. Squinting her eyes, she recognized a human with slender legs and a petite frame. Lynette held her breath and blinked. The moon shifted behind the clouds and the shadow disappeared into the darkness.

Lynette stared at the corner, begging the moonbeams to return. When they did, the corner remained empty, and she inhaled, feeling the air circulate throughout her body.

Lynette pulled her legs up into the fetal position and draped her mother's hand-crocheted blanket over her legs and torso. She sobbed into the pillow until her body stopped heaving and the liquid ceased to flow. Too tired to turn on the light, Lynette closed her eyes and prayed she wouldn't have any nightmares.

Chapter 8

This moment had played and replayed through Ruby's mind with every variation Mom could give. A hug, a cold shoulder, or an explosion were the first three reactions Ruby had practiced in her head. Mom had exploded and, although Ruby thought she knew how she'd respond, she wasn't ready for it. Knowing she should have kept in touch, she questioned the events leading up to her departure.

Ever since Ruby was ten, she wanted to be a model. Middle school and high school comprised binge watching America's Next Top Model and practicing how to walk down the imaginary runway in her bedroom. She loved makeup and fashion and beauty, and prided herself in adopting the newest trends first.

In her second year of college, she struggled with her advertising classes. Her head was always in the clouds, dreaming about high fashion. When Claudia, an old friend from high school, reached out about her life in L.A., Ruby had to go. Even if it meant taking a leave of absence during her studies.

When she had announced she was moving to L.A., her mother and father dismissed her dreams and shunned her, calling her selfish and out of touch with reality. Ruby left in the middle of the night, with nothing more than one packed suitcase and a goodbye note on the table. In Ruby's scratchy hand, she scrawled, "I can't stay. I'm going to the west coast because I KNOW I can do it."

When she arrived, she texted her parents, and Mom and Dad were a wreck. Constantly questioning her actions and decisions and harping on her lack of plans, she sent one last text saying she'd be fine, and then changed her number. She hoped by purging the negativity from her life, she'd be able to start a new life in Cali. Knowing she needed some connection to home, she contacted Auntie Lori and Mema, being careful not to share too much. She never asked them not to tell Mom and Dad.

She moved onto Claudia's couch until she secured a job and found a roommate.

When Auntie Lori shared the bad news that her parents had separated, Ruby had wailed heavy sobs and giant tears in the shower. It wasn't because they were now a statistic, but because she felt like an orphan.

When Dad admitted to having a girlfriend, Ruby cut him out of her life. Her heart broke for Mom, who could be a hard pill to swallow, but no one deserved infidelity. Dad claimed there was no one while they were living under one roof, but Ruby didn't believe him.

It was easy, being on the other side of the country. There were no reminders of her parents unless she allowed her mind to wander, and when it did, she indulged in a quick jaunt to the beach to ease her rocky thoughts.

Ruby had learned modeling and acting were the same. You had to turn on the emotion with a finger snap or flick of the wrist, and Ruby applied that on-off switch to her family. Learning that her family had fallen apart made her determined to show her independence and distance herself from the drama in Chicago.

Now, laying on Mom's old bed, a gentle, hollow knock sounded on the door before it squeaked open. "Can I come in?"

Auntie Lori moved to the edge of the bed and settled into the corner. She looked younger than fifty-five, with her sunny spirit, bohemian attire, and artsy eyeglasses.

"Hi." Ruby sat up and played with the seam on the comforter with one hand and hugged the pillow close to her chest with the other.

"Want to talk?"

It was a simple question and required an easy yes or no, but Ruby couldn't answer. "Uh, sure." She didn't meet Auntie Lori's eyes.

"Your mom. She means well. She was surprised to see you, and she's upset at me because I never shared our relationship with her."

Ruby tilted her head and gazed at her aunt, hearing the words roll around like a marble on cobblestone. "I thought for sure you would have told her by now."

"You need to talk to her."

Ruby's face tightened. "But—"

A slender hand appeared before Ruby's face. "Not now, Ruby. Tomorrow. It's late, everyone is tired, and the emotional event of Mema passing is weighing on us all. Tomorrow is a new day. We can all sit down and talk over breakfast like civilized humans. Like a family." She leaned over and embraced Ruby. "Try to get a good night's sleep."

Ruby swallowed the ping-pong ball bobbing in her throat. "What if I can't sleep? Then what?" she challenged.

"Then you go downstairs and have a cup of tea with me, because I will probably be up, too." Auntie Lori walked to the door, and Ruby scooted higher in bed.

"Hey, is my dad coming, do you know?"

"Yes, honey, he will be here for the wake and funeral."

Ruby nodded and stroked the pillowcase nestled on her lap. "Thanks, Auntie Lori."

The door clicked shut and Ruby remained alone in the guest room. The house still smelled like her Mema, a mix between Lipton tea and Polident. Ruby remembered sleeping in this room as a child, and she stroked the soft teddy bear sitting on the small night table.

Over the course of her life, Ruby had spent hours looking out the single window gazing at the ocean in the far distance. She loved spending summers with Mema and Papa, mostly because they made her feel safe and loved.

After Papa died, Mema lived alone, and Ruby did what she could to make sure Mema was okay. Spending summers here as a kid and spring break as a young adult helped her see Mema as the person she was, not just the grandma who loved to spoil her one and only grandchild.

By the time Ruby was sixteen, Mom and Mema had lost touch. They never lived close, and the distance created a natural wedge. Living halfway across the country made sugarcoating life easy, with no one there to validate its accuracy. Just like with Ruby and her parents, distance was an easy excuse to stop sharing.

Ruby remembered the hidden nooks and crannies in Mema's house where she used to hide her toys. Built-in drawers were the perfect spot for her books and journals, hidden under the extra sheets occupying the drawer. The long, thin closet underneath the upper stairs had been her favorite place to play house with her stuffed animals. It became a magical world where Ruby's friends came to life.

Crawling off the bed, Ruby opened the closet door and stared into the dark abyss. It appeared smaller than she remembered, and she pictured herself huddled beneath the staircase steps. Moving clothes hanging on the rod, she stepped further inside, nearly tripping on an old aquamarine suitcase wedged beneath the bottom two steps.

Ruby retrieved her flashlight, which remained hidden in the night-stand drawer for the past decade, and shined the light against the glistening metal hinges. She pulled on the vinyl box, surprised by how heavy it was against her powerful grip. Yanking it to the middle of the room, Ruby pushed on the latch, but nothing happened. A small lock held the suitcase closed.

Frowning and scrunching her forehead, she moved around the room searching for a tiny key in drawers, on shelves, and under furniture. Unsuccessful, she pushed the suitcase to the corner of the room and climbed into bed.

Imagining secrets and scandals, Ruby wondered what skeletons Mema had hidden in her suitcase. Her imagination ran wild. If she found Mema and Papa's secrets, would they make sense? Urging to remain close to Mema, she hoped so.

The next morning, Ruby sat at the kitchen table clutching a scalding mug of tea, with her mother to her left and her aunt to her right. No one said a word, and varying shades of blue eyes gazed around the room. Ruby didn't appreciate being attacked the night before, so she vowed not to speak unless spoken to.

"Loretta, what did the funeral home say?" Mom asked, buttering her bagel with quick strokes.

"The wake will be Thursday, and the funeral Friday. We need to get the obituary in the paper for tomorrow. It's due by two this afternoon. The wake'll run from four to six and the funeral is at ten. The three of us need to pull together some photos for a digital and physical collage."

Lynette dropped her bagel and raised her eyes to meet Loretta's. "Thank you for everything you've done." Ruby knew it pained Mom to admit weakness or show gratitude. Mom's eyes relaxed and for a moment, her old mom was there. As quick as it came, it was gone, and Mom's scowl returned.

Auntie Lori paced the room. "Of course. So Ruby, are you okay with collage duty? I think there are a ton of old photos in the attic. I'll pull them down later today."

"Sure, Auntie, whatever you need."

Auntie Lori turned to Mom. "Would you prefer writing the obituary or going through Mom's old clothes to pick out what she's wearing for the service?"

Ruby watched Mom balk at the thought of dressing Mema for her last hurrah. "I'll write the obituary."

Behind the safety of her mug, Auntie Lori grinned. "You sure? If you need help, let me know."

Annoyance creaked behind Mom's voice. "Yes, I'm sure. I work in academia for Christ's sake. I can write a damn obituary." She rose from her seat at the kitchen table and shuffled to the sink, dropping her full mug into the stainless-steel basin. "I'm going to shower."

Ruby and Auntie Lori watched Mom stomp out of the room in a huff.

"Okay, guess that solves that. When you're done eating, I'll show you where the totes of old photos are. You might have a hard time figuring out who is who, but make a pile of the good shots, and we'll go through it later. I'd rather have too many than too little."

Thankful that Auntie Lori hadn't lost it in the wake of her grandmother's death, Ruby said, "Of course. Whatever you need."

"The thing is," Auntie Lori said, "she lived a long life, right? She was in her eighties, her husband passed, her sisters passed, and most of her friends probably passed too. I would imagine twenty or thirty people will show. The wake will mostly be people from the community, and the funeral will likely be close friends and family."

Ruby admired Auntie's resolve during life's crappiest moments. "How are you keeping it all together?" she asked.

"I've been busy keeping it together for Mema. She deserves to have a nice last goodbye, right?"

Ruby squinted her eyes and nodded her head in uncertainty.

"Oh, don't worry. When I get back to Florida and pick up the phone to call my mom, it'll hit me like a ton of bricks."

"I didn't know you guys were that close."

Throwing her head back, Auntie Lori cackled. "Oh, we weren't. We weren't close until I got out of this town and moved as far away as I could. Thankfully, I was first, and your poor mother had to live in that house hearing how awful I was to leave for a man."

Ruby knew this skeleton version of the story, but had never pried for details. "Uncle Tommy, right?"

"You got it. We lived happily ever after until we didn't. I moved down to Florida for him, and then he up and left."

Without breaking eye contact, Ruby encouraged Auntie Lori to continue.

"No money, no relationship with my family, and trapped in the Sunshine State. He left, I moved on, and eventually I came around. It took about twenty years, but I surprised your Mema and Papa with a visit on my forty-first birthday. That's when we repaired the broken bridge from twenty-years before."

"And were you and Mom close?" Ruby thought she knew, but she wanted to hear it from Auntie Lori.

"Your mother and I," she began, "we were two peas in a pod. Told everyone we were twins, and most people believed us. We shared a room, dressed alike, and played with the same toys." Auntie Lori looked past Ruby's shoulder. "Then I went to high school and everything changed. I got my first boyfriend, whom Mema and Papa despised, and unfortunately, your mother got caught in the crossfire of the many arguments your grandparents and I got into." She leaned back in her seat, her mind seeming to be at a different time. "That was when things changed. High school. I had asked your mom to lie for me one night so I could meet Tommy at the lake, and she did. But we both got caught and grounded, and your mother pulled away, completely separating herself from me. She was so mad. Probably still is."

Auntie's story matched what Mom had told her over the years.

"So that was it?"

"That was it. We learned to be civil around each other. Most people wouldn't even know we used to be inseparable. Then your mom married your dad. They moved to Chicago, had you...out of sight, out of mind.

We're not *not* friends, we just aren't as close as we once were. And when COVID hit, it was normal not to see anyone. It's life, really."

Auntie Lori made it sound simple, but Ruby understood the complexity underneath her words. With the matriarch's death before them, no matter how fragmented that role had become, things shaped differently in Ruby's mind.

"Do you think I'll ever have a good relationship with my parents?" Ruby's voice sounded tiny, even to her.

"That's up to you. You have a lot to talk about, but yes, anything is possible."

Ruby picked up her phone and scrolled through her social media feed. She forgot to post for today, and her thumbs fumbled through her photos. Usually, she enjoyed this part of the job, collecting hearts and comments and words of affirmation.

Being in Maine felt like being in a different life. Although she was struggling, she needed to keep it together. One post at a time.

Chapter 9

By the time Lynette emerged from her room, the house had emptied. She listened to the steady drip from the bathroom faucet, letting it lull her chaotic mind. She peeked through the checkered curtains and saw a dry rectangle where Loretta's Civic used to be. The rain pattered against the window with slight taps. Relieved to be alone, she sat down with her laptop and her fingers moved across the keyboard. Typing, deleting, and retyping.

Grabbing her phone, she debated calling on Kate for details about Mom's most recent life. Lynette put the phone down and walked around the house for clues. An old recipe tin overflowing with index cards sat beside the electric kettle, bringing back memories from her childhood.

Flipping through the weathered cards, Lynette found her mother's recipes for meatloaf, roast beef, and lasagna. Script writing flowed like a lace doily, all intricate and loopy, covering the front and back of each index card. She traced the cursive letters with her finger, recognizing the similarity with her own handwriting.

Moving to the dining room, Lynette recalled all the Sunday dinners that had occurred in that room. A super-glued serving platter rested on Great Granny's sideboard, and Lynette fingered the crack. She was there that night, when the platter broke in half, and her mother locked herself in her bedroom. Loretta had just announced she was moving to Florida with Tommy the day after she graduated high school.

Stunned, Mom had slammed the platter on the table. Heavy with dinner, the middle hit the edge, fracturing the hand-painted ceramic. Like a volcano erupting, gravy had spilled down the table legs onto the floor. Loretta had grabbed her purse and left the house while Mom dashed to her bedroom. Dad disappeared behind her, and Lynette wiped up the mess. Like every 'emergency' that faced their family, she was the one to pick up the pieces.

With Loretta gone, Lynette had stepped around the house and scrubbed the floor free from sticky gravy. Careful to pick up tiny shards of glass that could slice when least expected, she washed the platter, dug through her father's tool kit, and glued the pieces together. It wasn't much, but at least Mom hadn't lost her daughter, her dinner, and her platter.

Standing alone in the dining room that held her memories captive, Lynette pulled her finger away from the dish and turned toward the window. A single tear slid down her cheek, and she sobbed into her reflection. Her mind was like a tripping electrical wire, with moments from her past fighting to connect the broken threads that once made her family whole.

Lynette grabbed a notebook and walked into her old bedroom. Ruby's suitcase lay open in the corner and the bedsheets rumpled into a messy ball with Lynette's old teddy bear wedged beside the pillows. An empty soda bottle, a half-eaten bag of chips, and a cell phone charger scattered across the bedside table top.

Ruby had made herself at home.

Lynette had lived in this room, however it looked nothing like this when she was a child. Now generic and bland, this room lacked any personality. Afraid to mess up the bed, she pressed her back against the wall and slid to the hardwood floor. Her joints, still sore from prepping her Chicago house for her departure, yelled at her for not taking it easy. Embracing the pain, Lynette stretched her aching legs and wondered if she'd be able to get up before Ruby came home. She hesitated to bother her daughter or appear intrusive, but being in her old room brought necessary comfort when reflecting on Mom's life.

The white-lined paper sat on her lap, and Lynette struggled with writing against her thighs. Looking to her left, she saw a large baby blue suitcase with two metal clasps and a leather handle. Just within her reach, she dragged it closer, and placed her paper on top. Lynette knew Mom was capable of understanding, compromise, and acceptance, even if she didn't show those attributes to her children. She quickly scribbled the words down.

As the morning wore on, Lynette recognized a handful of memories that exemplified Mom's character. She'd need some help, and trepidation toward asking Loretta and Ruby for assistance niggled at her. Lynette threw up her hands in surrender and put the paper beside her on the floor. She bent her knees to get up, but her body disobeyed her.

Rolling to her side, she managed all fours but couldn't quite move her knee to a half-kneel, half-squat position. She was stuck. Grabbing the mattress with one hand, Lynette pulled, but her knees cracked and her hips ached.

Racing her eyes around the room for something stable she could grab onto, Lynette placed both hands on the upright suitcase. She pushed her hands against the top, where the two sides became one, and heaved all her body weight through her arms.

Readjusting one foot forward, she pressed and leaned, and a loud crack sent her tumbling toward the floor. Her face smashed into the side of the suitcase, and her arms stopped midway in the center of the full container.

"Ow!" She slid her hands out of the luggage, careful not to slice her arms on the rusty latches, and touched her face. No blood, but her tender cheekbone was already swelling. Defeated, Lynette sat back against the bed, tipped her head toward the ceiling, and waited for her daughter and sister to rescue her.

Chapter 10

Shopping with Auntie Lori brought Ruby back to the first day of school, when wearing a brand-new outfit either made or broke your year. Especially in middle school. Auntie Lori, always the cool aunt, took Ruby shopping whenever she visited Florida.

Ruby had packed a dress for the wake and funeral, but had nothing warm enough for fall New England nights. With the help of Auntie Lori's credit card, she bought enough clothes to last her entire visit.

Walking into the house with two overflowing bags, Ruby scanned the empty kitchen. "Mom?" she yelled.

A muffled yell came from upstairs, and Ruby and Auntie meandered to the second floor.

"Mom?" Ruby asked again. She looked in Mema's room, but didn't see anyone. The bathroom door was open and empty. "Mom? Where are you?" she sang.

"In here."

Of course, she was in the room Ruby had claimed as home. *What is she doing there?* A scowl crossed Ruby's face as she followed Auntie Lori into the bedroom. Mom's legs sprawled like an isosceles triangle and her spine pressed against the wall. Her swollen eye held a purple gash just above her cheekbone.

"Mom! What happened?" Ruby noticed the punctured suitcase and all the clothes spilling onto the floor. She crouched down and touched

Mom's cheek, causing her to jerk her head to the side, trying to get away.

"Ouch, careful."

Ruby dropped her hand at Mom's disdain.

"That hurts." She grimaced as Auntie Lori chuckled in the corner.

"Geez, Lynette. We leave you alone for an hour, and you find yourself trapped in your old bedroom."

"I can't get up. I need help."

"Is it your arthritis?" Auntie Lori asked.

"Yeah, I was blessed with Mom's genes, I guess."

Mom smirked and Auntie Lori laughed. "Do we need to get you a lifeline, like we did for Mom?"

"What? Don't be ridiculous. Can you please help me?"

Auntie Lori and Ruby grabbed each of Mom's hands and yanked her forward. Mom stumbled, struggling to regain her footing, and she tripped into Ruby, pinning her against the wall. Ruby couldn't help but laugh at how old her mother suddenly appeared.

"Anytime."

Auntie Lori grabbed her shopping bags. "I've got to make some phone calls. I'll be back." She left the room and Ruby listened as her steps disappeared down the wooden stairs.

"Mom, are you okay?"

"Mm-hmm."

Ruby thought she heard her mom's voice crack behind her mumblings. "What were you doing in here?"

Pressing her lips forward, she touched her cheek. "I needed inspiration for the obituary, and I thought being in my old bedroom might inspire me. I didn't know I would get trapped."

Ruby couldn't help but giggle. "Well, the good news is, you got that suitcase open. Do you know what that is? I found it in the closet last night."

Mom shook her head. "No idea, but it has old clothes inside. The fabric prevented me from breaking my face or losing an eye."

"Want to check it out? It must be Mema's. It was locked, so I think it might have been precious to her. It's like finding a treasure chest, right? A treasure chest to the past, maybe."

Mom settled on the edge of the bed, and Ruby placed the suitcase and clothes between them. She pulled out clothes like a magician pulling a rabbit out of a hat.

Ruby retrieved a black blazer and a zap tingled up her arm. She dropped it quickly and spread it on the bed. "This is kind of cute," she said. "This is something I would wear." She slid the black jacket over her tank top, just as the lights flickered. Ruby admired herself in the full-length mirror. "I wonder why Mema has it."

Next, she pulled an enormous sun hat with a veil hanging off the edge. "Wow. Was this from Mema's wedding?"

Mom placed the hat on her head and the lights flickered again.

"That's so weird," Ruby said, gazing at the ceiling.

"Eh, this house is ancient. Maybe the lightbulb needs to be changed." She touched the rough veil and analyzed the intricate lacework. "I've never seen this before, but I recognize it from all the pictures. How do I look?" She pouted her lips at Ruby and Ruby pretended to snap a photo.

"Gorgeous."

Mom slid her hand in and pulled out an oversized maternity shirt with ruffles along the sleeves and neckline.

"Ew, this is the ugliest shirt I've ever seen. It looks like a tablecloth or curtains."

Mom furrowed her brows and checked the tag. "I don't recognize this shirt. It looks like something she would have worn when I was a kid. It says maternity. Huh, I wonder whose it is?" She slid the shirt over her head. "How do I look now?"

A pop sounded, and Ruby jumped.

"That light," Mom said, staring at the darkened globe hanging from the ceiling. "Ruby, would you mind turning on the bedside lamp?"

She clicked on the light and pressed her hand against her chest. "That scared me."

"We'll have to call an electrician. I hope it's nothing major."

"You look like you're wearing a tent. Take it off. I can't even look at you in that thing." Ruby laughed and held up her hands like she was stopping traffic.

Mom pulled the shirt over her head and placed it on the floor.

"There's one more." Ruby felt around in the box, and a rough, scratchy fabric rubbed against her skin. "It feels like a Brillo pad." She pulled out a hunter green dress with a long white ribbon sewed into the neckline. "What in the world?" Three buttons ran down the front and a white attached belt hung from the waist.

The radiator hissed to life.

"Okay, that looks like something from the eighties," Lynette surmised.

"How old were you in the eighties?" Ruby asked.

"Eh, teenage years."

Ruby grabbed the dress and held it up against her body. "This is actually kind of cute. The material feels scratchy, but I wonder if this'll fit. I could wear it in honor of Mema to her wake. Do you think that's disrespectful?"

"You know what they say. Fashion comes around every few decades. It's a dark enough color for the event. It's warm. Yeah, you can try it."

Ruby brought the old dress to her nose and inhaled, searching for remnants of Mema's perfume, but all she smelled was dust and time. Checking the tag, she couldn't find cleaning instructions. "I do want to wear this. If I drop it off at the dry cleaners, do you think it'll be ready for the services?"

"Three days from now? Maybe, but I would go today. You might be cutting it close."

Ruby hopped up and kissed Mom's cheek. Her heart slowed, and she pulled back, looking at Mom's tired eyes. She knew Mom loved her, but she didn't know how to bridge the gap that had grown since she left.

"Mom, I'm sorry, for before. For leaving and never contacting you. That was crappy of me, and selfish, and I shouldn't have done that." *Gosh, that was hard to say.*

Mom's hard eyes softened for a moment and a sad smile crept up her lips. "Thank you. It's not quite water under the bridge, but at least a stream is trickling."

Unsure of what she meant, Ruby hugged her. "Auntie Lori is busy on the phone, I think. Can you take me to the cleaners? You rented a car, right?"

Mom held out her hand and Ruby pulled her from the bed. "Sure. Let me grab my shoes."

When Ruby was a kid, she and Mom used to drive around and listen to the radio to pass the time. It was the only time they talked about friends and school. By avoiding eye contact, Ruby found it easier to speak her mind without being judged.

On the ride to the cleaners, the two women sat in silence. For something that had been natural and comfortable a decade before now ignited their painful past. There was a lot to say, but neither seemed able to start.

Chapter 11

By the time Lynette pulled away from the cleaners, Ruby was humming a cheerful tune.

"It sure is pretty out here." Ruby said.

"Mm-hmm." Lynette peered out the top half of the windshield and looked at the blue sky. "Not a cloud in sight." She faced her daughter and asked, "What's it like in California?" It was an honest question—no snark, no animosity, just pure interest.

Ruby thought for a moment and flipped her hair past her shoulder. "You know that movie Groundhog Day? It's kind of like that. Every day is nice. Warm, sunny, no rain ever. But it's so busy you rarely stop and appreciate the beauty. Life is in constant motion, so it feels like you're doing something wrong if you're sitting down or aren't working four jobs."

Perking up at the opportunity to get to know her adult-sized daughter, Lynette treaded carefully. "Is it expensive out there?" Lynette focused on her driving, knowing she was bordering on being the nosy mom.

"Yes, so expensive. I live in a five hundred square foot apartment with another woman, Shayla. Thankfully, we have our own bedrooms, but there's only one bathroom, and my bedroom's the size of our pantry back home in Chicago."

"Do you regret moving out there? It sounds like a hard life." She kept her eyes on the road to avoid confrontation by asking too many questions.

"It's hard. There's so much pressure to always look beautiful and happy. The industry is competitive, so I've been hanging onto this Jolie Belle contract like it's my life raft to success. But I do like it out there. The weather is to die for and I've found a good friend in my roommate."

Lynette's heart warmed when Ruby opened up and shared something about her secret life. "Is modeling for that company your full-time job?" She didn't want to sound too intrusive, so she added, "I hope you're finding time to enjoy your twenties."

"No, that's a side gig, but I've been trying to use it as a stepping stone to other contracts. And yes, I enjoy my twenties." Ruby giggled. "I'm fine," she rushed.

Lynette glanced at her daughter. "Are you dating anyone?"

Ruby's large blue eyes met Lynette's and for a moment Lynette saw the ten-year-old girl with pigtails who wanted to grow up and be a horse groomer.

"No, I don't have time for that."

Did Lynette sense an air of sadness? She hoped not. She wanted to ask how she had handled the divorce, but these last two minutes were enough for one interaction. The last thing she wanted was for Ruby to shut down or shut her out.

"Well, maybe one day," Ruby added.

Lynette opened the driver's side door and exited the car. The scent of chilly air rushed into her lungs and Ruby hugged her cardigan closer to her body. "Winter's coming," Lynette said.

Walking into the warm house, she found Loretta at the dining room table surrounded by notebooks, bills, and Mom's old Rolodex. For the first time since Lynette found out her mother had passed, she felt grateful that Mom hadn't named her the executor of the estate.

"Auntie Lori, do you need anything?" Ruby asked.

Without glancing up, Loretta adjusted her glasses and shook her head no.

Ruby crept out of the room and Lynette settled next to her sister. "Hey sis, do you want some help?"

"I feel a mess. Like a complete mess. I haven't been home to visit in what feels like forever, and Mom didn't know she was going to die. I can't find any of her documents or her checkbook or bank statements. I have this pile here of mail that needs to be opened, and I can't access her accounts." Loretta removed her glasses and wiped her eyes.

"What can I do to help?"

"I don't know. Nothing. I need the obituary submitted, so if you haven't finished that yet, please get that done."

Like a child scolded for not doing her homework, Lynette slinked away to her old bedroom. The notebook she had been jotting in lay next to the opened and emptied suitcase.

Ruby leaned into the mirror, reapplying her makeup. "What are you doing, Mom?" she asked.

Lynette smiled at the word *mom*. She hadn't heard Ruby say that word in years. Not realizing how much she had missed being a mom, she bit her lip to stop the emotion from betraying her nonchalance. "Finishing the obituary. Do you want to help?"

The two women sat side by side, recalling the positive characteristics of Penny Waller.

"She loved to cook," Ruby said.

"And she loved her tea. Tea and talking, that's what she did all day."

"She loved helping people...even if they didn't need or want help. Remember when she gave that stranger a ride home from the movies? Why would she do that? That's so dangerous. I think I was six or seven." Ruby's eyes enlarged as she recalled the memory.

Lynette fought a grin. "I was so mad at her that day." Her smile vanished and her eyes turned to Ruby. "What she did was dangerous, putting a young girl in danger like that. What was she thinking?" Like

61

a switch, the humor in the situation from almost twenty years before turned dark and angry. "She would do these things, you know? Just off the wall decisions that put people in danger. It was like you never knew who you were going to get. And sometimes she didn't know how her actions affected others. It was like she was living in her own perfect world, and no matter what people said or did, she was going to do it her way."

"She definitely beat to a different drummer. Maybe we could say she was spontaneous. That would be a good spin on emotional and impulsive, right?"

Lynette wrote the word down in her notebook. "When we were little, she'd lock us out of the house."

"What? Child services would be called if she did that today."

"Yeah, my dad was working, and she wanted us outside. She'd send Loretta and I outside for something. Maybe to take the trash out, maybe to put something in the car. Whatever it was, she'd immediately lock the door and tell us to find something to do until dinner."

Ruby narrowed her eyes. "Are you serious?"

"Yeah. It became a running joke, but I hated it. I was always afraid I did something to make her mad. As her granddaughter, you only saw her at her best, but she could be malicious. And locking us out was just one example."

"Wow. I can't picture it. What did Papa say?"

"Nothing. He was so burned out from work. He'd come home well after Loretta, Mom, and I ate dinner, excuse himself to his bedroom to change, and come downstairs for a microwaved plate. Unless it was Sunday dinner, he ate leftovers alone."

"Wow. Okay, how can we spin that? How about driven? Or motivated?"

Lynette laughed. "Yeah, I'd say motivated. Motivated to be in control." She read the words on the page. "I think I have enough.

It's just an obituary, not a eulogy. I'll summarize her early life, married life, and death with a few characteristics thrown in. Here, help me up. I'm too old." She held out her hand, and Ruby pulled, like a child pulling a wagon.

"Hey, Mom? Why did you and Mema stop talking? I mean, I know you weren't close when we lived in Chicago, but why'd you cut her out of your life?"

Lynette scrunched her nose and shifted her weight from one foot to the next. "You know, that's a good question. After my divorce, I no longer cared about what your grandmother or anyone else thought. She was mentally exhausting me, and I needed to focus on me without her voice chirping in my ear, telling me every decision I made was wrong." There was no sense telling Ruby it had actually started when she left for California.

Ruby's face fell and Lynette noticed regret glistening behind her pupils. She threw her arms around Lynette's neck and a small sob escaped Lynette's mouth. She had been dreaming of this moment for three years.

"I'm sorry you went through that," Ruby said.

Lynette didn't know what she was referring to and didn't ask for clarification. It didn't matter. "You know, she didn't want me to move away with your father. I did it anyway, and that was when the foundation fractured. The divorce was the final nail in the coffin, so to speak."

"I never knew. I'm sorry, Mom."

Lynette waved the notebook and left the room. "It's not your concern, honey. She was a good grandma. Probably a better grandma than mother. I promise it will be a positive obituary."

A reassuring wink led to Ruby's apprehensive smile. "I'd love to read it when you're done."

Lynette gave herself ten minutes to summarize her mother's life and death. It was generic, but complete, and despite its lack of detail, Lynette was proud she had pulled it together. The final product eliminated the moments that shaped her past, and she had once again reverted to the obedient daughter.

Chapter 12

After Mom had retreated to her room, Ruby struggled to comprehend the stories she had shared. She remembered the hitchhiker and how Mema welcomed him into their car with open arms. Ruby had understood Stranger Danger, and she wondered if Mema was exempt because she was an adult. Papa had been home, working in the yard, and he appeared unfazed. He always said things like, "You make friends everywhere you go," as if picking up a hitchhiker was a normal activity.

But as they drove the man home, Ruby had positioned herself by the car door and placed her hand close enough to the door handle to ensure a quick escape if needed. She avoided accidentally putting pressure on the handle, terrified she would fly out onto the highway.

Her heart had pounded in her ears and she felt the heat rise from her belly, but she misplaced fear with excitement. Her mom and dad would never pick up a hitchhiker, even if he wasn't a stereotypical hitchhiker with the thumb pointing toward the sky. This guy needed a ride, and for whatever reason, Mema thought it was safe. Maybe she'd seen him around.

Ruby had forgotten about that experience until that conversation with Mom, and with it came a series of emotions she had buried and forgotten. As an adult, Ruby looked back on that memory, recognizing its danger and the fear it produced within her. Mom had every right to be upset, and her reaction made Ruby feel like maybe Mom unconditionally loved her after all.

Shaking the feeling that maybe her grandmother was someone she didn't know or fully understand, Ruby walked into the kitchen and sat beside Auntie.

"What was it like living with Mema?" Ruby asked.

Auntie Lori removed her glasses and leaned against her bent wrist. "What do you mean?"

"I don't know. I have lots of memories with her, but now that I'm older, some of them seem out of character. Like the time she picked up the hitchhiker."

"Oh yeah. Your grandmother wore many faces. Sometimes she was serious, sometimes impulsive. Sometimes we were afraid of her, and other times she comforted us when we cried."

Ruby fingered the placemat. "Why do you think she was so unpredictable?"

Auntie Lori tilted her head for a moment. "Aren't we all? I mean, think of all the phases in your life. The good, the bad, and the ugly. As you grow and mature, you may behave in different ways to the same situation. I think life was hard for her. Sometimes I got the impression she never wanted to be a mother."

"Yeah?"

"But one thing she had was love. And your grandfather loved her with all his heart. His love is really what kept our family together."

Papa died when Ruby was thirteen. His memories had faded over the years, and an achiness settled on her heart.

"I miss them." Ruby wiped below her eyes.

"Me too, sweetie." Auntie Lori pointed to a stack of boxes under the dining room table, remaining fully engaged in whatever pile of paper she had found. "Want to help me with the collage?"

The scattered photos filled a variety of boxes and Ruby rummaged through, pulling out the ones that hadn't yellowed from decades of neglect. "Auntie, how many pictures do I need?"

"Eh, I don't know. Maybe forty? Thirty? Enough to cover a poster board."

With each woman responsible for some job related to the services, Ruby took her role seriously. She looked at every photo and made three piles: Mema, Maybe Mema, and Definitely Not Mema. As she emptied and analyzed the second box, she ended up with a small stack of keepers and a mountain of unusable photos.

Placing the pictures into a large Ziplock bag, Ruby dropped them on the table next to Auntie Lori. "Done."

Auntie threw her arms around her and squeezed. "Thank you. Your grandmother would've loved that you picked out these photos. And you saved me hours of work."

"I don't know if it's her, though. Some pictures are in rough shape."

Auntie Lori threw up her hands. "Oh, don't worry. I'll flip through them when I'm done, and you can arrange them later."

Mom trampled down the stairs with a ripped piece of paper covered in writing on both sides. "Mom's obituary is done," she announced.

"Thanks." Auntie Lori didn't so much as glance at the paper as it dropped onto the table.

"Can I read it?" Ruby asked, picking up the paper. Lines of scribbles, streaks of whiteout, and doodles in the margin decorated the page.

"Yeah, of course." Mom sat beside Ruby, leaning over her shoulder. "I did my best."

Ruby read the obituary to herself and smiled at all the amazing things her grandmother had been.

Penelope Waller (nee: Southby) was born on April 19, 1942, in North Eagleton, Maine, where she lived a full life taking care of her family and volunteering in the community.

Penny, as known by her friends and family, was a spontaneous, dedicated woman who loved her family and her husband. After her husband passed away in 2013, Penny threw herself into community service to help those in need throughout her community. She volunteered at the food pantry, organized coat drives, and was an active member at the senior center. Penny had a heart of gold and only wanted to help others.

She is predeceased by her high school sweetheart and husband, Harry, and survived by her two daughters, Loretta (Oceanside, FL), Lynette (South Haven, Illinois), and granddaughter Ruby (Los Angeles, California).

"Hey, Mom, no mention of Dad?"

"Eh, no."

Her services will be held on...

"Auntie Lori, when are the services again?"

"The wake is Thursday evening from four to six and the funeral is Friday morning at ten." She shuffled the pile of papers and pulled her glasses to the top of her head.

"Mom, I'll write that in for you." Ruby grabbed a pen and filled in the information. *In lieu of flowers, donations to Southeast Food Bank are encouraged.* "You did a great job. I think that sums it up well."

"You know, you, me, and Auntie Lori are her next of kin. I think we all should go up and speak on her behalf. Would you be okay with that? Loretta? Would you do that?" Mom looked at each of them and held their eyes.

"Fine. It doesn't have to be long, does it?" Loretta asked.

"No, just a few minutes."

A sour taste rose from Ruby's stomach and it churned like a small tornado ready to touch down. Public speaking wasn't really her thing, but it was her grandmother. She swallowed and gave her mom the most confident smile she could muster. "Sure."

Chapter 13

That night, the three women stood in the dining room where mountains of paper occupied every surface.

"I submitted the obituary.   It's running tomorrow." Lynette's voice couldn't hide her fatigue any longer.

"Thank you, sis. You did a great job."

Ruby's eyes danced between Mom and Auntie and she exited to the kitchen. "Anyone want a drink?" she yelled.

The two older women declined and Ruby returned with one glass of wine.

"Wine?" Lynette asked. "Since when do you drink wine?" It was a strange sight to see her daughter, always perceived as her baby, partaking in adult activities like drinking alcohol. Lynette leaned her head on her hand and fiddled with the tablecloth, staring at her daughter.

"Since I turned twenty-one." Ruby's curt response jerked Lynette back, and she bit her tongue from saying more.

Loretta changed the subject. "What time does Anthony come?"

"Who knows?"

The last time Lynette had seen Anthony was almost two years ago when the judge divided their possessions. Lynette got the house and Anthony got the cottage on the lake.

Lynette had simmered with anger for almost a year. Her daughter had left her and then her husband found a newer model. He completely uprooted the last leg of her life and suddenly she was standing on a pile of rubbish. Ruby was gone, Mom was a stranger, and Loretta had pulled away like a train rushing to the next station. She tried to focus on work but could barely keep up with the day-to-day responsibilities. She marked her life on paper with a giant red 'F', grateful Ruby hadn't witnessed her failing.

"He's not staying here, is he?" Loretta asked.

Lynette shook her head. "He'll probably stay at that fancy new hotel overlooking the marina." Sullenness emerged at the edges of her words; another reminder that he had sacrificed nothing. *Money and a new wife? Life couldn't be better.* "Ruby, how are you feeling about seeing your dad and his new wife?" She tried to keep her voice even, but the last word came out shaky.

Biting her bottom lip and picking at her cuticles, Ruby said, "Nervous."

"This is your first time, right?"

She nodded her head and leaned back. "Yeah, he offered to buy my plane ticket to the wedding, but I'd just started a new job. Plus, I was still mad at him for leaving you."

Lynette's head jerked up, her stomach churning at the memory of being alone in that big house, not knowing where her daughter was or whose bed her husband was sleeping in. "I wish you had contacted me," she whispered.

"I know." Ruby dropped her eyes to her hands and when their eyes connected again, Lynette saw a dam of water. "I'm a terrible daughter."

Without thinking, Lynette hugged her and breathed in her hair. "No, no," she said. "You are a great daughter on your own journey. Your job isn't to worry about me, but my job is to worry about you. And I've never stopped. I'm so glad you're here."

A sad smile pulled across Ruby's lips. "Thanks, Mom."

"Hey, I'm going to bed." Lynette kissed Ruby on her forehead, inhaling the scent of her cucumber melon shampoo. "You should too. We have a busy couple of days."

"You're right. I could use a good sleep. Night." Ruby placed her mug in the sink and gathered her belongings.

"Night. Sweet dreams and don't let the bed bugs bite." It was what Lynette said every night when Ruby was a child.

Quiet as a mouse, Ruby disappeared to the second floor.

"You have to watch out for her," Loretta said.

"I know." Shame at letting her anger prevent her from being there for her daughter seeped up from Lynette's neck. "I haven't been the best mom."

"Oh, please. You've been a mom. There is no good or bad. You did the best you could."

"I'm still upset you've been in touch with her all these years, Loretta." Tears pricked at Lynette's eyes. "I was a wreck, not knowing where she was. It was the tipping point between Anthony and me. He wanted to find her, and I was angry. It led to a fracture in our marriage that grew and grew until it was a precipice we could no longer traverse."

"Look at you with this lyrical language. You're definitely an English teacher," Loretta joked.

"I'm serious. Our relationship fractured before she left, but not severed. Now we're completely broken. He's moved on, and I'm just stuck in the same place I was when he left. And I couldn't even go to you. I tried, but you never returned my calls." Lynette slumped in her seat and rearranged the papers on the table.

"I'm sorry. I couldn't lie to you, and your relationship with Ruby was precarious. I asked Mom what to do, and she said to let it be and things would work out."

Wincing, Lynette rubbed her head. "Ouch. Mom knew? And you listened to her? That hurts. Since when did you ever listen to her?"

Loretta walked around the table and sat next to Lynette, their knees kissing. "I'm sorry. I really am."

"And Anthony knew," Lynette interrupted.

"If I could go back and do things differently, I wouldn't have ignored you and I would have told you. Because we weren't talking, I didn't know how desperate you were to find her. I was wrapped up in my life, and it was wrong."

Frozen and numb, Lynette didn't look at her. She couldn't. A pebble had formed in her throat, preventing her from breathing and swallowing. All the pain from the past three years rushed back at her like a tsunami, forcing her into a place where she needed to stop fighting in order to survive.

The only sound in the room was the ticking of the grandfather clock, loud and consistent. Lynette counted the clicks until ten seconds had passed and then she stood. Her heavy, stiff legs moved like wooden stilts as she excused herself from the room. "Good night, Loretta. I'll see you in the morning."

Like two acquaintances passing in the supermarket, Lynette left her sister to finish whatever still needed to be done. The past twenty-four hours had sent Lynette reeling to a place she didn't want to feel or experience again, so she did what she always did when uncomfortable. She left the conversation, stuck her head in the sand, and ignored it.

Stretching under the blankets, Lynette closed her eyes and listened to the muffled movements of her sister downstairs until she drifted off. One minute she was sleeping, and then she woke with a start. Her heart raced and her brain struggled to differentiate reality from the dream she'd just escaped from. All the images flashed before her. Lynette saw an image of Mom and Dad on their wedding. Mom wore that veil Lynette had found in the suitcase and her dress stretched around her midsection. *Was she pregnant? Wait, but Mom wasn't pregnant when she got married, was she?*

An image of Granny Southby's scowl, followed by Grandpa Southby's prim and proper stance, then Mom crying, and finally Dad smiling raced around her. In her dream, a giant bed moved toward her, blocking her view from the images, and the phrase, **You made your bed, now you must lie in it** etched in the background.

Nothing made sense, yet the emotions in her dream felt so real. Lynette woke feeling desperation and disappointment. She tried to piece together the images, but she couldn't differentiate what was real or fake. Was it truly a dream, or did she pull in stories she'd heard and pictures she'd seen to adjust the narrative?

An unsettled feeling came over her, and Lynette rubbed her eyes. She needed more sleep, less stress, and a time out from her life. Perhaps her brain was telling her she needed a break. *Yes, that must be it.*

Lynette climbed out of bed and snuck into the kitchen to make a cup of coffee. Outside, she inhaled the mixture of pine and salt water. Alone with her thoughts, Mom's distraught and pregnant image creeped into Lynette's mind. It was her wedding day, but not the joyous day Mom and Dad had painted throughout Lynette's life. Puzzled, she sipped her coffee, convincing herself it was just a dream.

Chapter 14

Ruby had loved Mema's quiet house when she was younger but now it made her itchy, constantly reminding her she wasn't in L.A. anymore. Over the past three years, she'd learned to love the sounds of sirens, cars honking, and ocean waves. Silence in L.A. didn't exist, and the constant noise soothed her like a hot cup of chamomile tea.

As a child, Ruby fell asleep to the sounds of Mema cleaning the kitchen after a large home-cooked meal, and the sounds of Papa snoring in the stuffed recliner downstairs. The comforting sounds had lulled Ruby to sleep and kept her safe when she was away from her mom and dad.

Laying in Mom's old bed, Ruby tossed and turned, struggling to rest her tired eyes. First, she focused on the sound of the wind blowing up against the house like a looming nor'easter, and then she focused on the pattering of feet downstairs. Auntie Lori didn't seem to sleep much, and although it wasn't quite the same as Mema and Papa's familiar sounds, it was better than silence.

Mom had retreated to bed hours before. Throughout the last twenty-four hours, a mixture of emotions had spun inside Ruby like a vintage washing machine. Seeing Mom again could have softened or hardened her, and at this moment, Ruby wasn't sure which way she wanted to go. Even though she missed her parents, she never quite got the feeling they supported her the way she needed.

Mema was the only one who pushed her to follow her heart, despite the consequences.

Ruby thought about Jolie Belle and the photoshoot she was missing in a few days. She had reached out to her agent, explaining this was a onetime occurrence and it wouldn't happen again. Not having that money put next month's rent in jeopardy, but when Auntie Lori called, she had no choice. She had to come home and say goodbye.

Although the modeling world never stopped, her life had stalled for the next week, and Ruby wasn't sure she'd have a job when she returned. She had signed a contract when they first brought her on, but did she read it? Of course not. All she cared about was that she was representing one of the biggest fashion companies of the year.

Her mind a jumbled mess, Ruby glanced at the clock on her phone and groaned. She threw the covers off and then tossed the throw over her legs. *What am I doing with my life?* She didn't know, but she needed to sleep before tomorrow's craziness began. Her mind went dark, and a void surrounded her. Ruby welcomed sleep with open arms.

Blackness transitioned to a light show, and images popped at Ruby like an amusement park funhouse. Mom and Auntie Lori as teenagers, Mema and Papa as parents, and an argument. Mema scolding Mom for her outfit and Mom's clothes morphing into the same outfit Auntie Lori wore. Looking like twins, they twirled until the house disappeared and a car surrounded them. Mema stroked Papa's arm, meowing like a cat. Papa barked like a dog. The car ride faded and refocused to a house party. Mom and Auntie Lori sat on a couch and all the adults resembled paper dolls. Mema stood in the center wearing the green wool dress, looking like a pageant queen. As she ate a hot dog, the ketchup dripped down her top and then disappeared. The party people slowed, and the couch transitioned back into the car. The words **Janice** and **Weaver** bounced from side to side. The words disappeared out the cracked window. The car filled with mist and blackness returned.

When Ruby opened her eyes, the sun beams warmed her face through the open window. She rolled over with a smile across her lips. For a moment, she thought she was still in California, but the rustic bed and wooden floor reminded her she was waking on the other side of the country. She rubbed her eyes and stretched her arms.

What a baffling dream Ruby had. She wondered if her grandmother had come to her last night in her dream or if the stress over the last few days had gotten to her. It made little sense, but it had to mean something.

Ruby grabbed a piece of paper and jotted down the details before they disintegrated from her memory. Maybe it was just a dream, but it felt so real, Ruby believed there was some level of truth behind it. She looked around the room, imagining the potential this room had and the secrets it carried.

When she was twelve, she dreamed of being a model like Kendall Jenner. Kendall was only a few years older than Ruby, and Ruby had watched her grow on reality tv. *If Kendall can do it, so can I*, Ruby had told herself.

Her freshman year of high school was a year of self-discovery, where boys were the only thing that occupied her mind. She stared at posters of Jake and Edward facing off for Bella Swan every night before bed, dreaming of finding the man who would fight for her.

Ruby had never thought about her mom as a teenager. She had always been the over-organized, uptight, safe woman who questioned everything. Ruby assumed that was what led her parents to divorce. Dad couldn't take it anymore, and Ruby couldn't blame him. Mom easily suffocated the people she loved.

Climbing out of bed, she padded downstairs to find Auntie Lori slumped over the dining room table with the forever growing piles of paper.

"Morning." Ruby sat beside her and watched her work. She hoped she never was the one responsible for organizing someone's life after death. It seemed like a never-ending cycle of stress.

"Morning. How'd you sleep?" Auntie Lori didn't raise her eyes, but continued examining old bills and documents. "Your grandmother kept everything, but not in an organized way. I feel like a detective trying to fit together the pieces to close out her life."

It sounded so businesslike and impersonal. "I slept okay. I had the weirdest dream."

"Oh yeah? What about?"

Ruby grabbed a croissant from the Pyrex container Kate had delivered the day before. "I don't even know. It had you and Mom and Mema and Papa. We all ended up at a Christmas party together. I can't really remember."

Auntie Lori hmmm'd noncommittally and returned to the documents.

"Do you think Mema was in pain when she died?"

"I'm sure she was terrified. She'd been laying on the ground for about three hours with a broken hip. I think when Kate found her, she was delirious and nearly unconscious."

Ruby watched the tears fill Auntie's eyes, and a large pit formed in Ruby's throat, making it hard to breathe. "I'm sorry. For asking."

Auntie sniffed. "It's okay. It's just so sad. I hate that she was alone for so long."

The heaviness in the air settled between them, and Auntie went back to sorting the papers. "Is your mom still sleeping?"

The gooey chocolate hiding inside the flaky dough smeared across Ruby's lips and a jolt of sugar zapped her awake. "This is so good. Better than coffee. And I don't know. I haven't seen her."

Right on cue, Mom walked through the door looking like a librarian. She wore a white button down top tucked into a black pencil skirt. Her feet nestled in black flats, and her hair rested in a low ponytail. Maybe not a librarian, but like a college professor. She looked like she was going to work.

"Morning Mom. Where are you off to?"

Lynette smoothed down her shirt and poured herself a petite cup of coffee. "Auntie Lori asked if I would secure a place for us to eat after the burial. I was going to head into the harbor and see if any restaurants overlooking the marina had availability. Want to come?"

Ruby looked around. "No, thanks. I might take this time to be alone. I have a lot on my mind."

"I'll be back in a few hours, then." Mom kissed Ruby atop her head and grabbed a croissant before leaving the house.

Ruby considered Mom's past. Maybe she had always wanted to set her own rules, but she learned early on she needed to obey. Obedience meant no conflict. And if there was no conflict, maybe things would never become uncomfortable.

"Auntie Lori?"

"Hmm?"

"How would you describe my mom?"

Auntie Lori took off her glasses and rubbed her eyes. "Dedicated, hardworking, and kind. Why?"

Ruby reflected on her dream and how Mom tried to wear clothes that didn't match her parents' expectations. "Was she always a rule follower?"

"Always."

"Why?"

"I don't know, honey. Maybe because I was such a rule-breaker. She saw firsthand how much strife I caused my parents, and she didn't want to do the same. Maybe she was jealous of all the attention I got as a kid—even though it wasn't positive. Maybe she felt that if she was perfect and did whatever was asked of her, she'd make people proud."

Ruby sat back and curled her fingers around her plate, analyzing the gooey frosting that smeared along the edges. "Do you think she regrets being so passive?"

"Maybe."

"I wonder if that's why her and I butt heads."

Auntie Lori's round blue eyes stared into Ruby's. "You're a good kid, you know. When you got into your teenage years, your interests developed away from hers and she couldn't connect with you as she once had." Her hands flew up to her chest in apology. "Just my opinion. Take it with a grain of salt."

Ruby swallowed and played with the swirl of chocolate. She licked the tip of her finger, savoring the taste.

"You broke free from her expectations and she didn't know what to do about that. It's natural. You're your own person and are now an adult. We don't live for our parents, but I think your mom thought if she did what our parents wanted, she'd automatically be in good graces. And life doesn't work that way, does it?"

They sat in silence, with Ruby staring out the patio door and Auntie Lori digging through papers. "What are you looking for?"

"Ah, I don't know. Anything of importance. Bank accounts, last will and testament, mortgage statements. It's all here in this mess. It'll take years to sort through with the lawyers, so nothing that can't wait until tomorrow." She pushed the papers to the middle of the table and her kind eyes warmed Ruby. "What are you up to today?"

"I don't know. Maybe I'll walk downtown, grab a coffee, and check out the shops. There has to be a bookstore down there, right?"

"That old bookshop with the café inside is still here. Cozy for sure. You should check it out."

Ruby kissed Auntie on the forehead and went upstairs to shower. A quick trip to the bookstore was exactly what she needed.

Chapter 15

Lynette traveled the twenty-minute car ride into Portland, lost in her own thoughts, and contemplating her dream from the previous night. Logical by nature, Lynette didn't believe in ghosts or spirits or people 'living' between worlds. No, when you die, you die. You go into the ground and are no longer here, and the people you leave behind learn how to live without you. It was cause and effect, and it made sense.

Even so, she couldn't shake the bride and groom and the pregnant belly. Nothing made sense. Loretta was born years after her parents married, so the dream was just that. A dream.

Lynette didn't understand how the hat and veil combo ended up in her dream. She tried it on for a moment, so why did it leave such an impression on her subconscious? She shook her head again. *You're tired. Overtired, overwhelmed, and in mourning.*

The Fresh Catch came into view, with its outside terrace overlooking the docks. Lynette knew not everyone liked seafood, but they must have other options, right? She recalled a few meals here with her parents when they first opened. Lynette had just graduated with an English degree and a dream of becoming a writer. She had spent the previous four years in Providence and came home every few months with her then long-term boyfriend, Anthony. This was the place her parents took them to celebrate her graduation.

Although closed to the public, she had made an appointment with Daniel, the new owner. Lynette had been out of town for so long, she hadn't stayed up to date with the local gossip, and didn't know if 'new' meant last month or last year.

A bell above the door rang as Lynette walked toward the hostess stand. Waiting, she looked around the unfamiliar space, not recognizing anything from the restaurant she remembered. Maybe she needed to find a new restaurant, or maybe it didn't matter, because her mother was dead. She needed a place with good food to feed family and friends, and this place had plenty of space.

A man with thick salt-and-pepper hair stepped through a swinging door from the back and Lynette's heart thudded. Unsure of why she had such a visceral reaction, she leaned on the podium to get a better look. Those eyes reminded her of someone, but she couldn't place who.

"Hello." He stuck out his hand and Lynette grasped it, noticing the callous skin and strong fingers. "Daniel Holmes."

Like a moth too close to a flame, Lynette dropped her hand. "Hello, Daniel. Lynette Franklin." She knew he wouldn't know her married name and hoped he didn't recognize her eyes. He'd stared into them long enough; they probably branded his heart. His gaze held hers for a moment too long and he ushered her to a table overlooking the water.

"First of all, I'm sorry for your loss." Always such a gentleman.

A heaviness flowed around Lynette as reminders of Mom and their current state presented themselves in every situation. Lynette's voice quivered, and she squared her shoulders. "Thank you. The funeral is on Friday and we're looking for a place to hold the reception. My mother frequented this place often, and with it next to the ocean, we felt it would be a good place to say goodbye." She kept her responses short and straightforward.

Daniel pulled out a notebook. "How many people?"

Lynette sighed because she didn't know. "Maybe twenty? Thirty?

It's hard to say." She should have a better idea of what was going on, especially since she was the one who always knew the details about everything.

Daniel pulled out a catering menu, and Lynette's eyes bulged at the prices. She didn't want to appear shocked or cheap, so she bit her tongue, swallowed her dismay and smiled. "Let's do one pasta dish, one chicken dish, and one seafood dish." She scanned the contents. "Fettuccine Alfredo, baked chicken with green beans, and baked cod with spinach. Perfect." If Loretta didn't like it, she could come down here and make the changes.

"Okay, and what is your name, your number, and the name of the deceased?"

Lynette knew she should have left when she recognized him, but she hadn't. She rattled off her name and number and when she got to her mother's name, a flash of recognition passed between his eyes. *Shoot.*

"Linnie?"

Lynette turned her shoulders away from Daniel, forcing the bile to stay down. "Yes." She heard the yearning behind her word, and her stomach tumbled with a desire for safety and familiarity.

He placed his hand on her arm, and his warm eyes drew her in like a magnet.

"I'm so sorry to hear about your mother. Why didn't you say something?"

So many words tumbled around Lynette's head and heart. She couldn't open a box that had tempted her many times throughout the years. There was no reason to dig up past regret. She didn't want to get hurt again or deal with the consequences of reliving the past. She had left this place a long time ago and never intended to return. "It seemed weird to bring up our past. My mom just died and you're a professional. I didn't want to deny you our business because you and I had a thing." By thing, she meant years of physical and emotional infatuation.

Daniel smiled his big toothy grin, and Lynette dropped her eyes, feeling a blush rise. Everything felt wrong. She was in mourning, not lust. She was here for her mother, not to reignite an old flame.

"You should have said hi," he said. "I should have recognized you sooner, but it's been what, over thirty years? Your voice sounded familiar, but I couldn't quite place it."

"Same." For the first time since she had arrived, a genuine smile crossed her face. "Do you think you can accommodate us?"

"Absolutely."

They finished up the order and Lynette stood to leave, but her wobbly legs stopped her. She grasped the chair back and regained her composure, hoping this, too, was a dream.

"Linnie, it was nice seeing you. And please send my condolences to your family."

Lynette waved the receipt in farewell and exited the restaurant. Her face dropped and big, fat tears rolled down her cheeks. Embarrassment wrapped itself in grief and heavy sobs shook her shoulders. Sitting in the parking lot for too many minutes, Lynette thought about her life and where things took a turn for the worse. Was it here? Or was it there?

The questions overwhelmed her and she drove home in silence, occasionally touching the menu Daniel had given her. Recalling his sweet eyes and soft smile, her emotions churned in a blender, and her confusion grew. Lynette couldn't quite figure out if her anguish was because she had lost her mom, Daniel, or her youth. Whatever it was, coming back here brought back too many memories she had wanted to forget.

Later that afternoon, Lynette sat with Loretta on their parent's three-season porch. The temperature had dropped and the leaves, once green and vibrant, were now painted with red, orange, and yellow hues creating a canopy of color. Lynette gazed through the storm windows, settling under her blanket.

"Tomorrow's the wake. Friday's the funeral, and Anthony comes tonight." Lynette slurped her spiked hot cocoa. Its warmth traveled down her esophagus in tiny waves, eventually reaching her toes.

"Yep. It'll all be over in less than two days."

Turning toward her sister, Lynette asked, "How have you been? Really been. I can't remember the last time we talked."

A small grin spread across Loretta's naturally bronzed face. "Florida's great. I left this version of me decades ago. Life in Florida isn't always sunshine and rainbows, but it's a hell of a lot better than here."

Lynette thought about her life in Chicago. Was Chicago-Lynette better than Maine-Lynette? She didn't know if there was a difference.

"How about you?" Loretta's blue eyes reached Lynette's and warmth overcame her body. It was honest sisterly concern that Lynette hadn't experienced in years.

"Uh, I guess okay. My life went to shit three years ago when Ruby left, but I've rebuilt it in a way that keeps me busy and keeps me out of trouble."

A slender hand rested on Lynette's. "You've never been in trouble, sissy. You've always taken the smoothly paved road. That's who you are, and that's what you do. You keep things even keel and steady. If you want exciting, you don't go to Lynette. You go to Lynette when you need a plan." Loretta pumped her arm, as if she were introducing Lynette as a candidate for president.

Lowering her eyes, Lynette watched a bug crawl across the floorboard. "Thanks. I guess."

"You know, I was always jealous of you when we were kids."

Lynette grunted at the ridiculousness her sister spewed. "What? Why?"

"Because Mom and Dad loved you more than me."

Lynette placed her mug on the coffee table. "What are you talking about? They did not. They gave you all their attention."

"I was the bad kid. The black sheep. The one that kept them up at night. You were the one they could lean on, the one they trusted." She grabbed Lynette's arm. "Do you remember that time I babysat you and they found out I had Mitch Donnely over? I got in so much trouble. You were two years younger than me, but after that, you were in charge any time they left."

"I hated obeying them all the time, but I think it's in my personality to be subservient. I wanted to be a leader like you, but didn't know how to break the mold. You never cared if you broke the rules or if people didn't like you."

Loretta adjusted the blanket over her legs, staring into the woods.

"All I wanted was acceptance and recognition," Lynette said.

Loretta leaned over and hugged her, her arms hanging loosely over Lynette's shoulders. "What happened after I left? You and mom used to be tight and then I find out you haven't spoken in years."

Rolling her eyes, Lynette leaned forward. "I told Mom no, and she didn't like it."

Cackling, Loretta raised her glass to clink. "Tell me more."

"It was when I met Anthony and his new job took him to Chicago. Mom didn't want me to go, but I went. She told me I was making the biggest mistake by leaving with him." Lynette raised her glass to the ceiling. "Cheers, Mom, you were right. Hear hear." She returned her gaze to her sister and continued. "She and I kept in touch over the phone a few times a year. Guarded by her judgment, I didn't share a whole lot. Then when Anthony left me, I couldn't go to her and listen to her 'I told you so,' so I never called her again."

"Damn, girl."

"By then, Dad was dead. Ruby had left. I tried to go to Mom when Ruby left, but Mom blamed her leaving on me, which was completely unfair. So, when Anthony left too, I was done."

"You know, I wish you had reached out to me during all that. I could have been there for you."

Lynette shook her head rapidly. "No, you couldn't. You were in Florida and I knew you and Mom talked often." Tears formed behind her eyes and she blinked them away. "I needed to walk this journey alone. Plus, you never called me and I got tired of reaching out to everyone."

"I didn't mean to hurt you," Loretta said. "You were always the preferred daughter. The one who made Mom and Dad proud. You seemed happily married, you had this beautiful child, lived in a gorgeous house. I was jealous that you got all the attention, so when we stopped talking, I didn't think about it. I was wrapped up in my life, and you were busy with yours."

Lynette dropped her mug on the table, the ceramic clanging against the coaster. "When my life went to shit, I fell into a deep depression. I couldn't get out of bed. I wasn't showing up for work and they put me on probation for six months. I had no one." She bit her quivering lip and rubbed her forehead. "That first year was the worst year of my life."

"I'm sorry, sis. I never meant to hurt you," she said again. "Do you understand why I pulled away?" Loretta blinked back the glassiness behind her eyes.

"I guess. Ruby, right?"

"Yes, I couldn't betray her trust. She felt alone and angry. She needed someone, and if something terrible ever happened, I promise I would have called you."

Lynette tried to reply, but a bitter laugh escaped. She rubbed the back of her neck, feeling her ribs tighten around her lungs. She had tried so hard to forget that terrible moment.

They sat side by side until the sun set behind the spectacular foliage, and a dark hue settled amongst the previously lit leaves. A light clicked on behind them and Ruby cozied up beside Loretta. "Hey, Mom. Hey, Auntie."

"I'm grabbing a snack. Be right back." Loretta left the porch, leaving Lynette alone with Ruby.

"Did you have a good day today?" Lynette asked.

"Uh, yeah. I went into town, got a coffee, and hung out in the bookstore."

"Bookstores are my happy place," Lynette mused.

"Mine too, although no one reads in L.A. so it's kind of like a lost cause. Mom, do you believe in ghosts?"

The tiny hairs on Lynette's arms prickled and poked against her cotton shirt. "I don't know. I never had before. Why?"

"Just wondering." Ruby settled back in her chair and Lynette thought about her dream.

Ruby's question hung in the air, with Lynette too afraid to ask more.

Chapter 16

A loud bang sounded in the kitchen, and Ruby sprinted through the house to see who had arrived. "Dad!"

Standing in front of the closed kitchen door stood a Hollywood-esque man wearing a black peacoat and an earbud in one ear. Behind him stood a petite woman with an apprehensive smile. Ruby recognized the upturned lips and smoky eyes from the wallet-sized wedding photo she'd received in her birthday card. It seemed Dad had traded in Mom for a younger wife.

He looked like a different person than the one she last saw three years before. His salt-and-pepper hair from three years ago had grown a few inches and turned black, from trips to the salon Ruby assumed. The ends curled slightly, and Ruby squinted, trying to decide if he had recently waxed his eyebrows. Instead of being closely shaven, he wore a neatly groomed beard and contacts had replaced his bifocals. He looked at least a decade younger.

"Rubenello!"

She hesitated in response to his childhood nickname for her, but leaned in and allowed him to embrace her.

"Is this Kai?" Ruby asked, glancing at the young woman next to him.

"Hi, nice to meet you." Her bird-like hand felt soft and malleable in Ruby's.

"Ruby. Congratulations on the wedding and everything. Sorry I couldn't make it."

An awkward pause settled between them, and Ruby kicked into hostess mode. "Tea? Coffee?" Without a response, she flipped on the teakettle and hurried to the coffeemaker to make a pot. "Take a seat. Mom and Auntie Lori are outside talking. They'll probably be in soon."

She watched Dad move throughout the kitchen, knowing where Mema housed all the necessary utensils. Retrieving the sugar bowl from the cabinet and some spoons from the drawer, he asked Kai if she wanted anything.

"No, Tony, I don't need anything right now."

At the word *Tony,* Ruby's body froze, and she furrowed her brows. She had never heard anyone call him Tony, not even close friends or family. This man that she was staring at was not the father she remembered. The father she remembered was overworked, underpaid, and underappreciated. He came home late at night in his suit and tie, a shell of a person. This person here was young in heart, vibrant, and laid-back.

Was it that easy to rewrite your future?

Ruby analyzed Kai from the corner of the kitchen, careful not to make eye contact. She drew a smile when caught staring. Kai looked like a nineties baby, Ruby decided. Somewhere between Ruby and Mom's age, Ruby understood Mom's disdain. She had been replaced by a younger woman with fewer wrinkles, more vibrancy, and untouched beauty. Kai's thick, curly, jet-black hair hung loosely around her face, and her petite frame was the exact opposite of Mom's broad shoulders, and tall build.

Ruby asked the right questions, inquiring about their life, dog, and work, and listened to them talk about a recent trip for Kai's twenty-year high school reunion, which confirmed her age as under forty. Ruby learned there were no children and Kai worked in advertising. Definitely in advertising, Ruby judged, scanning her smart shoes and freshly starched pants. Funny how Kai and Ruby could be work colleagues in a different life. Funnier, that Ruby wasn't doing anything with her career, and she wondered if Kai had ever wanted to model.

Checking her watch, Ruby slid out of the kitchen. "I'll be right back. I'm going to let Auntie and Mom know you're here."

Auntie Lori and Mom chuckled on the tiny sofa, fighting over the chenille blanket. The image warmed Ruby, and she wondered if maybe they could or would repair their relationship. "Hey, Mom," Ruby whispered. "Dad's here. With his new bride."

Lynette rolled her gigantic eyes and stood. The blanket dropped to the floor, and she stepped over it. "Thanks."

Back in the kitchen, the three women found Kai wrapped in Dad's arms.

"Ahem," Lynette announced.

Dad dropped his arms and stepped back, a smug smile emerging from his lips. Mom's face flushed, and she held her hands behind her back.

"Anthony," Mom said. "You look so...different." She gave him a weak hug and a slight wave to Kai. "I'm Lynette. You must be Kai. Nice to meet you." Ruby saw the angst in the lines of Mom's face and she fought an urge to hug Mom tight.

"You're here early," Auntie Lori said in an amicable-yet-accusatory way.

"Is that a problem?" Dad's voice cut through the room.

"No, no, not at all. Mom would have liked you here."

"Do you want a drink?" Mom pointed to the fridge. "We have water, beer, and soda. Coffee and tea." The coffee had stopped brewing and the familiar scent of hazelnut filled the room.

"I'm good. Kai?"

Kai stood beside him, her posture straight and narrow. She shook her head, looking at Mom.

No one spoke or moved. Auntie Lori widened her stance and leaned against the counter. "So, how've you been these past few years? How's the marriage? And the new wife?"

Kai's face pulled back, and Auntie smiled at her.

"Great." Dad didn't say more.

"You look good. I see you've been dyeing your hair." Auntie Lori's jab didn't weaken his confidence, and he ran his fingers through his thick mop.

"I see you haven't been dyeing yours," Dad retorted.

"Yeah, I've embraced my age."

Ruby didn't want to be privy to this exchange. She hadn't seen her father in a few years and she didn't understand why Auntie was being so rude. "Excuse me," she said, and hurried back to the porch to regain her composure.

She listened to the conversation ebb and flow in the kitchen. She occupied her mind by flipping through the magazines on the coffee table, but her ears remained attuned to the kitchen. Volume raised and lowered, and Auntie's voice carried the loudest. She didn't want to go in there, but she wanted the bickering to stop.

The door behind her clicked, and Dad stepped onto the porch. "Hey, can I sit with you?"

Ruby dropped the magazine and motioned to the seat beside her. "Sorry about them. It's been an emotional few days." She didn't know why she needed to excuse their bad behavior.

Dad leaned back, and crossed his leg over his knee. His pant hems rose above his socks, and Ruby saw green and red argyle escape from his ankle. "It's fine. I probably deserve it. Introducing your mother to Kai today of all days wasn't the smartest move."

Ruby looked toward the kitchen. "Where is Kai?" Panicked over Kai being alone with Auntie, Ruby considered rescuing her.

"She's fine. Believe it or not, your mom and aunt offered to go for a walk with her."

Ruby laughed. "Are you scared? Mom's in a fragile state."

Dad's smile lifted Ruby's mood. "Nah, Kai can handle it."

Ruby fiddled with her fingers, afraid to make eye contact with Dad. "Sorry about not going to the wedding. It...it wasn't a good time."

He placed his hand on her knee and she looked at him. Understanding, comfort, and possibly forgiveness looked back at her. "It's okay. You don't have to apologize."

Ruby didn't respond.

"I'm sorry I haven't been in touch," he said.

She waved her hands like it was no big deal. "The important thing is that you're here. You were in Mema's life for a long time."

Talking with Dad became easy after that. Dad had always been the easier parent. The more understanding parent who got her. They'd connected years ago over ice cream sundaes and rock collecting, which Mom had found frivolous and silly.

In the distance, a door slammed. "Looks like they're back," Ruby said.

The door to the porch swung open, and the intimate space became cramped. No one volunteered to cram on the small couch, so the three extra women stood in various corners.

Dad checked his watch and stood. "It's almost six. We should probably get going."

"Where are you staying?" Ruby asked.

"The Seaside Inn. The drive up was brutal."

The group transitioned to the kitchen, where Dad and Kai bid their farewells.

Mom raced to the door and grabbed his arm. "Thank you, Anthony, for coming. It means a lot to me."

He touched Mom's arm in sympathy, and a pained expression crossed Mom's face. Ruby hugged him, feeling his powerful arms and protective stance surround her. Like a gracious host, she hugged Kai, feeling her bony shoulder blades rub against Ruby's forearms.

Ruby watched them leave as the mood in the house shifted. Mom and Auntie, exhilarated from the past hour, jabbered like two teammates who won the match. Ruby didn't share in their excitement and excused herself for the night.

While in bed, she focused on the emotional blender from seeing Dad for the first time in years with his new wife. Breaking into heavy sobs, she allowed the weight of the world to crush her. She'd lost Mema, but did she find her parents? Ruby knew that bad moments eventually transitioned to good, but she'd lost Mema without saying goodbye. When her chest stopped heaving and the tears ceased to flow, Ruby asked Mema to stay with her and she fell into a peaceful sleep.

Chapter 17

The day of the wake came quicker than Lynette wanted. She took her time waking, unable to expel the heaviness holding her prisoner to her mother's former bed. She had made sure to drink enough liquor the night before to fall asleep before her demons could come out and play.

She moved downstairs in a fog and found Loretta sitting by the empty fireplace.

"Hey, sis."

"Hey, how'd you sleep?" Loretta's messy hair poked out at odd angles, and Lynette smiled at the newfound comfort they had with each other.

"Better than the night before. Do you need anything?"

Loretta handed Lynette a cup of coffee. "Nothing. Whatever we haven't done, we haven't done. It's no big deal. How are you feeling after seeing Anthony?"

Lynette sighed, with her ex-husband's sudden presence filling her mind. "God, it was so weird. He looks ten years younger, while I look ten years older. Maybe I need to find a man half my age. I bet that's his secret. Hot sex and no kids." The black, bitter coffee slid down her throat.

"You're way hotter than she is."

The corner of Lynette's lips rose, and she stifled a chuckle. "Yeah, she's the complete opposite of me, isn't she? Dark-haired, petite, wrinkle-free, pretty. No wonder he left me." The interaction with Anthony was short, but just long enough to remind Lynette of all her inadequacies. "You know, that was the first time I'd seen him in almost two years. I'm surprised he showed up for Mom, actually. I assumed when he divorced me, he divorced the entire family."

Loretta's deep eyes studied Lynette's face, and she moved to the couch to sit beside her sister. "He did it for you and Ruby. He may not be in love with you anymore, but he loves you and he loves his daughter. It's called respect, and even if he is a jerk, he still has respect for you and our family."

Lynette stared at the fireplace, watching the embers smolder orange and then turn black. "Sure."

"I mean, would you have gone to his mother's wake or funeral?"

"Yes, I would." The indignation in her voice surprised her. "But I wouldn't bring my new spouse. I'd leave him at the hotel."

Loretta narrowed her eyes. "Really?"

"Yes, really." Lynette rearranged her legs into a pretzel and tightened her ponytail. "Thank you for standing up for me."

"I love you," Loretta said. "And I owed you one."

Lynette let the words float around her. "Thank you." She audibly swallowed and checked her watch. "What time do we have to be at the wake?"

"Three."

They sat side by side in silence, lost in their own thoughts. Lynette didn't want to think about Anthony or Kai. She knew she had to face them tonight, but maybe they would drop in and drop out, like every other guest paying their respects. There was no reason for him to stay and mingle.

About an hour later, Ruby walked down the stairs in her pajamas. Her hair looked just as messy, and Lynette couldn't help but wonder how she had slept the night before. "Morning, honey. How are you?"

Ruby opened her mouth wide into an exaggerated yawn and flopped onto the couch. She leaned against Loretta; their obvious comfort would have bothered Lynette in the past, but today it put her at ease.

"So tired. Can you drive me to the cleaners, Mom? I have to pick up that wool dress. They open at twelve."

Lynette checked her watch. "Yep, I'm going to hop in the shower. We'll leave in an hour."

Pleased to have something to occupy her time, Lynette carried her coffee upstairs and sat on the ruffled bed. Her mother's dresser remained lived in, with overflowing drawers and a smattering of makeup along the top. Lynette pulled out her mom's favorite cardigan and breathed the soft cashmere. Hints of floral perfume poked at her nostrils, and Lynette's eyes watered.

"Oh, Mom." She couldn't muster any other words, but her regret remained clear.

Lynette pulled the teal cardigan over her sleep shirt and dug through Mom's jewelry box. She found a beaded necklace that matched the sweater and pulled it over her head. Matching earrings sat in the top drawer of the large stand-up jewelry box and Lynette pushed the studs through her earlobes. Even as a woman past the half century mark, Lynette recognized her elderly mother staring back at her from her reflection.

Angry at how the last third of their relationship had unfolded, Lynette ripped off the earrings and tossed them on the dresser. "Why, Mom?" Lynette asked the mirror. "Why'd it have to end like this?"

The radio faintly playing in the background increased in intensity until the static overpowered Lynette's words. She ran to the alarm clock and punched buttons until the noise stopped.

Memories lingered in the room, and she closed her eyes to keep them out. She rocked on her heels and inhaled, trying to stop the lightheadedness. Somehow, the warm cardigan calmed her racing mind.

The sweater wasn't black or traditional death attire, but it brought Mom's cheerfulness to an otherwise depressing day. If Ruby could do it, so could Lynette, and she vowed to wear the sweater in honor of Mom.

When Lynette emerged from the bedroom, she felt her mother on her skin. Apprehension about the next twenty-four hours carried her down the stairs to start her final goodbye to a mother she had watched drift away until they stood on opposite islands without a raft.

Her shoulders shook and her mascara ran as tiny streams of liquid coated her cheeks. If she could've relived the past twenty years, she would have done it differently, and she hoped Mom had felt the same.

Chapter 18

Ruby climbed into Mom's rental and extended her long legs under the dash. The top half of her legs burned under the heater vents while the bottom half chilled in the cool, fall air seeping through the undercarriage. "Do you think it will fit?" She rubbed her hands together and shoved them in her pockets. The sherpa lining of her new parka reminded her of winters in Chicago.

"We'll have to try it on and see," Mom said under her breath as she pulled into the parking lot.

They entered the narrow store, filled with rows and rows of clothes hidden under plastic. "I have to pick up for Franklin," Ruby said.

The clerk sorted through the racks, searching for the dress. "Ah, yes," he said. The plastic wrap crinkled and dragged along the floor. "This is vintage. Really nice. It was popular in the eighties when women wanted to get back into the workforce and needed an outfit for interviews."

Ruby leaned closer, remembering her dream, and Mema wearing the dress. "Interesting."

Mom pulled out her wallet to pay.

"Oh, you know, I tried to get this ketchup stain out, but the stain must have been there for decades. I got it out of the wool, but not the ribbon."

Ruby widened her eyes and peered closer. Her heart rate slowed and her fingers turned clammy. "Oh, I hadn't even noticed."

"Yes, I tried. You won't notice it if you tie the ribbon a certain way. I'll take off twenty percent for my apologies."

Ruby took the dress and studied it. Yes, there certainly was a small stain on the white ribbon. Unbelievable. Mom handed the cashier a twenty, and Ruby followed her back to the car. The dress sat across her lap like a blanket and Ruby fingered the clear, thin plastic.

"You okay? You look like you've seen a ghost." Mom glanced at Ruby and pulled the car out of the parking lot.

Ruby's head shot to the left. "Wh-what?"

"You look surprised." Mom's tender eyes looked at Ruby. "You okay?"

Ruby sighed loudly and leaned her head against the window. A small headache formed between her eyes and she blinked back tears that spontaneously appeared. "Yeah, I just had a feeling of déjà vu."

"Mema?"

"Yeah, with this dress." She wanted to tell Mom about the dream, but it seemed so strange and incomplete.

"I don't think I've ever seen that dress before," Mom said.

Like sticky Velcro, Ruby struggled to move her tongue. She pursed her lips and swallowed what little liquid she could muster. "Well, the guy said the eighties, right?"

"I can barely remember family vacations from that time. There's no way I'd remember one random dress."

Ruby changed the radio station and turned up the heat. "Mema didn't work, did she?"

"No."

"Did she ever have friends?"

Lynette squinted her brows and looked out the window. "Um, yes, she did. When I was a teenager, Mema joined this women's club. I guess it would be like a book club these days. A bunch of housewives would get together while their kids were at school and do stuff together. Tea parties, book parties, Tupperware parties...any party and she was there. Oh, and she and one friend volunteered around town. I think that was when she got involved with the food bank."

Ruby bit her thumbnail and flakes of polish fell on the clear plastic. "Do you remember her friend's name?"

"Oh, huh. She became friends with someone from Papa's work. I think it started with a J. Janice, maybe? Or Janet? Joyce? J-something."

Ruby's heart thudded and stopped for a quick moment. "Was her last name Weaver, by any chance?" Ruby glanced at Mom, recalling the letters floating around the car, but her face remained blank.

"I can't remember. It was so long ago, but I think my dad worked for a Weaver."

Ruby rubbed the plastic bag and smoothed out the dress. Her dream was not a coincidence...but what message had her grandmother sent?

When they got back from the cleaners, Ruby got to work on the photo collage. Auntie Lori needed it ready for the funeral home and she only had forty-five minutes to get it done. She pulled out the three stacks of photos and quickly sorted through them.

Finding Mema's high school graduation photo and wedding photos were must-haves, and when Ruby found them buried at the bottom of the pile, she arranged them within the center of the board. A few photos of teenagers and young twenty-somethings filled one corner, and photos of Auntie Lori, Mom, and Papa dotted the remaining space. Ruby found a photo of her and Mema at her high school graduation and tucked it in the top corner. Pleased with the aesthetic, she placed the poster boards face up on the table.

"Mom?"

Mom stepped out of the downstairs bathroom. Hot rollers lined her head like the streets of New York City. Her makeup-free face revealed splotches and dry spots and Ruby pulled back, shocked at how old Mom appeared. Even in the three years since she'd left, Mom had aged a decade.

"I finished the posters. Do you want to see?"

Mom trailed behind, wiping day cream into her wrinkles. Ruby raised the posters and Mom stared at the wedding photo. "That looks nice." Her voice cracked and Ruby gave her a sideways glance.

"Was that Mema's wedding?" Ruby asked. Instead of wearing the hat-veil combo Ruby had retrieved from the suitcase, Mema held it in front of her belly. The veil hung to her knees, and Papa smiled like he'd just won the lottery.

"Yeah. Do you think she looks happy?"

It was a strange question to ask, and Ruby tipped her head to the side. "I think so."

"Yeah, I guess she does." Mom turned away and headed toward the bathroom. "You should show it to Auntie Loretta if she hasn't seen it yet."

Ruby found Auntie in the other bedroom. On the phone, she held up one finger, said farewell, and then closed her phone. "Sorry. There's so much to coordinate. What's up?"

"I finished the posters in the nick of time. Do you want me to ask Mom if she can drive me?"

Auntie Lori checked her watch. "Eh, no, I got it. I have to run down there and drop off a check."

"I'll meet you there at 3:30." Ruby kissed Auntie's cheek and then hurried upstairs to get ready.

Mema's green dress was a tad tight. Ruby's hips seemed wider than Mema's and the stiff fabric stretched and slid over her thighs, resembling a matchstick. The skirt settled a few inches higher than where it sat on Mema's legs, from what Ruby could remember, and her bosom filled out the top with a tiny crest of cleavage poking through. For an interview dress from the 1980s, this dress was more risque than Ruby expected.

She squatted, sat, stood, and bent, teasing the seams to rip or pull, but they didn't. Ruby tied the white ribbon into a loose bow and the ends dangled between her breasts. She admired herself in the mirror and readjusted the bow to hide the ketchup stain.

Moving down the narrow hallway, she called, "Mom? Can I come in?"

"Sure."

Ruby opened the door and slid through the crack. "Does this look okay? I need a sweater. This dress is cute and I want to wear it, but it feels a little tight. I'd feel more comfortable if my boobs weren't hanging out."

"You look fine, but your boobs are a little distracting." Mom dug through her suitcase and pulled out a white pullover. "Here you go. This'll look good on you."

Ruby slid it over her head and pulled the ribbon out from under the sweater. A tiny smidgeon of red ketchup remnants splattered the top, so Ruby flipped it over. Now, instead of a dress, it looked like a skirt and top. She fastened a Jolie Belle necklace to complete the look. "Perfect. I'm going to put on black tights and then I'll be ready."

After she pulled on her tights, Ruby secured the straps of her shoes and went downstairs. She had only been to a few funerals in her life, and the idea of seeing her dead grandmother caused butterflies to take flight in her belly. Channeling Mema's courage, Ruby took a swig of wine and grabbed her purse. She needed to erase the grief that was building and ready to erupt. Her brain had been in overdrive for far too long, and it was fracturing and breaking her heart.

She took another gulp and hurried to find her family.

Chapter 19

"I'm so sorry for your loss." Like a loop, the sentiments traveled at every frequency, speed, and decibel level as men and women moved along the perimeter of the tiny viewing room.

Mom's rigid body lay in the mahogany casket with her hands folded under her breasts. Her rosary beads weaved between her knobby fingers and across the top of her left hand.

She looked better than Lynette imagined, although the foundation on her skin highlighted every wrinkle and crevice, marking the full life she had lived. The funeral home had dotted her cheeks with a mauve rouge and a pink lipstick. She looked like everyone's favorite grandmother, but still resembled the mother Lynette had remembered from twenty years before.

"Thank you." Lynette didn't recognize most of the people who passed through the line, for they must have been friends from after Lynette had moved to Chicago.

Lynette scanned the line and her eyes stopped on the tall man with silver-streaked hair who stood alone. A blush traveled from her chest to her neck and she fanned herself with the wake card. *Why does Daniel look so young? And what is he doing here?* Feeling like an old hag, Lynette unbuttoned the top button of her blouse.

"Is it hot in here?" she asked Loretta. Loretta stood on her left, and Ruby stood on her right. No one else appeared bothered by the current temperature.

"No, are you okay?" Loretta's voice carried an ounce of concern, and Lynette wiped her brow.

"Yeah, it must be a hot flash." She waved her arms like a chicken and pulled at her shirt's collar. "I need to get some air. I'll be back."

She scooted between the rows of empty seats at the back of the room and slid out the back door. Just as she approached the threshold, she heard a deep, familiar voice say her name and she froze.

Turning to her left, she made eye contact and stepped toward Daniel. Behind him stood Anthony and Kai.

"Hi, Daniel." She mustered a smile and touched her hair, ignoring the stares coming from behind him. Babbling, she thanked him for allowing them to use his restaurant. Suddenly hyperaware of Anthony and Kai, she blushed and lowered her eyes. Her muscles quivered, and she needed fresh air now. "Excuse me," she said, as she walked past. Her hands shook and her smile wavered under the circumstances.

Like a light switch, the tears blurred her vision, and she wiped maniacally. She had cried on and off all day, not because she missed her mom, but because she missed the mom she didn't know. And now it was too late.

Anthony glanced at her with a puzzled look and pulled Kai's waist closer to him. Lynette wasn't sure if he did that to show possession of his new prize, or if he felt uncomfortable watching Lynette converse with the man who got away. Anthony had seen pictures of Daniel from high school, but that was more than thirty years ago. There was no way he would recognize the man beside him as the man who had held and broken Lynette's heart.

Turning to Anthony, Lynette said, "Thank you for coming. It means a lot to Ruby."

Anthony's friendly face fell, and he pulled Kai tighter to his side before turning his attention to the front of the line.

"Excuse me." Lynette hurried back to the reception line before her chest exploded with shock. Her ex-husband and ex-boyfriend stood side by side at her mother's wake. This was what they made movies about.

"Loretta, do you have a cigarette?" Lynette whispered.

"No, I quit years ago."

She raced out of the building and into the cool night air. Her body twitched as the scent of nicotine floated in the distance, and she found herself pulled to find the source. Walking around the parking lot like a hound dog, Lynette spied a couple in the back huddled around their car. She needed something to calm her nerves, and the little nip in her pocket had emptied down her throat long before. As she got closer, she recognized Kate and her husband, Nick, leaning against their car. Her legs carried her to them, despite her previous claim that Kate needed to stay in her lane.

"Kate," she called.

Kate immediately pulled Lynette into a tight hug, and Lynette's body stiffened.

"Thank you for all the help you've given Mom. She always loved you." Lynette's words sounded rehearsed because they were.

"Of course." Kate's warm eyes calmed Lynette's spastic heart.

"I'm having a hard moment right now." Tears filled Lynette's eyes and she couldn't stop them from dripping down her cheeks. "Do you have a cigarette I can bum? I don't smoke, but I need something."

"I don't, but Nick does. He keeps them in the car for emergencies."

Kate's husband dug through the glove box and handed Lynette a cigarette and lighter.

Relief swept through her as she inhaled the sweet but bitter taste. Her brain slowed and her lungs stopped hurting. "Thank you."

While she savored each drag, she watched Kate and Nick walk arm in arm into the funeral home.

Daniel exited the large double doors, and Lynette watched him climb into his truck and pull out of the semi-circular driveway. Her heart raced as she hid in the shadows. Unsure of what she feared, she went back inside to find her family.

Ignoring the unexpected emotions Daniel stirred in her, Lynette walked through the front door with her head held high. She smiled at the few people huddled around the guest sign-in book and stepped past them. Glancing into the main room, Lynette saw Anthony and Kai talking with Ruby. Two people sat in the chairs before the casket and Loretta was gone.

To give her daughter space, Lynette analyzed the photo collage Ruby had created. She studied Mom's facial expressions from the previous decades of her life. The wedding photo still monopolized her attention, and Lynette analyzed Dad's expression. A giant smile decorated his face. Mom appeared happy, but Lynette knew better because of her sneak peek into their story. It hadn't been a wedding of desire, but a wedding of obligation. Maybe that was why they never had a relationship with her maternal grandparents. Mom never spoke poorly of them, just reiterated that a two-hour drive was too far, and Lynette never questioned it. Funny how when Lynette lived a two-hour plane ride away, Mom gave her hell for not visiting.

After looking at the photo more closely, Lynette noticed small creases around Mom's eyes, angst in her tight-lipped smile, and fear in the way her body pulled away from Dad. Lynette had paid attention to this photo earlier, but now she couldn't help but wonder if they built their entire family and life on regret and big secrets.

"She was a beautiful woman," a voice said. "I wish I had a relationship with my mother the way I had with her."

Stung by Kate's words, Lynette pulled back and threw her a sideways glance. "Oh." Kate and Nick had bought their house after Lynette and Anthony left for Chicago.

"We spent most holidays together. Your mom would bake delicious cookies and pies and cakes and join us for dessert. I cleaned her house and ran errands with her every Saturday. We got to know each other well during those times."

"Well, I'm happy she had you."

"Happy for what?" Loretta joined Kate and Lynette at the photo collage.

"Happy that Mom had Kate," Lynette clarified. "Kate was quite the helper for Mom during the last few years."

Loretta's pinched smile didn't reach her eyes. "Yes, Kate. Thank you. Lynette, are you ready to go in? Poor Ruby is up there alone."

Lynette and Loretta excused themselves and joined Ruby, shaking hands with strangers and accepting half-hearted hugs. Anthony stood beside Ruby and accepted condolences, too. Her anger from the day before had subsided, and Lynette leaned into him. "Thank you for being here."

He half nodded. "I'm her dad. It's my job."

Lynette settled herself beside her daughter and side-hugged her tightly. Without thought, more tears flowed, and all the regret Lynette carried about the way she treated her daughter puddled at her feet.

Ruby pulled away, and Lynette wiped her eyes. "Are you okay?" Ruby asked.

"Yes. I've missed you so much. And I'm happy you came." She wanted to say more, but it didn't feel like the right place. There were too many prying eyes watching their relationship either crumble or mend. Lynette sensed Loretta's listening ears, but her eyes remained fixated on the casket.

Ruby grabbed her hand and the two women remained as one until the last person passed through. Kate and Nick sat in the back row of the room until they were the only guests left. When the funeral home employees turned off the music and turned up the lights, Kate and Nick had gone.

Even if Kate acted like the daughter Mom had always wanted or if she talked about Mom as the mom Lynette always needed, she couldn't shake her burning chest or constricting lungs. Knowing Kate had replaced her as a daughter made her hands twitch and her eyes squint. It wasn't fair.

Chapter 20

When the last guest exited the funeral home, Ruby's back was on fire and the blisters on her feet from her new shoes rubbed and stung with every step. No one had noticed her dress, but her dad did comment that she looked beautiful. She knew the green skirt complemented her tanned complexion and accented her blue-green eyes. Her Jolie Belle beads pulled the ensemble together, and she quickly took a selfie for future posts.

Still a tad too tight, she maneuvered with precision every time she sat down. She liked this dress, but there was no way she could wear it again. It would have to go back into the mystery suitcase.

Dad hugged her and said he'd see her tomorrow before saying goodbye to Mom and Auntie Lori.

Ruby helped pack up the flowers, photos, and guest book and kicked off her shoes in the car. "That was a really long day." Leaning her head against the chilly headrest, she closed her eyes.

Mom sat behind the steering wheel and pulled out of the parking lot. "Yes, it was a lot." Ruby detected sadness and grief in her voice.

"It was nice that Kate stayed as long as she did. I feel bad that I didn't keep in better touch with Mema once I got to California. We had such a great relationship, but once I got to L.A., I needed to focus on work."

Mom winced. "Yeah, it's good she had someone to look out for her. And don't feel guilty. Life happens."

Ruby knew exactly what Mom meant by that. Life happens. You make choices and never know the consequences until it's too late. Usually, you don't recognize the impact until you're too far gone to make a change. 'Life happens' seemed to be the mantra for all her imploded family relationships.

By the time they got back to the house, Auntie Lori was already in front of the television with an overfilled glass of wine. "You ladies want a drink?"

"Sure, but let me get out of this dress. It wasn't my smartest move."

"Oh, honey, you look beautiful," Auntie Lori said.

"Yeah, but it's too small. I just want to throw on some pajamas and loosen up." Ruby went upstairs to change and when she came down again, a glass of wine waited for her on the wooden coffee table.

"Thank you," she said, before settling beside them on the couch. The television ran an infomercial, but the only role it filled was background noise.

"You ready for tomorrow?" Mom asked.

Ruby's shoulder came up and down, contradicting her verbal response. "Yep."

"I can't wait for tomorrow to be over," Auntie Lori said. "Although, then I'm stuck with all the estate stuff. Ugh, why me, Mom, huh? I can barely manage my checkbook and you expect me to manage your life?"

"Yeah, it should have been me." Mom's matter-of-fact voice turned Auntie's eyes steely.

"What, you don't think I can handle it?"

Mom took a sip before responding. "Yes, you can. But I imagine you're overwhelmed. Remember that time you begged me to research your English final? You tricked me into writing it because you *obviously* couldn't write after having your wisdom teeth pulled." Mom rolled her eyes.

"Whatever. I'll figure it out. And for the record, I had an infection, and the meds knocked me out."

Ruby watched the animosity grow between Mom and Auntie. Being an only child, Ruby didn't know if this was a sisterly squabble or something deeper.

"At least Kate isn't doing it." Mom jutted her jaw and sneered.

"What's that mean?" Auntie Lori asked.

"Nothing, just that she claims to have had this great relationship with Mom. She makes me feel like she was more of a daughter to Mom than we were."

Auntie Lori shifted her weight. "You're ridiculous."

Mom creased her lips. "Maybe, but that's how she makes me feel."

A silence fell upon the room, and Ruby focused on the infomercial selling knives on the television. After a few minutes, she checked her watch and carried her empty glass into the kitchen. "I'm heading up. We have to wake up early tomorrow and I need to get a good night's sleep. Good night." She blew kisses to the other women and left them to bicker.

Climbing into bed, she noticed the black blazer laying across the chair in the corner. She slid it over her arms and back and admired how the cut accentuated her waist. A tingly sensation flowed through her body like a shot of whiskey, and Ruby stumbled back. "That wine must be strong," she mumbled, and dropped the blazer on the chair.

Climbing under the blankets, she closed her eyes and when they opened the next morning, she felt broken inside. A melancholy pulled her into an abyss, as she acknowledged today as the funeral.

She'd had the strangest dream, and she couldn't quite shake how real it felt. Papa was sick in the hospital and Mema was fluttering around like a bumble bee hopping from flower to flower. The black blazer Ruby tried on earlier hung from Mema's plump frame.

She snuck him chocolate candies, which he shoveled in his mouth and swallowed without chewing.

He begged her to call their kids, but she refused. He accused her of being stubborn. The words *stubborn* and *wrong* bounced off the walls like a ping-pong ball.

She disappeared. He disappeared. And she reappeared in their home with Kate beside her. If Ruby didn't know better, Kate looked like she lived there, too. The kitchen disappeared and Mema appeared in Papa's study. A glowing baby photo of Ruby lit up the room.

"Beautiful girl, I miss you."

And that was all she remembered. Ruby furiously scribbled it down in a notebook, trying to connect the two dreams. The only thing they had in common was the clothing from the suitcase.

But it was just a dream, right?

If it was just a dream, why did Ruby feel so broken inside?

Chapter 21

The morning of the funeral, Lynette stared at the ceiling, willing her body to move. Rolling out of bed, she gazed outside. *For such a cold time of year, it sure is pretty.* In the far distance stood a hint of blue where the ocean water hit the sky. The trees had turned into hibernation mode and the dotted leaves reminded her of a bountiful cornucopia. *A beautiful day for a funeral.*

Lynette pulled on her black pantsuit, followed by her mom's cardigan sweater. As she gazed at herself in the mirror, she made a face at the rather nondescript outfit, wishing she could do better. Lynette brushed back her blonde hair and secured it in a ponytail. *Mom's dead. Her opinion doesn't matter anymore.* She spun away from her reflection and sighed, her neck and shoulders falling forward.

In the kitchen, Lynette found an already brewed pot of coffee, so she poured herself a liberal cup. Ruby raced through, wearing black pants, a white top, and that black blazer they found in the suitcase. Loretta sprinted around the house, grabbing the flowers and photos from the night before.

By the time they arrived at the church, the pews had already filled. Most of the people were over the age of sixty-five and hadn't attended the services the night before.

"It seems like Mom knew many people," Lynette said to her sister, nodding at the crowd.

"There's Kate." Loretta jerked her head toward the front of the church.

Kate sat beside Nick, looking fashionable in her pinstripe pencil skirt and black blouse. "Look, she even has a matching hat. Definitely Mom-approved," Lynette sneered.

"Don't let her affect you, Linnie." It was more a warning than a request.

Loretta placed the flowers next to the altar and waved to Kate amicably.

Sliding into the front pew, Lynette sat directly in front of Anthony and Kai. She turned around, gathering all the manners Mom and Dad had taught her. "Thank you for being here."

"Of course. We're heading out after the services because Kai has to work tomorrow."

"Of course, of course." Lynette turned and faced the closed casket covered in flowers, wondering why it bothered her so much that Anthony was leaving early.

Making the sign of the cross, she prayed to God, asking for his forgiveness and to help her repair all her relationships. Anthony included.

Ruby and Loretta joined Lynette in the first pew and Lynette watched the priest move around the altar.

"Family and friends, now is the time to celebrate Penelope. Would the family please step forward?"

Lynette's body froze, and her heart pounded against her brittle spine. Scrunched in her seat, she tried to disappear into the wooden pew. She had forgotten all about the eulogy and had nothing prepared. During the chaos of coordinating the services and writing the obituary, time had raced by like a fifty-meter dash.

The priest's eyes bounced from Loretta to Lynette to Ruby, and finally Loretta rose. She grabbed Lynette's and Ruby's hands and pulled them to the altar.

"Hello." The noise traveled up and down the church, creating an echo amongst the tall ceiling and stained-glass windows.

A murmur of responses bounced back at them.

"My name is Loretta, and this is my sister Lynette and this is my niece, Lynette's daughter, and Penny's granddaughter, Ruby. We don't have a speech prepared, so I thought we'd come up and wing it."

The crowd chuckled.

Loretta continued. "My mother was one of a kind. She was multi-dimensional, and you never really knew who you were going to get. Sometimes she was serious and determined and other times she was silly and spontaneous. She ran the house with an iron whip. My father was so in love with her, he'd do anything to keep her happy. She'll be missed." Loretta stepped back and looked at Lynette.

Lynette stepped forward, her mind a blank notebook. She willed her mouth to move. There were too many hurtful memories creeping forward and she didn't know if she could keep them at bay. "She would have loved having all of you here. Thank you for coming." It sounded hollow and impersonal, but if she gave any more, she'd unleash the demons or break down in regret. Both those options were not acceptable, and if Mom was alive, she'd tell Lynette to keep moving forward.

Ruby stepped forward and cleared her throat. "I am the only grandchild of Penelope Waller. I have wonderful memories of growing up with her, and I loved coming to Maine. Both she and my Papa created a safe, fun place for me to escape to, and we forged a beautiful friendship. I miss her every day. My biggest regret is living across the country because I wasn't here for her when she needed us." Ruby's eyes filled with tears and she blinked them back. "I love you, Mema. Thanks for everything."

The three women returned to their seats, and the priest asked,

"Would anyone else like to share a word or two?"

Kate stood from her pew and made her way to the altar. She carried a folded piece of paper and set it on the podium. Lynette watched her unfold the paper, straighten her posture, and smile at the audience.

"My name is Kate, and I live–ehr, lived–next to Penny for the past twenty years. When I moved in, she and her husband, Harry, welcomed us with homemade cookies and a nice home-cooked meal. Coming from New York City, I had never been exposed to such open, loving neighbors."

Lynette shot her sister a look and a half-smile.

"Over the years, we became very close. Penny taught me how to cook, and I taught her how to garden. She connected us with people in the community and we connected her with resources when Harry got sick."

Loretta hit Lynette's thigh but Lynette couldn't move her eyes from Kate.

"When Harry had his stroke, my husband got him into the best rehab hospital in the state."

Loretta squeezed Lynette's knee and darted her gaze from Kate to Lynette without turning her head.

Lynette's ears perked up at the word *stroke*. When did Dad have a stroke?

"When Harry died, we helped Penny with all the arrangements and stood by her side."

The dagger within Kate's words lodged in Lynette's side. She had offered to help with the services, but Mom refused, saying she had everything taken care of.

"And now she is with the love of her life, safe in his arms again." Kate folded the paper and stuck it in her skirt pocket. "Thank you, everyone, for coming. Penny would have loved to see you. Like she often told me, don't weep about what we've lost, smile at what we've gained. Thank you."

The guests attending the funeral clapped and Lynette slid further down in her seat. The rest of the service went by in a blur.

After the burial, about twenty people drove to The Fresh Catch for a Celebration of Life. With the restaurant open to the public, Daniel had prepared the back room with half a dozen tables for the guests and a series of banquet tables for the buffet.

Lynette placed the photo collage up against the wall in the far corner and Loretta dropped the flower baskets around the photos. She followed Loretta to the bar, where Daniel stood filling water pitchers.

"Hi, Daniel. Good to see you again. What's it been...twenty years?" Loretta was always good at small talk. Lynette stood behind her sister, unsure if she had ever shared her relationship with Daniel to Loretta. By the time Lynette and Daniel became a thing, Loretta was long gone.

"At least. Maybe more. I'm sorry about your loss."

His eyes moved from Loretta to Lynette and a small blush crept up Lynette's neck. She gave a meek smile and grabbed a full pitcher. "I can bring this out." Turning toward the dining area, she left Loretta to square away the details with the luncheon.

Placing the water pitcher on the first round table, she walked to Ruby, Anthony, and Kai, who had already settled themselves at a table overlooking the water. "Is there room for me?" Lynette asked.

Ruby scooted her chair closer to her father and Lynette sat down.

"Is everyone doing okay?" It was a fair question, considering they had just attended a funeral.

"Yeah. I'm getting a drink. Does anyone need anything?" Anthony's gruff voice cut through and he stood abruptly.

"I'll have a glass of chardonnay," Lynette requested.

"Water is fine with me," Kai replied. "I'll drive," she confirmed with Anthony.

"I'll come with you," Ruby said and rose from the table.

Alone with her ex's new wife, Lynette couldn't help but acknowledge the dread that was slowly clawing its way through her. Her skin prickled at her ex-husband's happiness, and she wondered why she had gotten the short end of the stick.

"Thank you for coming," Lynette repeated for the hundredth time that week.

"You know, Lynette. I'm glad we came." Kai's syrupy voice drenched Lynette.

Lynette unrolled her napkin and placed it on her lap before raising her eyes.

"You look good. I'm glad you're doing well," Kai said.

Inside, Lynette guffawed. *Doing well? I'm a mess. I'm lonely and living life on autopilot. How is that doing well?* "Thank you. You look like you're doing well too." There was too much polite conversation happening, and bile fermented in her stomach.

Anthony and Ruby returned with a small tray of drinks and passed them out to the table.

"Linnie," Loretta called from behind.

Loretta turned.

"You never told me you dated Daniel."

The blush from earlier exploded on Lynette's face, and Anthony leaned back, observing her with inquisitive eyes.

"Yes, after you left, he and I dated for a while. Maybe a year or two; I can't remember." She did remember, but didn't want to reveal that intimate part of her history with Kai beside her. Lynette remembered his tender kisses, his hard abdominal muscles, and his protective arms. She couldn't remember why they broke up, but it happened slowly, like beach erosion after too many storms.

"He was asking about you."

"Who was?" Ruby asked.

"Daniel. The guy who owns this place," Loretta clarified. "He and your mom used to date."

Ruby stood and scanned the bar. "Oh, that guy? He's cute, Mom."

Lynette gave her sister a warning glare. "Yes, he is, and yes, we used to date. Your grandmother loved him."

She glanced at Anthony to see if he caught her jab, but his eyes remained on his drink.

"Food's ready. Do you mind if I grab a plate? We really have to get going soon." He grabbed Kai's hand and led her to the buffet table, where a small group of people had already congregated.

Loretta stood and clinked her wine glass, addressing the crowd. "Thank you, everyone, for coming. My mom, Penelope, would be thrilled so many people came out to celebrate her life. Please enjoy your meal."

The rest of the room rose to the buffet, except for Lynette. She remained seated, watching Daniel's head bob behind the bar. She licked her lips, remembering his body underneath his basketball uniform. It was a history she had buried, but just seeing him again brought the memories to life.

Chapter 22

When the celebratory dinner was over, relief swept over Ruby. She hadn't thought about work over the past few days, but a series of text messages from Shayla reminded her that life hadn't stopped. Instead of answering the string of texts, Ruby checked her watch and called her roommate. In California, it was two in the afternoon, which was prime audition time. Ruby hoped Shayla wouldn't answer, but needed to stay connected.

Shayla answered on the third ring. "Hey," she whispered. "Is everything okay?"

"Yeah, are you in an audition?"

"Yeah, can I call you later tonight?"

"Sure, bye." She pulled the phone away and then yelled into the receiver, "Good luck."

The phone call disconnected and Ruby retrieved her new sweater from the brown shopping bag before heading downstairs. Auntie Lori sat in the same chair in the dining room, surrounded by the same pile of papers that had buried her over the past few days.

"Auntie Lori, go rest."

"I can't until this is done. I don't want to bring it home to Florida with me."

"Is there anything I can do?" Ruby didn't think she'd be much help, but she followed directions easily.

"Nah, I'm getting the last of it together for the lawyer. I need to drop it off Monday before I head home."

"Okay, I'll leave you alone then. Do you want a drink or anything?"

"No, thanks."

Ruby retreated to the living room, where Mom sat reading a book on the couch.

"What are you reading?" Ruby sat on the middle cushion and Mom passed her a small blanket.

"The newest book by John Clapper. It's a thriller. You know, to escape from the past week."

Ruby leaned forward and grabbed the magazine off Mema's coffee table. "I'll let you read," she said, flipping through the magazine. "When things get hard, I like to dive into celebrity life. It feels so far from my own problems, you know?"

"Even though you want to be one?"

"I don't want to be a celebrity; I want to model. They're different."

"Whatever you set your mind to, I know you'll excel."

Her body slightly recoiled, questioning Mom's sincerity, and she focused on the pictures in the magazine. "Thanks," she said.

Mom remained focused on her book and turned the page.

They stayed like that for a few minutes, quietly reading, getting lost in their own worlds. Ruby flipped the page and read a headline about a horror film being made. On the next page, Ruby saw herself on a half-page advertisement. "Mom, look," Ruby said, holding up the magazine.

Mom peered closely. "Is that you?"

"Yeah, pretty cool, huh?"

"That's amazing," Mom said. "You did it." A proud grin swept her face.

The dream-like vision of Mom as a young girl flashed through her mind. "Hey Mom?"

"Mm—hmm?"

"When you were a kid, did you have trouble creating your own identity?"

Mom dropped her book on her lap. "Yes, your grandmother had a tight leash on us girls. She dictated what we looked like, what we wore, and how we acted. You're lucky you didn't have her as a mother."

Dropping the magazine on her lap, Ruby asked, "What do you think happens after we die? Like, where do you think Mema is?"

"I don't know. Hopefully, she's happy."

"Do you believe in the afterlife?" Ruby kept her eyes on the magazine.

"What do you mean?" Mom placed her book face down on her knee.

"Like, do you believe in ghosts?"

Ruby wasn't sure, but she thought she saw a flash of recognition cross Mom's face. "Um...I didn't, but I think maybe I do now."

"Me too. I keep having these weird dreams," Ruby started. The last thing she needed was Mom laughing or minimizing her dream, so she treaded carefully.

Mom removed her glasses and rubbed her eyes. "Me too."

Ruby blinked rapidly, hearing Mom's admission on repeat in her head. A tingle and a zap erupted in her chest. "You are?"

"Yes. Well, I've had one dream since I've been here. It was kind of weird."

"Like weird with Mema, right?"

"Yes."

"Me too. What do you think it means? Do you think she's trying to tell us something?"

Mom leaned forward. "I don't know. If it happens again, I'll let you know. How many dreams have you had?"

"Two, so far. One took me back to when Mema wore that green dress and the other took me back to when she wore the black blazer."

"And I dreamed about her wedding." Mom's eyes bulged and her

122

face elongated. "That suitcase, Ruby. Do you think it's that suitcase? Or the clothes within it?"

"I don't know, but I don't think it's a coincidence."

Mom leaned back on the couch and stared at the fireplace. "It's so weird."

Ruby couldn't help but think of Mema, the dreams, and what it meant. Maybe Mema wanted her to figure it out or learn something, but what?

Ruby walked into the dining room and gave a bowl of pretzels to Auntie Lori. "You should eat something while you're working."

Auntie Lori crunched the pretzel between her teeth. "Thanks. I'm almost done."

"Hey, Auntie Lori, can I ask you something? I promise it'll be quick."

Auntie Lori dropped the paper she was holding and held Ruby's gaze. "What's up?"

"Do you believe in ghosts? Or spirits? Or do you believe that when we die, we leave this world?"

Auntie Lori answered without thinking. "I think when we die, we die. Our body dies and our soul goes to heaven or hell or purgatory. So no, I don't believe in spirits or ghosts. I believe when our body dies, our soul no longer has a vessel to be in this world, so we leave."

Unsatisfied, Ruby kissed Auntie on the cheek and sat in the chair beside her.

"Why do you ask?"

"I was just wondering. I'm going to read. Call me if you need me." She walked out of the dining room and returned to the couch.

"Mom, do you think Mema's trying to tell us something?"

Mom shrugged. "Right now, I think it's a coincidence. If I have a dream about that ugly maternity dress, I'll let you know."

"You know that ketchup stain on that dress? The one the cleaner couldn't remove? I dreamed about how that happened before I knew there was a stain. That's kind of weird, right? That couldn't have been a coincidence."

Mom scrunched her mouth. "I don't know, honey. It's rather strange, but the idea of her here in this house freaks me out more. Like, why is she between worlds?"

Ruby didn't know, so instead, she asked, "When are you heading back to Chicago?"

"I need to return to work by January. I took the rest of the semester off, which is only about a month more. I don't have a plan."

Shocked, Ruby opened her mouth wide. "You? Without a plan? Blasphemy!"

Mom threw a sideways glance at her daughter. "You don't know me like you used to. A lot can happen in three years. I lost you, your father, and my sense of self. Planning didn't exactly get me far in life."

Ruby scrunched her eyebrows.

"I fell into a deep depression. Thank God I had Martha."

Questions about the life she left behind in Chicago flooded her.

"What about you? When are you leaving?" Mom asked.

"My flight is Wednesday, so I have a few more days to help you and Auntie Lori do whatever needs to be done."

"Do you have a busy week ahead of you?"

"Ugh, I'm actually missing a big job on Monday. I emailed my agent, but I've been so busy here I haven't been able to check in. I'm sure they gave it to another model." Ruby's voice dropped. She really needed that money.

Ruby's phone rang, and she glanced at the screen. "That's my roommate. I'll be right back."

She ran up to her room, glancing at the suitcase in the corner. "Hello?"

"Ruby! You will not believe this," Shayla exclaimed.

"What?" Shayla's excitement penetrated Ruby and her fingers tingled while anticipating the latest gossip.

"I got a job with Jolie Belle. A series of social media videos, because no one watches commercials anymore." She squealed into the phone and Ruby squealed back. Shayla had represented a variety of small fashion companies but never got the BIG one.

"Congrats!"

"Yes, so when are you coming home? They were asking about you... or not asking, but talking about you. Are you missing a big shoot or something?"

Ruby's brows knitted together. "Yeah, Monday. What did you hear?"

"I don't know, really. They said they sent you an email."

She hadn't checked her email since she'd arrived. With Shayla on the phone, Ruby pulled up her email and methodically searched. Buried in the salesy emails from all the companies she wore, she found one email from her agent. "Found it. Hold on, let me skim it. Dear Ruby, we are sorry for your loss, however, we need to end your contract. As stated in the contract, you are to be available three-hundred-sixty-five days starting June 15th. You are not available during this difficult time, which means the contract has been broken. Your contract with Jolie Belle is now considered null and void." Ruby stopped talking and choked on her tears.

"Oh shit," Shayla said. "But..."

"Wait, did you know? What did you hear?" Ruby asked again.

"Nothing really, just that they needed to find a replacement for that shoot and that they sent you an email." Her voice trailed at the end of the sentence, and Ruby waited to see if she'd add more.

Devastation ate at her chest, making it hard to breathe. "Shayla, I have to go. I'll call you later."

She hung up the phone and curled into a ball on her bed. *Mema died... how can they hold that against me?*

Everything she had sacrificed to get to L.A. just blew up in her face.

Chapter 23

Reliving her dream, Lynette recalled the pain in Mom's face and the excitement in Dad's. Pregnant and married at eighteen, yet no kids until twenty-four. It had to have been made up. There was no way her parents would give a child up for adoption...would they?

But Ruby had dreams too, and it seemed the dreams revolved around that locked suitcase. An unfamiliar suitcase filled with random clothes. It seemed unusual, but why would they both have strange dreams about those clothes? It didn't add up.

Lynette shook her head and reopened her book. She tried to immerse herself in the world of police procedure and murder, but the words didn't connect in her mind. Instead of paying attention to every detail about every character, images from Lynette's dream poked at her brain and pulled her out of the story.

She placed the book face down on the table and rubbed her eyes, thinking about how every relationship had slipped through her fingers. Overtired and overwhelmed, she still harbored negative emotions about Loretta, the wild child, being in charge of the estate. She couldn't wait to get home, but home to what? Her life had ended three years ago.

Pulling on her sneakers and stepping outside, she walked up and down the neighborhood streets with her phone to her ear.

"Hi, Martha," she said into her cell.

"Oh, Lynette. I am so happy to hear from you. Did you get my flowers?"

Distracted by her family turmoil, Lynette hadn't even noticed the beautiful flowers decorating the viewing room. "Yes," she said, "they were beautiful."

They chatted about the bookstore and work, and Lynette gently broached the subject of dreams. "Hey Martha, do you have any good resources on dream analysis? Like, what they mean?"

"I can check tomorrow and send you a list. I love that stuff."

"Oh yeah? What do you find so fascinating about it?"

"That your subconscious is communicating with you during your most vulnerable state."

"Huh." Lynette huffed as the cold air filled her lungs. "What do you mean by communicate?"

"Like, they help you process things you've been dealing with for years. It takes all your childhood trauma, experiences, and emotions and creates an image that your brain can handle to process and store the information appropriately. Why? Have you been having weird dreams?"

"Kind of. Do you believe spirits can contact you through your dreams?" She felt silly asking such a woo-woo question, but the coincidences with the clothes and the dreams were too much.

"I don't know much about that," Martha said matter-of-factly, "but there is someone you can talk to."

"Like a psychic?" Lynette didn't believe in psychics.

"No, like a medium. They bridge the gap between the living and the dead. Maybe she can help you interpret your dreams."

"Thanks Martha. I feel silly because I don't really believe in this hocus-pocus stuff, but ever since my mom died, weird things have been happening." She confided in Martha about the locked suitcase, the old clothes, and their dreams. "I don't know if it's true or fake because my mom never had a baby at eighteen, but it felt so real. And I can't shake it from my mind."

"That is strange. Your dream was in pieces, right? Or at least what you remember?"

"Yes. My memory is foggy, but she looked pregnant and unhappy. That was clear as day."

"You can do one of two things. Do some research, talk to a medium, and see if there's a reason, or ignore it and chalk it up to a bad dream."

Lynette hesitated. "You know, my mom and I had an awful relationship once we moved to Chicago. I have this guilt hanging over me for not being there for her. I didn't even know my dad had a stroke, that's how distant we were. I found that out at her funeral." Lynette recovered her shaky voice. "From Kate, of all people. I keep thinking there are more secrets, more to her story, and maybe it will help me handle her death and how things ended between us."

"Then I think you know what you need to do," Martha said simply. "Other than that, how are you? I miss our coffee dates and book talks."

Lynette rounded the corner back to the house. "I don't know. Loretta is overwhelmed with the estate, so I feel like I can't really leave until it's sorted. It's not fair that she's stuck with all that crap when I have nothing."

"You have me!"

"I have you."

"You have work."

"Yeah, so what? I don't even like work. I just do it for a paycheck and the health benefits. There are so many terrible memories in Chicago, maybe it'll be good to escape from it for a while. I told work I'd be back by spring semester, so I have some time to figure it out."

"Oh! Sorry to interrupt, but you got mail."

"Can you send it to me? I'm not sure when exactly I'll be coming home."

"No, Lynette, I mean mail. A fat envelope from the Illinois Post."

She thought back to the photo contest she took part in and a small glimmer of hope wrapped its arms around her. "Oh yeah? Do you have it with you?"

"Yeah, I'm here now."

"Open it up. I submitted a picture in a photo contest."

Lynette heard rumbling through the phone.

"Let's see. Congratulations, your photo has been included in the top ten photos. The winner will be selected by December thirty-first for an all-expenses paid trip to Los Angeles, California."

Lynette's spirits rose, both at the sound of her good friend's voice and also at the news that her memory was worthy of winning. "That's great!" In a strange way, it validated the pain she endured when everyone left.

"There's more. There's a second page addressed to you. Dear Lynette," Martha read, "We tried to contact you via email but we haven't heard from you. Please check your spam folder and move us to your inbox so we can continue sending updates regarding the contest. Thank you, The Illinois Post."

"I'll have to do that. Hey, I gotta go, but thank you. That piece of mail brightened my day...and so did talking to you. I can't wait to see you."

With a smile Martha couldn't see, Lynette said goodbye and stuffed her phone in her pocket. She jogged to the old house, escaping the raw, gray air. She wanted to share her good news, but didn't want to jinx it. She tucked her secret close to her heart and breezed into the kitchen. With the services and the stress of seeing Anthony over, she welcomed the time with her family.

Later that night, Lynette lay in her parent's old bed, huddled under the massive pile of blankets. Suddenly spooked by the shadows in the room and the anticipation of sleep, she pulled the blankets to her eyes and closed them tight.

Her heart raced when her body jerked at the sound of a tree branch breaking outside. *It must be an animal or the wind.* Lynette flipped on the bedside lamp and scanned the room. The closet doors remained shut, the hallway light spread from under the door, and a pile of dirty clothes sat in the far corner. Nothing looked amiss.

She closed her eyes again, and thoughts of ghosts, spirits, and mediums infiltrated her mind. Freaking herself out, she turned on the tv at a low volume and focused on the sound of the eleven o'clock news.

When her eyes became heavy, she closed them for a moment, praying that morning would arrive fast. When she opened her eyes, her body bolted upright and her fingers gripped the sheets. Tiny beads of sweat formed along the nape of her neck. She wiped her neck, closed her eyes, and rubbed her temples.

It was only a dream. The thought didn't calm her mind, but solidified her hunch that Mom and Dad were expecting when they married, but in this dream, Mom was pregnant. Like, really pregnant and wearing that awful top from the suitcase. Dad stood at a grill, cooking outside, and Mom sat in a chair knitting. *Knitting...was that Loretta? But Dad called the baby Lorraine. Lorraine, Lorraine...there was no Lorraine. And Mom looked sad, always sad.* Lynette felt her unhappiness, which solidified her assumption that Mom didn't want to get married. *Whatever happened to Lorraine?* Worst-case scenarios popped through Lynette's mind. *And why was she kept a secret all these years?*

Unable to handle her thoughts any longer, she hopped out of bed and ran to her old bedroom. "Ruby." She barged open and through the door, finding her daughter fast asleep. Gripping and shaking her shoulder, she said, "Ruby, wake up. I need to talk to you."

Chapter 24

As if lightning had struck the house during a violent storm, Ruby jerked from her side to her back and sat up, straight as a rod. She placed her right hand across her chest and adjusted her sleep shirt with the other. "Jeez! Mom, you scared me." Her heart pushed against her sternum and she listened to her heartbeat bump against her eardrums.

"Ruby, I need to talk to you." Mom's voice flowed like a record on double speed, high pitched and fast. "I had a dream." The word dream stretched for miles, like Ruby was the only person who knew what the word meant. "Did you have a dream?"

Ruby shook her head. "No, not last night. What was the dream about?"

"About that maternity shirt. That enormous shirt you called a tent? It was in my dream. Mema wore it. She was pregnant with Loretta, but Papa called her Lorraine. I don't know a Lorraine."

Ruby sat up straighter and slid to the corner of the bed, patting the space beside her. "Here, sit down. Do you want some water?" She pointed at the water bottle on the bedside table.

"No, no. Listen, I need to tell you before I forget. The first dream I had was the day they got married. My mom was pregnant. But it made little sense because Loretta wasn't born until a few years later. So, in this dream last night, Mema was pregnant and sad. Dad kept referencing a baby named Lorraine." She clapped her hands and jerked her head toward Ruby. "Did they have another baby? And if so, where is she?"

Ruby tried to hang onto every word, but Mom spoke a million words per minute and it was difficult to hang onto the details. Instead of requesting clarification, she listened while Mom flubbed through the sequence.

"At their wedding, Mema was pregnant but looked depressed, and Papa seemed excited. Then, she was pregnant again, but Dad kept calling the baby Lorraine. In my wedding dream, it seemed like they only got married because they were pregnant, but they didn't have Loretta until years later." Mom's round eyes studied Ruby. "Am I going crazy?"

"I don't think so. I don't know what's going on, but I think Mema's trying to talk to us and tell us something."

Mom stroked the edging of the blanket. "I talked to Martha."

"Martha? From Chicago?"

"Yeah. She thinks we should talk to a medium. Maybe the medium could give us some insight into these dreams."

As much as Ruby believed in signs and spirits, she didn't know if she trusted contacting the dead. "I don't know, Mom...that stuff scares me. And it's always scared you, too. Why are you willing to risk it now?"

Mom grabbed Ruby's hands. "You're right. It terrifies me. But this is so strange, Ruby. I don't understand it, and that also scares me. I can't leave here without knowing why Mom is communicating with us."

Ruby had never seen Mom act this erratic, and it worried her. If the dreams hadn't affected Ruby as well, she would believe Mom was delusional. But she was right; Mema was trying to tell them something, teach them something, or maybe even say goodbye.

"Okay, Mom. I'm here for a few more days. If you find a medium, I'll go. I'll go for you, because this whole idea of spirits stuck between worlds scares me. But I trust you."

Mom grabbed Ruby's hand and placed it on her chest. The rhythmic thuds penetrated her fingertips. "I can't decide if I'm scared or excited. Want to go to the bookstore with me later? Or the library. We can find something about dreams and the afterlife."

Ruby pulled her hair back. "Sure, Mom. Let me shower and get ready, and then we'll go."

She left Ruby's room, and Ruby stared at the vinyl suitcase wedged in the corner. It seemed possible, but not plausible. She shoved it back into the closet's corner where she found it and closed the door.

Ruby missed Mema, but she didn't want Mema to haunt her dreams any longer.

"Auntie Lori, have you ever struggled to pay your rent?" Ruby doodled on the notepad and slowly raised her eyes. "I'm asking for a friend."

Auntie Lori adjusted her gaze from the television to her niece. "A long time ago, back in the 2008 recession. I was in the middle of a divorce and had just lost my job. Your uncle moved out of the house, and I needed to pay the mortgage. At least until the divorce was finalized."

"So, what did you do?"

"I got a job wherever I could. I went from working in an office with vacation and benefits to working at Walmart as a greeter on the weekends. When I still couldn't pay the mortgage, I put an ad in the paper for a roommate."

Back in 2008, Ruby was in third grade. With Auntie Lori in Florida and Ruby in Chicago, she didn't know what hardship Auntie Lori journeyed through. At eight years old, it wasn't a problem she should have been aware of. More concerned with whether she'd get a Furby from Santa or the newest iPod, she assumed her family was perfect.

Ruby's eyes returned to the notepad. "Sorry you went through that. It all worked out, right?"

Auntie Lori chuckled. "Oh yeah, my new roommate robbed me one night and never returned. I was too nice and didn't create a lease that held up in court, nor could I find her, and my husband lost all trust in my sensibility. It was not a good time. Why do you ask? What's going on with your friend, I mean?"

Unsure of what kind of life she was returning to in L.A., Ruby licked her lips. "Just wondering. Mom and I are going out for the afternoon."

"Where to?"

Good question. If she told Auntie Lori the truth, she may think they had a screw loose. "Out to Portland. We both really like bookstores, so we thought we'd go check out the shops downtown." Pleased that she hadn't given too much away, Ruby smiled at her aunt.

"Pick me up a coffee on your way home, will you?"

"Rubes, you ready?" Mom's voice cut through the room and Ruby grabbed her jacket and pulled on her hat.

"Yeah. Auntie, we should be home in a few hours."

She followed Mom to the car, and they drove to Portland, parking on the street and walking the rest.

"Books Encore. Have you been here before?" Ruby asked.

"I haven't walked these streets in about twenty years. I've never heard of this place before."

"I came in the other day. It's cute and cozy."

A young woman, a few years older than Ruby, stood behind the desk holding an e-reader. "Welcome. Can I help you find something?" She bounced on her toes and smiled.

Ruby said, "No," as Mom said, "Yes."

The woman turned from Ruby to Mom. "What can I get for you?"

Mom leaned on the counter and lowered her voice. "Do you have anything on dream interpretation? Or, do you have a recommendation for a medium who specializes in dreams? That would be even better."

The clerk walked Ruby and Mom to the back of the room, where a tall stack of books leaned against the bathroom door frame. "Here are our metaphysical books. You'll find dream journals, dream interpretation, and dream references here." She pointed to a narrow section on the shelf. "As you're looking, I'll be googling mediums. I've lived here my entire life, so I have some connections," she said.

She walked back to the front desk and Ruby squatted, running her eyes along the bottom third of the stack. She removed four books of different thickness and height and carried them to a small round table. "Let's start with these."

Mom picked one up and flipped through. "This one talks about common dreams and what they symbolize, but I don't think this is what we need. We need information about paranormal communication." She threw the book beside the stack and grabbed another. "This one's a journal. This isn't what we need, is it?"

Ruby took the journal out of Mom's hands and flipped through. "This might be good. I feel like every time I wake from a dream, I remember all the details, but as the day progresses, I forget. We could use this to document our dreams with Mema. Maybe we'll find a common theme or something to figure out what she's trying to tell us." Ruby tucked the book under her arm and continued looking at the shelves.

It was a small bookstore that lacked the impersonal feel of the big box stores. Since the space was smaller, the options in each category contained fewer books, and it didn't carry exactly what Ruby and Mom needed.

"I'm getting these," Ruby announced. She walked to the front of the store, carrying a handful of resources, and the woman behind the desk gave her a piece of paper.

"Like I said, I've lived here my entire life. Ms. Eleanor Smith is a medium. I haven't been, but a lot of my friends have. They said she was excellent and gave closure to whatever questions they had. Give her a shot. Her shop is about a half hour south of here right on the beach."

Ruby noted the woman's name and phone number. "Eleanor Smith?" She had a hard time visualizing Eleanor Smith. Her mind pictured a typical grandmother with gray curly hair, chocolate chip cookies, and a jar of candy sitting on the table.

"Yeah, that's her name, but she calls herself Nora," the woman said. "She's excellent. A little quirky, but I've only heard great things."

Ruby doubted she'd find a website, but maybe a google search would reveal some reviews. "Thank you so much." She tucked the paper into her inner coat pocket.

As they drove home with two dream journals and a few books, Ruby said, "I'll call Nora when we get back. Maybe we can see her before I leave on Wednesday."

"Sounds good. I hope she has an opening."

The rest of the ride home was quiet. If there was one thing the Waller/Franklin women had in common, it was fighting their demons alone. Maybe instead of ignoring their past, Ruby and Mom could talk it out. Ruby wondered if the road to forgiveness had been paved, but she needed to trust the path. Maybe that's what Mema was trying to do.

For dinner, Ruby joined Mom at The Last Catch. The dream journal and metaphysical books sat in a pile between their water glasses.

"Okay, dreams," she instructed. "Tell me everything about your dreams." Ruby held the pen in her hand, ready to jot down the details.

Mom summarized the wedding and explained Papa's excitement and Mema's reluctance, Mema's parents' anger, and Papa's parents' joy. Lorraine. Random words dotted the lined page with moons and stars decorating the margins.

"Lorraine?" Ruby asked. "All I can think of is Marty McFly."

"Yes, I think that was it."

Ruby flipped the page and shared what she remembered. Papa in the hospital. In big letters she wrote **STROKE?**, **Kate and Mema**, and **Papa's**

wish that Mema call.

She recognized the missed opportunity on Mom's face. "Sorry."

Mom wiped her eyes and her mouth scrunched up in a tight ball. "Ugh, I wish I'd known. I carried so much anger toward her."

Ruby touched her hand. "What exactly happened between you two? All I remember is that when I was little, we traveled to Maine for the holidays, and then when I hit high school, I went alone."

"Well, we couldn't send you alone on a plane as a young child, could we?"

Ruby leaned forward and kept her eyes down. "So, what happened?"

Mom folded and refolded her napkin. "Nothing, really. Mema wasn't supportive of me moving away with Dad. I think she relied on me for too much, and that's how it was for most of my life. So, I put my foot down, moved away with Dad, and our relationship became strained and eventually non-existent."

"I kind of saw that, in my dream," Ruby said. "You came downstairs in this crazy get-up. Like those weird high-top sneakers with the Velcro across the top and crimped hair, and Mema made you go upstairs and change."

"Sounds about right," Mom mumbled.

"It seemed like Auntie Lori did her own thing, but knew how to act around Mema."

"She always got me in trouble. She'd pull me into her shenanigans and when we got caught, she always blamed it on me. My parents believed her, so I learned early on that I needed to behave and oblige in order to get their love and acceptance. That was also when I pulled away from Loretta. I was tired of taking the brunt for her mistakes."

The server brought over a plate of bacon-wrapped scallops and Ruby and Mom ordered fish and chips. "A perfect meal in honor of Mema," Ruby said to Mom.

"So that dream I had with the dress...do you remember that night?

You were there, in my dream."

Mom shook her head. "Not that I recall, but maybe. I mean, Papa worked so much. I remember lots of work events. Some were for he and Mema and some were for the family. I remember Mema having more social events when we were a little older. Loretta babysat me, and that's when all the trouble started. Sneaking boys in and out of the house, smoking, and pushing back any time she could."

"Is that why you felt you had to be the perfect kid?"

Mom stirred her water glass. "Who said I had to be the perfect kid?"

Ruby raised her eyes to the ceiling. "Come on, Mom, you've always tried to be perfect. Perfect house, perfect job, perfect family."

"Not a perfect family. Broken marriage. Estranged kid. Falling out with family. Nothing says perfection like being alone in the world."

"But don't you think some of those things happened because you tried to hang onto this 'do-good' persona for so long? I remember you doing everything for everyone. Working and being in charge of PTA. Cleaning the house and chauffeuring me around. You liked people to see us a certain way, and I feel like that personality quirk came from somewhere early on."

"When I was a kid, it was easier to not make waves."

Ruby turned the page and wrote *KATE*. "Do you think Mema thought of Kate as her own kid?"

Mom rolled her eyes. "I mean, Kate knew about Papa's stroke and I didn't. I'm not a psychologist, but that has to say something."

Ruby summarized the dream about Mema, Kate, and Papa, and how Papa requested Mema call their kids. "He wanted you to know."

"One thing about your grandmother," Mom said, "was that she had a mean streak. She always hung onto past disputes and that anger came out when you least expected it. She probably never called because she wanted to punish me."

Ruby wanted to change the subject because their conversation had turned against Mema, and Ruby wasn't sure she wanted her view of her grandmother tainted by Mom's bitterness.

"What do you think is going to happen with the house and all her stuff?"

The server filled their water glasses, removed the appetizer plate, and placed their fish and chips on the table. Ruby immediately reached for ketchup and created a small volcano for her fries.

"She allocated Auntie Loretta as the person in charge, but I'll help her. I'll stay until January or as long as she needs me. Mema was buried yesterday and Auntie Loretta seems a bit overwhelmed. I'd like to help her, however I can."

They ate the rest of their meal in silence, and Ruby flipped through the dream journal again. "There are no more clothes, Mom. Is this it? Is this all that Mema had to tell us?"

Mom shoved a French fry into her mouth. "Let's try to get an appointment with the medium. Maybe she can tell us. If that suitcase is it, then so be it. But maybe it isn't. Maybe there's more we need to see."

Chapter 25

The server dropped the check, and Lynette scanned the total. "Uh, excuse me." She waved the paper back and forth. "This isn't right."

"Yes, it's on the house." The server flashed a cheerful smile. "No one argues with the owner." She winked, and Lynette's face flushed.

"Oh, okay. Thank you." Lynette tucked the paper back into the receipt folder and placed it on the table with a twenty-dollar bill sticking out. "For the tip," Lynette said.

"What's up?" Ruby asked.

"Oh, you know. Just a little discount. It's very kind." Lynette's voice turned meek and her mouth turned dry.

"Was it Daniel?"

"Yes. He is the owner."

Lynette rubbed the back of her neck and glanced at Ruby. Tiny butterflies living in her stomach took flight at the thought of seeing him again.

Ruby whooped and held her hand up to give Lynette a high-five. Instead of celebrating, Lynette gave a wistful smile.

"Come on, Mom. Don't leave me hanging!"

Lynette's hand shot up, tapped Ruby's, and shot down. Then she looked around the room, ready to wave a polite thank you, but Daniel was out of sight.

"I want to see him again. Size him up," Ruby said.

"Didn't you meet him after the funeral?" She hugged her purse to her chest.

"Not really. I mean, I saw him, but we never actually met."

"Oh, I don't know. Our history is kind of complicated."

Ruby shoved another French fry in her mouth. "Yeah, what's the story? I don't ever remember hearing about a Daniel."

Lynette sighed. "He was my high school sweetheart. I was a junior and he was a senior. The summer after he graduated, we broke up and got back together. He was a few hours away, and I tried my best to keep our relationship alive, but he never returned any of my phone calls. Then I met your dad and the rest is history."

"That's it?"

"That's it."

Lynette stood and pulled her arms through her jacket. "It's been over thirty years." She threw her purse over her shoulder and marched toward the door, but standing at the host stand was Daniel. Lynette's eyes ran around the perimeter of the restaurant like a pinball machine, searching for another exit. No luck.

"Lynette." His deep voice evoked memories of a simpler time. "Did you enjoy your meal?"

"Yes, thank you for your generosity. That was very kind of you." She grabbed Ruby's arm. "Daniel, this is my daughter, Ruby. Ruby, this is Daniel."

"Thank you for dinner," Ruby said. "It was delicious." Lynette watched her eyes crinkle with mischief. The last time Lynette saw those eyes filled with wonder was when Elfie showed up for Christmas twenty years ago. It was a look of magic and opportunity.

"We must be going," Lynette said.

Daniel's hand grabbed her arm and tiny sparks traveled from her wrist to her shoulder. Her belly fluttered with memories.

"How long are you in town for?" he asked.

"Eh..."

"January," Ruby announced. "She'll be here until January."

A warm smile erupted from his lips. "Great, hopefully we'll see each other again." Sparklers exploded in Lynette's stomach, and she pulled her arm away.

"Yes, we'll be in touch." Breaking from his concentrated gaze, she headed out of the restaurant with Ruby close on her heels.

Back at the car, Ruby whooped again. "He's cute, Mom. I want to hear everything about him."

Lynette wasn't ready to share her feelings. Hell, her feelings scared her, and until she sorted the sparklers lighting up her insides, she wanted to keep Daniel to herself. "Right now, there is nothing to say. Just an ex-boyfriend from years gone by. There's no story."

She glanced at Ruby as she turned her shoulders to reverse out of the parking spot. Ruby's eyes glowed with questions as she looked at Daniel's silhouette in the tall restaurant window.

When they arrived back at the house, Ruby excused herself to call the medium.

"Hey Loretta?" Lynette called, but no one answered. She sneaked into the house and found her sister asleep on the couch.

Lynette settled at the dining room table and sorted through the short stacks placed neatly in the center.

Although Loretta hadn't asked for help, Lynette was curious what type of obstacles Mom had left.

Lynette spied a large envelope with Kate's name on it. Careful not to disrupt the pile, Lynette removed the 8X11 typed document. "The law offices of Studebaker," Lynette read. Her breath caught in her throat, as if she'd just found treasure in a buried pirate's chest.

She skimmed down the document, ignoring large, unfamiliar words. It was her last will and testament, and it appeared Kate was the benefactor of all her assets except for the house and her life insurance.

Lynette skimmed quicker. All her assets?

Her life insurance was to be split by her next of kin. That would be Lynette and Loretta. Her bank account and stocks, which Dad worked tirelessly to maintain, went to Kate, and the house went to Ruby.

What a disaster. Ruby won't want this house. No aspiring model made their career while living in Portland, Maine. Mom wasn't stupid, so why would she make these choices? And how much was in her life insurance? Hopefully, enough for Lynette to escape her sad life in Chicago.

She heard rustling in the other room and shoved the paper back into the envelope. Her nerves rattled at the mess her mother had left them. *Kate got almost everything.* Taking deep breaths, Lynette paced the room, thinking. She needed to talk to Loretta.

"Mom, I got an appointment for Monday." Ruby barreled into the dining room and her bright eyes flashed at Lynette. Lynette forced a smile.

"Great." She fumbled with the piles, making sure nothing looked out of place.

Ruby's smile fell, and she sat beside Lynette. "Are you okay?"

Lynette didn't like lying, but this last will and testament was not worth worrying Ruby, especially when Loretta hadn't confirmed Mom's wishes. "Yes, just tired. I might lie down for a bit."

She stepped into the kitchen and pulled a mug out of the cabinet while the water boiled. "Tea?"

"No thanks. I'm going to give Shayla a call."

"Who's that?"

A flash of red crossed Ruby's face and her relaxed posture stiffened. "My roommate."

Sad that she didn't know the name of her daughter's roommate or how long they had been living together, Lynette nodded.

"Mom, I have to tell you something. I lost my job."

Lynette dropped the mug on the counter with a clatter. "What? No."

"Yes."

"How?"

"Modeling is a fluid career. There's no loyalty. I mean, I work part time at the bookstore—"

"The bookstore? I worked at a bookstore when I was your age." Memories of Lynette and Martha from twenty years before filled Lynette with warmth. God, life was so much easier back then.

"Yeah, and that's fine, but it doesn't pay my rent. It pays for quick trips for coffee or a night out at the bar."

Lynette tried to picture Ruby at a bar, flirting with attractive men, and having one too many. She hoped she was safe. Biting her tongue, Lynette stopped all the worries she'd carried for the past three years from spilling onto the kitchen floor. "Oh."

"Yeah, so because I broke my contract with Jolie Belle, they emailed me, saying I no longer represent them."

"Oh, I'm sorry."

"Their new spokesperson might be my roommate, Shayla. She didn't say that, but she called to tell me they hired her."

Lynette's eyes bulged, feeling Ruby's disappointment. "I'm sorry," she said.

"It's okay. I was upset at first, but that's the modeling business. I have to call and see if she has some other leads for me when I get back." Instead of looking worried, Ruby looked relaxed, like maybe Jolie Belle wasn't right for her. Lynette scrunched her forehead. *Wasn't modeling Ruby's life?*

"Good luck." Lynette raised the steaming hot water to her lips to prevent unwanted motherly advice from pouring out of her mouth.

She watched her grown daughter move out of the kitchen and down the hallway. Lynette returned to the dining room table to see what other key information she could find.

Mom's last will and testament looked like it would be a mess. If Ruby got the house, but Kate got everything else, did that mean she received all the furniture and items in the house? Lynette hoped that wasn't the case, and if it was, Kate would understand why it wasn't her place to take ownership of the family's memories. *She wouldn't want that stuff, would she? She wasn't family.*

Curious about the life insurance, Lynette gently leafed through the piles. At the top of the fourth pile, she found a statement from the insurance company. Lynette's breath hijacked, and she coughed into her fist. *$500,000. Wow! Thank you, Mom.*

Lynette dreamed about what she would do with a quarter of a million dollars. She could rebuild her life somewhere away from Chicago, that's what. She could move to California, or here even, and restart her life with Ruby. *God, she missed her.*

Their relationship appeared to be improving, even though they hadn't fully addressed the tough issues that had caused problems for the past three years. Still hurt, Lynette tried to ignore the past, but Ruby's leaving seemed to be the catalyst that destroyed her life. Maybe it was unfair, but coincidences didn't lie.

Lynette crept upstairs and watched a television show on her phone. The tea had cooled, and the pile of cookies she confiscated from the kitchen left a pile of crumbs, proving she had no self-control. Lynette swiped the sheets and lay down with her head pressed against the pillow.

She closed her eyes and listened to the sounds of quirky television dialogue and laugh tracks infiltrate her mind.

Images, words, and emotions flooded the darkness behind her eyes. Mom, in the same cardigan Lynette had found in her closet, glowed like a Christmas tree, with Kate standing beside her. Hugs, smiles, and a general air of happiness. A beep, Mom's cell phone, and the word **Loretta** in the air. "Later," Mom had said to her phone. "I may not have my girls, but at least I have you." Another embrace, theatrical music, and then nothing.

Her eyes opened to another day in Maine and her desire to embrace Mom ached in her heart. An overwhelming urge to tell her she was sorry flooded her eyes and ran down her cheeks, but it was too late. It appeared Kate had taken over the role of daughter.

Chapter 26

The rest of the weekend dragged on, with Ruby spending most of her time in front of the television watching cooking shows that required little attention. With all this time on her hands, she stressed about modeling and money. Or lack thereof.

Shayla told her not to worry, but Ruby heard the sugar-coated stress in her voice.

Ruby changed the channel, convincing herself not to fret until she returned on Wednesday.

Mom walked into the living room and sat at the edge of the couch. "One o'clock, right?"

"Yep. Want to head out around lunch?"

Today was the day.

When Mom told Ruby about the cardigan and the dream with Kate, Ruby didn't show any surprise. Ruby had seen their friendship in her own dream and she understood how friends turned into family. Shayla had been that person for Ruby.

Kate hadn't been around since the funeral and Ruby wasn't sure if she'd see her before she returned to L.A. Auntie Lori had spent many hours alone and hyper-focused on the will, because she wanted to have everything settled or partially settled by the end of the week. Time was not on her side, and Ruby knew not to bother her.

"I'm ready to go whenever you are," she said to Mom.

"Ten minutes." Mom left the room and Ruby closed her tablet.

In the car, on the drive toward the New Hampshire border, Lynette broke the silence. "What do you think of Kai?"

Ruby snorted. "She's young, pretty, and probably someone I would be friends with. Dad looked good. Happy."

Mom sighed. "Yeah, he did. Sometimes I wonder how we lasted as long as we did."

Ruby's vision blurred, remembering when their little family of three was perfect in her mind. It wasn't until middle school when she started to notice the cracks. "I know how. You were too busy to notice. You both worked. Dad was never home, and you had a kid. Until I left, you never had time to question your marriage."

Her mom blinked back the tears. "Yep, I would say things crumbled after you left."

Ruby had never been good with feelings. She grew up in a household where everything was go-go-go. If those little feelings of mismatched intentions popped up, her parents encouraged her to bulldoze past and move on. It's what they did and what they taught.

Mom's hand dropped on the edge of Ruby's seat. "I don't regret a thing."

Ruby's throat thickened. "I do," she muttered.

Mom glanced at her from the side. "Yeah?"

"Yeah. I don't regret moving to California, but I regret cutting you out of my life. It was so hard in the beginning, without a job or an actual apartment. I was crashing from couch to couch. The first thing I did was get a cell phone with a new number and I purposefully didn't tell you."

A thin line appeared where Mom's lips used to be. "I tried to call you, but your number was disconnected. It was a slap in the face, after everything we did for you and how our life had crumbled after you left."

A tiny pebble grew in Ruby's throat as she listened to Mom's voice falter. "I'm a horrible person."

"No, you're not. You're a young adult trying to make her way into the world. We built you to be independent and strong. You're exactly who we raised you to be. You know, regret is a part of life, so you better get used to it."

Ruby half smiled.

"Plus, you weren't all to blame. I did the same to my parents." They pulled into a small strip mall near the beach. "Is this it?"

"Yeah, I think so." They climbed out of the car and walked along the storefronts.

In the center of the building stood a tiny shop with holiday lights illuminating the display window. The door jingled when they walked in and a woman with long, frizzy black hair greeted them. She wore a flowing, flowery, crinkle skirt with a beaded belt wrapped around her waist. The ends hung to the middle of her thigh and jangled like a lullaby. Golden bangles lined her forearms, and a giant stone covered the space between her upper knuckles on her pointer finger.

This was not how Ruby imagined Eleanor to look, but her eccentricity put Ruby at ease. Her outside persona matched the image Ruby had conjured in her mind, giving her credibility in this mystical field.

"Hello," she said. "My name is Eleanor Smith, but you can call me Nora." Double dimples poked through her cheeks.

"Hi. Lynette and Ruby." Mom spoke with authority. "We have an appointment today."

"Yes, wonderful. I didn't realize there were two of you. Each appointment is individual. Who would like to go first?"

Ruby and Mom looked at each other. "I'll go," Mom said.

"Please follow me." Instrumental music played gently in the background, and dim lights along the back walls cast long shadows within the room.

Nora led her through a beaded curtain and Ruby settled in one of three leather chairs lining the wall. She browsed the room for magazines, but found herself in front of the bookshelf filled with gemstones and tarot card prints.

Twenty minutes later, the beaded curtain swooshed and Lynette's pale face exited the dark room. She smiled faintly and sat down next to Ruby.

"How was it?" Ruby asked.

"Good." Her face washed of all color. "I'll tell you about it later."

"Ruby?" Nora's friendly voice and smile pulled Ruby out of her chair like a magnet and her tight shoulders relaxed. She gave Mom one last look and walked into the darkness.

Nora sat across from her and pulled out a stack of tarot cards. Ruby's chest squeezed, knowing she'd always been afraid of dabbling in the afterlife.

"Okay, Ruby," Nora started. She shuffled the cards. "Have you ever visited a medium?"

Ruby shook her head, eyeing the large deck of cards.

"When the spirits come to me, they are in their optimal state, which means there is no embarrassment, shame, or anger. They may share things that are uncomfortable for you, but neutral to them. Their emotional state is what you and I would call balanced. And free of judgment. Are you prepared to learn things that might unsettle you?"

Ruby's fingers turned cold. "Yes," she said.

"To get started, please shuffle and cut the cards."

Ruby did as she was told, and Nora flipped over the top card, scrutinizing the upright image of a woman holding a star.

"Ah, the star card. There are opportunities in front of you, but you must see them to access them." Nora closed her eyes, concentrating.

Ruby's heart raced and her body felt like it had been struck by lightning. Everything tingled, and Ruby's breath caught in her throat.

Without opening her eyes, Nora whispered, "There is someone here for you. She is drinking a cup of tea."

Ruby shivered and leaned forward.

"Please ask me specific yes-no questions and understand that you can ask anything and you will get an honest response."

Ruby lost feeling in her fingers and she rubbed her clammy hands on her thighs. "Is it Mema?"

Nora leaned forward and crossed her hands. "I see a coin. A penny. Does that mean anything to you?"

Ruby gasped and nodded.

Nora gazed past Ruby's right shoulder and she slowly turned toward Ruby. "I'm seeing cookies. And smelling gingerbread."

Ruby cocked her head to the side. They always made cookies whenever she visited. Ruby wasn't positive about what the intention was, but in her mind, it was a joyous moment.

"Okay...sorry," she said to Nora, "I've never done this before." Her voice quivered.

"Take your time, my gem."

Ruby flew to the back of her chair like a speeding bullet. The heavy sobs escaped her as her mouth fell open. She tried to respond, but her dry tongue stuck to her lower jaw.

Nora gently patted Ruby's shaking hand. "Take your time, dear. These things can be difficult."

"My gem," Ruby said quietly. "Why did you say that?"

"It's what she said."

Ruby may not have believed it before, but she did now. The only person who called her Gem was Mema. "I'm sorry, I can't do this." Her heart racing, Ruby rose from the table and stumbled back to the waiting area.

Nora's voice called to her but Ruby didn't hear.

"Ruby, are you okay? You're white as a ghost." Mom covered her mouth with her hand. "I'm sorry. I didn't mean that."

Throwing on her jacket, Ruby tripped toward the door. "It's okay, let's go. This thing is freaking me out." Ruby held up her shaking hands to show how her body had responded to Nora's news.

Nora stepped out of the back room, and Mom apologized for their sudden departure. "Thank you, but we have to go."

"I will see you soon," Nora said and the door slammed.

Back at the house, Ruby and Mom sat down for a cup of tea to discuss their experience. They had said little during the car ride home, both caught up in the silence of their thoughts.

"How was it?" Ruby asked. "With Nora?" Unable to make eye contact, she fumbled with the sugar bowl.

Mom inhaled and held her breath. "Did she pull a tarot card?"

Ruby nodded. "Yeah, it was the star."

"What does that mean?" Mom asked.

"I don't know. She said something about opportunities that need to be recognized. What'd you get?"

"Upside down judgment."

"Yeesh, that doesn't sound good," Ruby said. Maybe she didn't want to know.

"Yeah, that has to do with guilt. It's all about feeling guilty for the past and asking for forgiveness and accepting forgiveness from others."

Feeling like an unwelcome voyeur in Mom's heart, Ruby slinked away from further discussion. "Would you go back to her?"

"Yes. She made me think about things. Like the past, the dreams, and forgiveness. Maybe that's what those dreams are about." Mom sipped her tea and stared out the window.

Ruby pulled out her phone and scanned her social media. No one seemed to realize she was gone. She placed her phone face down on the table and moved toward the living room. "I'm going to rest for a bit," she said through the doorway.

Lounging on the worn couch, Ruby thought about which opportunities may present themselves. A sudden noise pulled her away from her thoughts, and Auntie Lori flew through the front door with Kate directly behind. They appeared to be arguing, and Ruby scrunched down lower on the couch.

"Lori, I didn't know," Kate whined.

"Sure, it's fine. It's what Mom wanted." Loretta zoomed past the back of the couch and Ruby held her breath. She peeked her eyes over the arm of the couch toward the dining room.

"Are you sure? I feel terrible."

Auntie Lori spun on her heel, her nose practically touching Kate's chin. "It's fine. It's what she wanted."

It didn't sound fine.

Mom stepped through the threshold. "Hi, you're back."

"Yep. I'm back. Things with the lawyer are in process. Sit down, I have to tell you something."

Mom settled in a chair.

"Where's Ruby? I need her too."

Ruby popped up from the couch and rubbed her eyes, pretending to have just woken up. "I'm here." She meandered to the table. Kate's head lay in her open palm, and Auntie Lori flipped through the documents.

"I saw the lawyer. With Kate."

Mom narrowed her eyes. "Why were you there, Kate?"

"Well," Auntie Lori said, "Mom left Kate quite a bit in her will."

Mom's eyes darted between Kate and Auntie.

"Here's the deal in a nutshell. Kate got Mom's savings and assets. Ruby, you got the house, and Lynette and I got her life insurance."

Ruby leaned forward, her arms and legs stiff. "What?"

"The house, Ruby. The house. It's all yours."

Ruby looked around, processing Auntie's words like they were a hodge-podge of different languages Ruby had never learned. "The house?"

Annoyance crept into Auntie's voice. "Yes, the house. Kate got the bank account and stocks. At this time, I don't have a clue what it's worth, but Dad took care of Mom, and Mom had no expenses, so I assume it's around half a mil. Lynette, you and I get about two hundred and fifty thousand each."

Ruby watched Mom's face pale at the recognition and realization of so much money.

"Kate," Mom interrupted, "no offense, but how did you weasel your way into the will?"

"Mom!" Ruby couldn't believe how rude her mother could be. Ruby knew exactly why Kate had been included. Kate was the only one who showed any interest in Mema over the past twenty years.

Kate swallowed and picked at her fingers. "I don't know. I really liked your mom and dad. We got along well."

Mom huffed. "Really."

"Really. I thought of your mom as a mother figure. She always looked out for me, and I for her."

Ruby touched Mom's arm. "Mom, it's true. The black blazer. From the suitcase. It's true." She tried to communicate the relevance of the black blazer with her eyes, but it didn't seem Mom understood.

"Well, I'm glad she had you." The stiff compliment fell and Mom pulled up her lips into a forced smile. Kate smiled back.

"Anyway," Auntie Lori said, "it will be months to years before the estate goes through probate. Ruby, you can sell the house, but not until things are finalized."

"Like, in years?"

"Yeah, I don't know."

Confusion around her additional responsibility made Ruby's knees weak. *A house, just like that?*

"The good thing is that the mortgage is gone, so you could live here for free if you wanted."

Dollar signs flew toward Ruby's face, and she imagined Mema throwing her a Get Out of Jail Free card. Maybe she could turn it into a vacation home and rake in enough money to survive L.A. rent.

Confused by the turn of events, she wondered if returning to California in two days was the smartest move.

"Although I am the executor, Kate knew Mom best. And I have to get back to work eventually, so Kate and I will work together until things are done."

Ruby saw Mom's shoulders tighten, probably because her organizational skills had been overlooked again. Or because Kate was treated more like family than her. Ruby understood how overbearing and difficult Mom could be, but she also understood how hurt Mom may feel by not being included. It was as if Kate or Auntie Lori were more deserving of Mema's time.

Mom stood from the table and placed her eyes on Ruby. "Ruby, seeing as how this house is yours, are you okay if I stay here until January?"

Ruby nodded. *Her house.* It was now her home. The weight of the extra obligation made it difficult to breathe. "Sure, Mom."

"Kate, Loretta, I'm here if you need help." With that last statement, Mom left the room.

Kate and Auntie Lori spoke quietly amongst themselves using legalese terms Ruby didn't understand, so she sneaked out of the dining room and back onto the couch.

Mema, why? She didn't want to be tied to a haunted house in Maine. She wanted to be in L.A., modeling and struggling like she had been. She didn't want someone to give her a handout, and this house was the most unnecessary handout someone could have given her.

"What time is your flight?" Shayla's boisterous voice popped through the phone and Ruby couldn't help but smile.

"I get in around six. I'll get a cab or something."

"Nah, I'll get you. A cab during rush hour? That'll cost you hundreds."

Ruby packed her clothes into her suitcase, cramming the extra sweaters she had bought on top. The hunter green dress remained in the closet, shoved deep into the busted open suitcase. She liked that dress, but there was no way she was taking it home. "Thanks. How was your week?"

"So busy, but good. I got another job."

"Congrats!"

"Yeah, nothing big, but enough to pay for groceries. I think it's a three-day shoot for a series of commercials."

"Good for you." Ruby thought she wanted to go home, but she didn't want to leave Maine with so many loose ends.

"How about you? How was it seeing everyone?"

"So weird. I can't really get into it now," she said.

"Oh, someone nearby?"

"Yeah," Ruby lied. She didn't know what to think about Nora and she wasn't ready to share that vulnerable yet scary experience with Shayla.

"I miss you. I'll see you tomorrow."

Ruby hung up the phone and shoved her small toiletry bag into the front pocket. The zipper threatened to bust open, so Ruby sat on it and bounced to ensure its strength.

A slight knock vibrated through the door, and Ruby turned. "Come in."

Mom entered with short, quick steps and sat beside her. "Are you okay?"

Ruby slid back and rubbed her eyes. "Sure."

"No, really. It's a lot to process."

Ruby huffed. "What part? Mema talking to us from the grave, seeing you and Dad, or inheriting a haunted house?"

"Yeah, it's a lot, isn't it?"

Ruby didn't know how to feel.

"I wanted to tell you about the dream I had," Mom said.

Ruby paused and straightened out her pillows.

"Mema came to me in another dream, except it wasn't from an item we found in the suitcase. It was the cardigan I wore at her funeral. I had found it in her bedroom. In my dream, she was wearing it. Anyway, it was after Papa died. I saw her and Kate in the kitchen."

Ruby narrowed her eyes. "Wait. What are you saying?"

"I'm saying that the suitcase isn't the magic item. She's communicating through other clothes. I think the suitcase was the avenue to show us she meant business...like, she knew we'd go through it out of curiosity. I think she'll keep communicating with us as long as we wear her clothes. Any of them."

Ruby didn't want to believe her, but her gut told her it could be true. "What? That sounds crazy." The room tilted as Ruby realized there could be more memories just waiting to be unleashed.

"I'm saying that if she isn't done talking to us, we can't leave her hanging."

"What did Nora say, exactly?"

"She told me to only ask yes or no questions, so I asked about my dreams. Ruby—." Mom grabbed her arm. "She got married because she was pregnant. Not because she loved Papa."

Ruby squinted her eyes. "What happened to the baby?"

"The baby died at birth. So—and I'm assuming here—Mom got pregnant, got married even though she didn't want to, and then lost the baby but was still stuck in the marriage. Can you imagine how isolated and bitter she must have felt?"

Ruby nodded.

"Papa, though, he always seemed so happy-go-lucky. I think he really loved her and I think she settled. That could explain so much. Her mood swings, her unpredictability, and how Papa always defended her. I know it's crazy," she repeated, "but I know there's more to the story."

"So who was Lorraine?"

"The baby who died. My second dream when Mema was pregnant must have been when she was pregnant with Loretta."

"Mom."

Mom held out her hand. "I know it sounds crazy. Now, I'm going to ask you something. Something important because I don't know if you are the key. Without you here, everything may fall to crap. I mean, you found the suitcase. Not me. You. Without you here, she may stop and I need her. There are too many questions that have gone unanswered."

Ruby's heart thudded and her blood raced. *This cannot be happening right now.*

"Stay here. With me. At least until January."

"No."

"Please. Mema isn't done yet."

Ruby threw her pillow on her luggage. "What? How do you even know that?"

Mom's eyes raced back and forth. "I don't. But I have a feeling. You and I have a lot of history to unpack. Don't you think you owe it to me? Don't you think I owe it to you?"

Entrapment wrestled with a desire to help and Ruby's heart tugged in every direction. She shook her head and yanked at her hair.

"This is your home now," Mom coaxed.

"No, it's not."

"But it could be. Can you give me two months? You don't have a job, right?"

"Maybe not modeling, but I have to return to the bookstore next week."

"But, isn't that just a part time gig? I mean, it's not your career, or anything."

"No, but Mom, I have an apartment. I have a car. I can't just leave my roommate and boss hanging. I'm not that kind of person."

Mom grabbed Ruby's hand and rubbed it. Ruby watched her mom's long, burgundy nails trace the lines across her hand. "Okay. Just think about it." She rose from the bed and walked out of the room.

Ruby couldn't believe Mom had asked her to uproot her entire life to chase the ghost of her dead grandmother. It felt wrong, but the adventurous side of Ruby emerged. Adventure combined with closure may be good for their family.

Maybe L.A. wasn't the place for her. She certainly couldn't pursue her modeling dream in Maine, but maybe she could make it work. Social media reached the world. If she got creative, she could build something for herself. A new brand persona, like the great outdoorsy girl. There had to be other ways to build a modeling career, and she wasn't looking hard enough.

Ruby eyed her luggage and checked her email. Nothing from Jolie Belle. She closed her phone and remained stiff on her bed. Trapped and frozen, she knew her life had changed. And Mema still had an influence over her, only this time Mema was pulling the strings like a puppeteer.

"Mom, wait."

Mom turned, holding a full mug of coffee.

"Where are you going today?"

Mom sipped her coffee and looked out the window. "Nowhere. To the airport to drop you off. Have you said goodbye to your father?"

Ruby shook her head. "No, I wanted to talk to you. Before my flight."

Mom leaned against the counter and Ruby saw excitement and nervousness mix in her blue eyes. Ruby knew it was bold, but money was a hard cold fact about life, and currently, she couldn't afford to live.

"Mom, if I stay here until January, can you pay my rent? It's the only way this will work."

She had thought about it all night, even begged Mema to come to her in her dream, but the only thing she saw behind her eyes was darkness. Without some sort of confirmation from Mema, she didn't know if staying or leaving was the right decision.

It didn't matter. Her gut told her to stay. Besides sunshine and pretty bodies, what else did California offer her?

"You need me to pay your rent? How much?"

Ruby knew this was the kicker. Once she gave Mom the total cost of her share, she would laugh and say no. "Um, $2300." Her voice fell to a whisper, embarrassed that she had escaped to a place known to run people out with the high cost of survival.

"What?" Mom's voice hissed in a half-whisper.

"My rent is $2300. And parking for my car is $500...a month."

"So, three thousand dollars." Mom raised her head to the ceiling and inhaled and exhaled like a well-practiced mindfulness exercise. "I knew it was expensive, Ruby, but nothing like that."

Ruby watched and waited, but Mom never answered her question.

"Mom, you know what? Forget it. I have to be at the airport in three hours. I'll go grab my stuff."

"Oh, no. Let me talk to your father. I'm sure he owes you some money."

Mom topped her mug with fresh liquid energy and the scent of hazelnut swirled toward Ruby's nose. Ruby bit her lip and watched Mom march out of the kitchen.

Ruby still wasn't sure if she was making the right decision, so she paced the kitchen, eating tiny bites of homemade blueberry muffin Kate had dropped off the day before. Her car was in L.A. and without a car, she'd be trapped in this neighborhood. Auntie Lori was leaving,

Mom hated Kate, and winter was coming. Staying here seemed like an all-around bad idea, yet Ruby couldn't quite settle on the biggest reason not to stay.

Without confirmation from Mom, she was heading home. She may be unemployed, but at least she had an apartment and a friend. Ruby grabbed her luggage from the upstairs bedroom and dragged it down the old, rickety stairs.

"Hey, are you leaving?" Auntie Lori's cheerful voice cut through the hallway.

Ruby threw her arms around Auntie's strong shoulders, her puffy hair pressing into Ruby's face. The curly strands tickled her cheek and Ruby sneezed.

"Bless you."

"I'm leaving soon. Just getting ready."

"Okay, expect something in the mail, and make sure you stay in touch. I don't have time to track you down with all this lawyer crap."

"Yes, ma'am."

Auntie's eyes narrowed playfully. "Don't call me ma'am. I'm too young for that."

"I'll stay in touch, I promise." Ruby settled her luggage next to the front door. Looking out the front window, she saw Kate raking Mema's yard.

"What in the world?" Auntie Lori asked, coming up behind her.

"Should we help her?"

"Why is she doing that? I swear, she has something up her sleeve."

Ruby pulled on Mema's boots, which lay haphazardly near the door, and pulled on an overcoat she found in the back closet. "I'm going to help. When Mom comes downstairs, tell her I'm outside."

The leaves crunched under Ruby's heavy boots and a gentle breeze pushed cold air against her face. "Hi, do you need some help?"

Kate rested against the stick of the rake and shook out her free arm.

"Yes, that would be great. I promised your grandmother I would take care of her yard, and just because she isn't here anymore doesn't mean I won't keep up my end of the deal."

"Here, let me rake, and you can put it in the bag." Ruby grabbed the rake out of Kate's hand and swiped the leaves into a pile. "Tell me about your relationship with Mema. It seemed you were close."

A small smile spread across Kate's face and she removed her glove before wiping her eye. "Have you ever been so alone, you never thought your heart would heal?"

Ruby nodded. She had felt like that when she moved to California. She felt like a naïve idiot, making the biggest mistake of her life, yet somehow it had worked out.

"I married my husband when I was thirty-five. All my friends had married and had kids by the time they were thirty, but I was independent. I didn't need a man until I did. I loved living alone and being in charge of me and only me, but life got lonely. After we got married, my sister died in a car crash. My mom died. And my best friend lived in Texas. I loved my husband, but I felt disconnected from female influence and support."

Ruby focused on the leaves, slowly building a pumpkin-colored glacier in the middle of the yard.

"We moved here for Nick's job, and I met your Mema and Papa. They loved you so much, Ruby."

"Why don't I remember you? I came here often when I was younger."

"We didn't become close until after your Papa got sick. Your grandma needed me just as much as I needed her. With your mom and aunt far away, they couldn't give your Mema the support she needed."

A tiny ache poked at Ruby's heart. She knew what it felt like to be alone, or that everyone you loved was against you.

"Life is too short, and sometimes you need whoever you can find to fill that void. That was how it started, but it became more. Over the past ten years, your grandmother became my support and cheerleader, while I became her caregiver."

"And now you're doing her yard?"

"Yes, and I will until I don't have to."

"Ruby," Mom hollered from the doorway. "Time to go. I'll meet you in the car in five minutes."

Ruby handed Kated the rake and hugged her gently. "I've gotta get to the airport. It was nice getting to know you."

"Yeah, safe travels."

Ruby trudged to the house and retrieved her luggage. For such an emotional week, she thought for sure she'd be itching to get home, but maybe L.A. wasn't the home she had always imagined. Ruby wrestled with staying in Maine or returning to California.

Either way, her life would never be the same, but which life was best?

Chapter 27

A strange melancholy filled the car as Lynette maneuvered through the small, twisty back roads, eventually leading to a major thoroughfare.

"Boston, right?" Lynette asked.

"Yes, it was the closest airport with a direct flight."

Traffic wasn't too bad for a Wednesday, and the GPS lady navigated them through the maze of narrow highways and old bridges.

Lynette needed Anthony to get back to her, but so far, nothing. She bit her bottom lip and drummed her fingers on the steering wheel.

If Ruby had wanted to stay, they wouldn't be driving right now. She would have said yes and they would have figured out the logistics later. Instead, Lynette had found her outside with Kate cleaning the yard. Instead of thinking about staying, Ruby had fraternized with the enemy, as Lynette watched from the upper bedroom window.

Lynette prayed to Mom, asking for Anthony to come through.

She'd been on an emotional roller coaster the past few days. Grateful to Martha for watering her plants, collecting her mail, and monitoring the furnace when the temperature dropped, Lynette let the financial worries around work float around her. She had to go back to work in January if she wanted to keep her job and her home.

Lynette redirected her attention to Ruby. "So, L.A., huh? Does that mean I won't hear from you for the next three years?" She tried to sound witty, but apathy bounced around the car.

"What's that supposed to mean?"

Lynette sighed. "It means I miss you, and I don't want to miss you anymore."

Ruby looked out the window, looked at Lynette, and changed the radio to another song. "I'll be in touch."

It wasn't a promise, but a declarative statement. Being an English professor, Lynette knew the difference.

As they pulled into the arrival lane at the airport, a beep sounded deep within Lynette's bag. Her heart stuttered, and she said, "Ruby, can you grab that? It might be Auntie Loretta." She hoped it wasn't, but didn't want Ruby to know she needed Anthony to contact her before Ruby disappeared through the terminal.

Ruby dug through, pulling out a travel sized bag of tissues, a wallet stuffed with so many receipts Ruby could barely wrap her hand around it, and a mini-water bottle. "Geez, Mom. You have everything in here except the kitchen sink."

"Try the side pocket." It dinged a second time.

Pulling out the phone, Ruby asked, "What's your passcode?"

"0430."

"My birthday," Ruby whispered.

"Yeah, your birthday. Every time I use my phone, I think of you." Even though her heart fluttered, she kept her eyes on the road.

Ruby wiped the corner of her eye as she unlocked the phone and read the message. "It's from Dad. It says, 'Sure.' That's it."

Lynette pulled to the sidewalk and secured the car in park. Ruby reached for the door. "Don't get out," Lynette said, and she hit the automatic lock button. All the doors clicked.

"Huh?" Ruby turned and her beautiful blue eyes had reverted to the six-year-old with stuffed animals on her lap. Hope was what Lynette saw, and it motivated her to explain.

"Your father and I. We're paying your rent until January. If you want to stay, and I hope you will, we will cover your expenses. I will not beg, but I think your Mema would like it. And I would like it. Plus, you need to figure out what's going on with the house." Lynette threw up her hands in surrender. "Your choice."

Ruby checked her watch and looked outside. The doors bustled with people coming in and out. Luggage dragged and dropped, and police officers directed traffic.

A car horn sounded behind them.

"Oh shit," Lynette said and waved in her rearview mirror. "I know you have an apartment out there, but you can live here expense free. What do you say?"

Ruby hesitated and fiddled with her fingers in her lap. Her face contorted into confusion. The passing seconds felt like a decade and a horn behind them sounded.

"Well? What do you say?" Lynette asked again.

A slow smile spread across Ruby's face. "Fiiine. But I'm doing this for the house, and only because I was fired."

Lynette threw her arms around Ruby's neck and leaned her forehead against Ruby's. "Thank you." She pulled out of the drop-off lane, careful not to hit any pedestrians. "I promise we'll be great roommates. You're an adult and so am I. No nagging from me."

Lynette owed Anthony a big thank you. He wasn't the greatest husband, but he was a wonderful dad. Lynette couldn't fault him for that.

Chapter 28

When Ruby walked into the kitchen, Auntie Lori's face lit up like the Cheshire Cat. "My my my, what are you doing here?"

"Eh, long story." Ruby dropped her suitcase at the door.

"Ruby and I decided it might make the most sense for her and I to stay here together until January. That way you can go back to Florida without a worry and we'll take care of the house for the time being."

Ruby knew Mom wasn't being fully honest. Part of her wanted to explore the clothes to unlock Mema's memories.

"Wonderful!" Auntie Lori threw her arms around Ruby and squeezed her tight. "I knew you two would come around."

"Hey Loretta." Mom's voice broke up the embrace. "Do you think Mom was ready to die?"

Auntie Lori leaned against the table. "I would think so. I mean, her body betrayed her. I'm sure Kate feels massive guilt for not finding her sooner, but things happen for a reason."

"But Auntie, do you think she'd still be alive if Kate came over sooner?"

Auntie Lori adjusted her glasses. "Maybe, I don't know."

"So, you think maybe she wasn't ready to die..." Mom repeated, with a faraway look in her eyes.

"No, that's not what I said."

Ruby interjected. "What you're saying is that we don't know."

"Right."

"Which means maybe."

"Maybe? I don't know."

Mom poured a glass of wine.

"Geez, Lynette, a little soon, isn't it?"

"Four o'clock? Never too early. You want one? Ruby?"

Auntie Lori shook her head no while Ruby grabbed a glass and extended her arm.

"Loretta, do you believe in ghosts?" Lynette asked.

Auntie Lori rolled her eyes. "What has gotten into the two of you? No, I do not believe in ghosts."

Mom ignored Auntie Lori's disbelief. "Mom hasn't come to you?" Although a question, it sounded more like an accusation.

"No, Linnie, she hasn't. Or maybe she has, but I didn't recognize the sign."

Mom leaned close, peering into Auntie Lori's eyes. "Okay." She pulled back and took a sip of her wine. "When do you head back to Florida?"

"Well, since you and Ruby are staying, I'll fly home Friday if I can get a decent price. I'm meeting with the lawyer one last time, and I can do the rest through email."

Mom kissed her on the cheek. "Thanks for all the work you've done for Mom. At first, I was upset that Mom chose you over me, but my life is such a mess. She probably didn't want her death in my hands."

"Well, I'd love to share the responsibility." Auntie Lori's eyes glazed over, and she swiped at them vigorously.

"That's what Kate's for, right?"

Ruby had already finished her drink, so she grabbed Mom's glass, sitting on the counter, and took a swig. The sweet, wet liquid reminded her of all the times she yearned to simplify her life.

"Oh please, what does Kate know about Mom?"

"More than you can imagine," Mom said.

They prepared dinner together, moving around the kitchen and pulling leftovers out of the fridge.

"Loretta, did you know when Mom and Dad got married she was pregnant?"

Ruby recognized the superiority of holding secrets behind Mom's eyes.

"No, they got married before I was born," Auntie said.

"No, they married because they were pregnant. Mom lost the baby. Stillbirth, I think. They called her Lorraine."

Auntie Lori pulled back, her face surprised, with a hint of apprehension. "And how do you know that?"

"Mom came to me. In a dream."

Auntie Lori laughed. "Sure, Linnie, whatever."

Ruby wanted to interject and defend Mom's story, but she didn't want to get involved. It wasn't her dream to tell.

"Lynette, you've always done this. Tried to be Mom's favorite. You're ridiculous if you think I believe Mom is coming to you in your dreams. Please." She stormed out of the kitchen, leaving Ruby and Mom alone.

"I tried to tell her," Mom said, "but I guess Mema doesn't want her to know."

Mom threw a plate into the microwave and pressed the thirty-seconds button. They watched the plate spin until a beep echoed in the kitchen, and then they ate dinner in silence.

On Friday, Auntie Lori left, leaving Ruby and Mom in the big house, with Kate peeking through the windows.

"Why is she always around?" Ruby wondered out loud. She turned to Mom with a curious glance. "Every time I look outside, she's there, doing yard work, organizing Papa's tools, or standing near the mailboxes. It's weird, isn't it?"

"Just give her the benefit of the doubt," Mom said. "Now that Mema's gone, I feel like she's lost."

They sat on the couch, watching Food Network for the thousandth time.

"Mom, why did I stay again?" She had been thinking about Shayla lately, and how she had left her in a lurch with their apartment. Ruby had texted her from the car as they left the airport, apologizing. She promised she'd explain later, and reassured her she'd be home in January.

Shayla responded with a shock emoji, asked if she was okay, and told her to keep in touch.

So far, they hadn't spoken on the phone. Ruby had called a few times, but there was no answer. Perhaps Shayla was busy with Jolie Belle, or perhaps she was upset Ruby ditched her. Clara had been more understanding of Ruby's situation. She told Ruby to take care of what she needed and call her when she returned.

"Well," Mom said, "I was thinking we could experiment a bit. Loretta will be back up for Thanksgiving, and I told her we would clean the house out. So, you and I have to go through the attic and basement before she arrives. I was also thinking we could go through her closet. Maybe the magic of the clothes will continue."

Ruby considered Mema's closet. Nothing in there would fit her, and nothing was in her preferred style. "Why are you so motivated to keep the dreams coming?"

Mom raised her eyes and scrunched her mouth. "I wasted so many years by distancing myself and feeling angry toward my parents. And now that she's gone..." Her jaw tightened as she fiddled with the hem of her sweater, pulling at a loose thread. "If I can just hang onto her a little longer, maybe a part of me that broke can slowly repair itself."

Ruby understood. She was only twenty-three, but she had lost valuable time with her own parents. And for what? A wing and a prayer?

"You know, I think I'm going to get a job," Ruby announced.

"Really?"

"Yeah, not in modeling. Obviously." She rolled her eyes, like modeling in Maine was commensurate with surfing in Colorado. "Unless I want to be the spokesperson for the great outdoors...which I don't. There really isn't any opportunity for me up here to model, but maybe I can find something else." Ruby's brain continued to move on speed dial and her thoughts poured out of her mouth. "Like a regular job. Just something to keep me busy. I can't watch cooking competitions and eat snacks for the next two months. Plus, I always work better under pressure."

"But you're only here for two months."

"So? They don't need to know that."

Mom didn't respond right away, and Ruby saw the wheels inside her brain moving. "Where do you want to work?"

Ruby tapped her chin. "Somewhere where I can meet young people. Maybe that bookstore? That woman who helped us with Nora seemed nice. I can try it. Have you considered getting a job?"

"I'm an English professor. That's been my identity for the past thirty years. I can't get a job at a college for eight weeks. What else would I do?"

"I don't know. Aren't you're paying a mortgage for a house you aren't living in?"

Her mom looked at the tv. "I can't get a job with ill-intentions. I can't accept a job knowing I'll be quitting in two months' time."

"Don't you have any friends here? Maybe they know of someone who needs help. Even if it's under the table."

"Here?" Mom's voice rose an octave. "No, they're all gone. People moved on. No one wanted to stay here."

"Do whatever, Mom, but I feel like down time isn't great for you.

Between working part time and taking care of the house, it'll be January before you know it."

An image of Mom, red-faced and nervous around Daniel, sprung to Ruby's mind. "I know. Apply at Daniel's. That'll keep life interesting." Ruby winked.

Mom's lips curled into a smile, and she shook her head. "I can't do that, can I?"

Ruby's phone dinged and a message from Shayla popped up. "That's Shayla. I feel bad leaving her in a lurch, but if Dad's paying my rent, I guess it doesn't matter."

"Don't feel bad. He owes you. Come on upstairs. I should start going through Mema's room."

Ruby grabbed a trash bag and followed Mom up the steep staircase. "Trash, donate, keep, right?"

"I think we need to clean out the garage and turn it into a mini-estate sale. Mema had boxes upon boxes of holiday decorations I don't want. Do you?"

Ruby thought back to the beautiful lights Mema and Papa strung from the gutters and draped over the bushes. She remembered making gingerbread houses when visiting. It never looked like the picture on the box and it brought out the worst in Ruby as she tried to secure the walls from falling. Every time she'd yell in frustration, Mema would ask what piece was giving her trouble, and when Ruby pointed it out, Mema popped it in her mouth and said, "Problem solved."

As if life's problems could be eaten away...

"Maybe a few things here and there, but not much."

"We'll have a Thanksgiving weekend sale. That'll give us a month. We can invite Auntie Lori up so we don't throw away something she wants. We'll clean out the garage and store stuff in there, in case it snows."

"Do you think I can drive Mema's car? Or can we share it? I don't think having a rental for the next two months is in your best interest."

"Yeah, I'll make sure the insurance is up to date. We can share it."

Ruby couldn't believe they were getting along so well. It made her jumpy, like she wasn't quite ready to trust the kindness and compassion Mom was showing.

Up in Mema's room, Mom emptied the drawers. "Underwear, socks, and bras." She held up a large beige bra. "Trash." Catching flying undergarments, Ruby stuffed them into the bag.

"You sure you don't want to try these on for magic?" She chuckled.

"Ha! I don't need to know what went on behind closed doors."

"Yeah, some things deserve to stay hidden." Ruby tied up the bag and said, "That was easy. I feel better already."

Mom pulled open the next drawer. "Nightgowns. Hmmm...do you think any of these hold magic?"

They looked worn, but still in decent shape. "No, donate." The nightgowns went into another bag.

They worked around the room, emptying drawers and filling bags.

At the end of their scavenger hunt, a small pile of potential items that could bring Mema back from the dead rested in the corner. Handbags, scarfs, fancy shoes, and old sweaters. On the top shelf in her closet, Ruby found a box of aprons with costume jewelry wrapped inside.

"Mom, look at this," she said, holding out the crumpled apron.

Mom came over and analyzed the contents.

"Clip-on earrings and chunky pendants. They're definitely magical."

Ruby placed the items in Mema's empty underwear drawer, where they continued to store potential. "Safe and sound." Soon the drawer overflowed with budding magic, and Ruby and Mom shared a look of hope, like maybe it wasn't too late to start over.

Chapter 29

Over the next week, Lynette hadn't been able to relax because the constant flux of dream montages and magical clothes wouldn't stop. Her jumbled brain needed a rest, so she drove to Nora for some answers.

The door jangled and Lynette walked into the dimly lit room. "Hello?"

Quiet music played in the background, and scents of cinnamon and cloves danced through the air.

Nora hurried out of the back room, adjusting her hair. "Hello." Her eyes scanned Lynette, up and down, clear that she didn't quite remember her.

"Hi, are you available for a reading? I was here about a week ago. With my daughter."

Nora leaned forward, peering into Lynette's eyes, and grabbed Lynette's icy hand. She stroked the tennis bracelet Lynette had found in Mom's jewelry box. "This is beautiful. Yes, follow me."

Lynette's confidence with this experience had grown, although it still felt somewhat unnatural and wrong.

Nora motioned for Lynette to sit across from her.

"How can I help you?" Nora's finger lay on top of the table, and Lynette admired her bedazzled nails of all different colors.

Ignoring the little voice reminding her not to give away all her secrets, she sputtered, "I'd like to communicate with my mom. The one who recently passed."

The music merged into the background and Nora's hands fiddled with a deck of tarot cards. Instead of one card, she flipped a few cards and stared at the pictures. Lynette watched her facial muscles twitch and move, but couldn't infer the meaning behind her expressions.

"I see a big house. And laughter. I see a jokester. Someone or something making people laugh."

"That's my dad. My dad always tried to make us laugh."

"I see regret. And sadness. I see someone who left without saying goodbye."

Lynette's heart fell into the pit of her stomach. "Is that why she's still here? Haunting me?"

Nora tipped her chin upwards. "Not haunting. She's communicating."

"It feels like haunting," Lynette mumbled.

Nora ignored her comment and closed her eyes. "I see a fire."

"Fire?" Lynette didn't know of any fire. She racked her brain. Wouldn't a fire be something she recalled or had heard about?

"Yes," Nora said.

Lynette needed to know. "Why is she still here? Shouldn't she be with my dad?"

Nora swayed her hands over the cards. "I need more direct questions, my dear."

Lynette's mouth turned dry, afraid to voice the fear in her heart. "Is she stuck between worlds?"

Nora's eyes shot up from the table and met Lynette's with authority. "My dear, she is perfect. She is okay."

A shiver ran up Lynette's spine. When Nora didn't say more, Lynette gripped the checkered scarf wrapped around her neck.

"She is with you," Nora said.

Lynette sucked in a breath. She couldn't think with her emotions overpowering her, and she found herself frozen.

Nora gazed past Lynette and closed her eyes, crooning, and touching the tarot cards on the table. Lynette leaned forward, her heart racing and her blood running through her icy veins.

"Do you have any other questions?"

Lynette swallowed. "Yes. Are her clothes magical?" Hearing the words made her lower her shoulders fully knowing how crazy she sounded.

Nora tilted her head and placed her hand in a bowl of crystals. She pulled out a sky-blue crystal and placed it in Lynette's hand. "Celestite," she said. "Hold this." She closed her eyes and hummed. "I see her everywhere."

Dissatisfied with the vagueness of Nora's response, Lynette tightened her grip around the stone. Keeping her voice steady, she asked, "Did she regret how things ended? Between us."

Nora hummed and rearranged the cards on the table. "Yes."

"And Kate. Did Kate replace Loretta and I? Because that's how it feels."

"No."

Relief washed over Lynette. "Will Ruby and I repair our relationship?" Lynette swallowed down a sob, feeling the rock in her throat widen. Her mouth dried up while she waited for a response.

"I see...nothing of certainty. See, the person here with us can only reflect on her past, not your future." Nora touched her hand. "It is uncertain. We cannot predict the future, only identify past pain and joy that may shape the future."

Lynette wiped her eye. "Okay, thank you." She needed to get home, call Martha, and talk to Ruby. Lynette threw her money on the table and stood.

"Wait, we aren't done," Nora protested, but Lynette didn't hear. She had already raced out the door.

Chapter 30

That afternoon, Ruby borrowed the car and approached Books Encore, pulling into a spot directly in front. Nerves raced through her body as a feeling of deceit crept up Ruby's spine. Maybe Mom was right. Maybe it wasn't fair to apply or accept a job when she had no intention of staying.

She checked her makeup, climbed out of the car, and sauntered into the store. "Hi," Ruby said to the same woman who had given them Nora's card.

"I remember you," she said. "Did you end up seeing Nora?"

Ruby nodded. "Yes, um, that's kind of why I'm here. I was supposed to return to California, but seeing Nora made me rethink my plans." There. It was a half-truth, at least. "Are you hiring? I worked at a bookstore out in L.A. for about a year."

"Oh, yeah?" the woman said. "What else could you bring to the business?"

Ruby shifted her weight, unprepared to answer such interview-like questions today. "Um, I have a degree in advertising, I know my way around social media, and I am a model. I know how to build a brand and create an online presence."

The woman stuck out her hand and shook vigorously. "Yes. I'm Stella. I own this place."

"Ruby. Nice to meet you."

177

"Do you like to read?" Stella asked.

"I love it." To avoid an opportunity for Stella to ask about her long-term plans, Ruby quickly added, "I grew up reading."

"What's your favorite genre?"

Ruby knew this was a trick question and would reveal her integrity as an avid reader. "Paranormal romance. Shifters. Werewolves are my favorite."

Stella grinned. "You're hired. It's important that we highlight those books that aren't sold in the big box stores. I need someone who can work part time, just a few hours a week. Do you think that would work?"

Ruby couldn't believe Stella hired her, just like that. "Absolutely." She grabbed a business card, knowing Mom would be pleased.

"So you're good with social media?"

Ruby's smile grew with confidence. "I'm practically a social media guru."

"Oh, good, because I need someone to hype up this business. Maybe organize local author events, book sales, and make recommendations. Anything online that will talk up this business and make it the best bookstore in Portland."

Ruby leaned against the counter, her voice animated. "Absolutely. I am a whiz at creating content and I love engaging with an audience."

"Perfect. What's your availability?" Stella asked.

"I'm open." Ruby knew she'd have to run it by Mom because of the shared car situation, but she didn't want to lose this opportunity.

"Can you start tomorrow?"

"Yes." Ruby turned toward the door and spun. "No. I'm sorry, but my birth certificate is in California, and I don't know where my social security card is. All I have is my license." She scrunched her forehead and bit the cuticles around her thumb.

"No problem. It'll be fine. Show up tomorrow at nine-thirty and we'll get you set up."

Ruby couldn't believe how easy it was to get a job. Sitting in Mema's car, she scolded herself for not asking about pay, but from the sounds of it, it might be under the table.

She puffed her chest and bellowed a loud laugh. *This was too perfect.* She knew all this experience in managing her modeling career would pay off. Ensuring the windows were up, Ruby sang every song that rang through the speakers on the way home. Today was exactly what she needed to get her life back on track.

As she made her way into the house and up the stairs, Mom stood in the bathroom wearing a red and white checkered scarf around her neck.

"Nice scarf." Ruby said.

"Thanks, it's Mema's. I found it in the back of one of her drawers." Mom tightened the scarf.

Ruby couldn't hold her excitement in any longer. "I got a job!"

"Congratulations! At the bookstore?" She pulled a handbag from the towel holder. "Here, put this on."

"Yeah. She wants me to start tomorrow." Ruby adjusted the leather cross body bag hanging across her torso. She posed in the mirror, checking herself from all angles. "It's cute."

"I think it's from the forties."

"Very vintage," Ruby said. "It's perfect for Jolie Belle." Her face reddened, realizing her mistake. She no longer needed to curate the perfect look for Jolie Belle.

The soft leather rubbed against Ruby's fingers and she pressed the permanent creases, clearly well-loved and often used. She dug through the inside, pulling out a matching leather wallet. "This is cute. I like it. Stella, the woman at the bookstore, hired me on the spot."

Mom pulled at the scarf. "I love bookstores. Every time I'm in a bookstore, I feel at home."

Ruby nodded.

"Do you like this? I remember Mom wearing it in some old pictures when I was little. I'm hoping it brings back a positive memory of them... not like that wedding scene."

Ruby flipped through the wallet, searching for any of Mema's forgotten treasures. Stuck in the credit card slot was a yellow, weathered picture of Mom and Auntie. "Check it out," Ruby said, waving the photo in front of her.

Mom grabbed the photo and held it up to the light. "Look at that. I think I was two and Loretta was four. We looked like twins back then."

Ruby peered over Mom's shoulder to get a closer look and smelled her flowery perfume. Two toddlers wearing matching dresses hugged each other in front of a black backdrop, clearly taken in a photography studio. Auntie Lori flashed a toothy grin and Mom's thin, blonde curls rested against her neck.

She stroked the picture and smiled. "Two of my favorite people."

Mom ducked her chin, trying to hide a smile, but Ruby saw it, and grinned back.

Just like every other dream, a cloud of smoke erupted. When it cleared, Ruby opened her eyes, and images flashed before her in no sequential order. Two toddlers wearing matching dresses. A large Buick with bench seats. A photographer. A tantrum. Mema and Papa in frustration. The word **kweam** and **cream** floating around the car. Then **sowwy** and **sorry.** Mema distraught. Papa yelling. First yelling at the girls, then yelling at Mema. The girls crying and constant flashes of light.

Mom's crumpled baby face, stooped posture, and Auntie Lori's taunting words weaved in and out of her memory. Ruby wondered how much of those early memories shaped her mom as an adult.

Maybe Mom always felt responsible for Mema's unhappiness. Whether Mom knew it or not, her unresolved issues fell onto Ruby. Ruby never followed the path Mom set out for her and Mom never hid her disappointment. Growing up pretty, seeking the spotlight, and always fishing for compliments, Ruby had created a competitive desire to be someone important and desirable. The traditional mold Mom and Dad had shaped for her was impossible to squeeze into, and maybe Mom was never able to squeeze into the mold her parents had created either.

So many complicated feelings morphed into one. Ruby didn't like the unease she felt after waking from that memory. The images didn't tell a complete story, but the distress on little Mom's face told Ruby what it was like growing up with Mema, Papa, and Auntie Lori.

Ruby retrieved the picture from the nightstand and shoved it back in the wallet. She stuffed the wallet in the purse and shoved them both into the broken suitcase. She didn't want to relive the chaos that moment brought. That picture hadn't captured love, joy, and affection; it was a moment of frustration, yet anyone looking at that photo would never know.

It seemed our memories never painted the true picture. It only painted the truth we wanted to believe, and somewhere the real truth got buried under layers of perception. Ruby pulled out her notebook, capturing the truth she observed in her dream.

Chapter 31

Ruby was right. Lynette was lonely and needed something other than Nora and dreams to occupy her mind. She strummed her fingers on the table, practicing what she would say to Daniel.

Hi, I'm looking for a job.

Hi Daniel. I thought maybe if we spent time together, we could see if we were meant to be.

Are you hiring?

I have nothing else to do, so I wondered if you needed help.

Her words sounded foolish in her head, so she took a deep breath and closed her eyes. *It's now or never.* She opened her eyes, touched the numbers on her cell and a deep voice she'd recognize a mile away answered. "Thank you for calling The Last Catch. Daniel speaking."

"Hi Daniel, this is Lynette Franklin, uh Lynette Waller," she stumbled.

"Hi Linnie, what can I do for you?"

She opened her mouth, but nothing came out.

"Linnie? Hello?"

She cleared her throat to start again. "Hi, yes, I'm here." Closing her eyes, the words flowed like a fire hose. "I know it isn't tourism season, but I was wondering if you needed any help. I'm open to anything, really."

She heard a chuckle behind his words. "Are you looking for a job?"
Straightening her back, she said, "Yes, yes, I am."

"I think I can find something for you. Come on down and we'll chat."
Lynette hung up the phone and clapped her hands. She didn't mention it was only for a few months, but she'd be sure to tell him if he asked.

A few days later, she got her schedule. Three lunches a week seating guests. Pleased with the distraction and easy money, it felt like she and Ruby were two ships passing in the night, but the distance created a comfortableness that both women needed.

Instead of enemies, they were roommates, and a mutual respect emerged. They weren't together all the time, but when they were together, the positive vibe carried them further than the negative memories or emotions they had obsessed over for far too many years.

October turned to November, and Lynette tried to make her parents proud by taking care of their property like she owned it, but she knew she couldn't compete with Kate's green thumb. Kate had planted bulbs for the following spring, and reseeded and winterized the yard. Lynette knew Mom would smile down at Kate's master plan, but she could make Mom proud, too.

Wearing a winter hat from the front closet, she dragged and pulled the long, thin rake, feeling her body warm from the repetitive work. She welcomed the tiredness, knowing she'd sleep well.

A voice behind her echoed through the bare trees, and Lynette's body jumped. Her hands rose to her chest, and the rake clattered to the ground.

Kate approached from behind.

"You scared me!"

"Sorry about that. Nice hat." Kate wore the same hat that sat snuggly on Lynette's head.

"Thanks. I found it in the hall closet."

"Your mom and I made them. She taught me how to knit and we made hats together. We donated most of them to the hospital for the newborns. Your mom really liked it."

Lynette didn't know if Kate was bragging to get a rise out of her, but it was working. Every time Kate was around, Lynette felt inferior, like the child hidden in the back room to prevent the family from sharing their shame with others. Never good enough. Never really wanted.

She picked up the rake and said, "What brings you over today?"

Kate shuffled closer, the leaves dancing below her feet. "I'm here to help. This is a big yard, and it's supposed to snow tonight."

Lynette's heart softened at Kate's generosity. "Thank you. I'll get the bag."

The two women worked in silence while Lynette focused on raking the leaves into a pile. In the quiet and with the monotonous movements, her mind drifted. She didn't understand why Loretta asked Kate to help with the estate, while she had been forgotten.

"How are things going with Loretta and the estate?" Lynette asked. She kept her voice even, hoping it didn't sound accusatory. Keeping her eyes on the leaf pile, she transferred it into a brown paper bag.

"Good. You know, I wanted to talk to you about that."

Lynette looked up and waited.

"I didn't know your mom was leaving me anything, and I was just as surprised as you were. I could use the money, for sure, but I don't want to complicate all your family stuff. She wasn't my mom, and although I loved her with all my heart, it doesn't seem like you guys knew about our friendship. It just feels weird, you know?"

Lynette nodded. She knew. Lynette didn't know Mom at all, it seemed.

"I talked to my husband, and we have what we need. I have a photo of your mom and I on her 70th birthday. I told Loretta and the lawyer we don't want any money."

Lynette's head snapped up, giving Kate her undivided attention. "You should take it if she wanted you to have it." She placed her hands on her hips and bit her bottom lip. "I don't dislike you, Kate, I'm just surprised at how close you were to her. The way she treated you isn't like how she treated us." A hot, angry tear poked Lynette's eye, and she blinked it back. "But I'm happy she had you."

"I'm sorry she didn't treat you well." Kate's eyes fell to the ground. "She was always kind to me."

"Yeah, you probably saw her at her best."

"I'm sorry," Kate mumbled.

They worked side by side in silence. Too many questions formed behind Lynette's closed mouth, but she couldn't seem to voice her words. It took too much effort, so all she managed was the occasional grunt as she picked up the leaves.

Kate rolled up the last bag and dragged it to the driveway. "I have to go, but if you need anything at all, I'm right next door. We don't have to be friends, but we can be neighborly."

Lynette forced a smile and collected the rakes. "Thanks for your help. I owe you one."

She walked into the house and pulled off the hat, throwing it on the steam radiator hissing in the kitchen.

There were so many secrets in the house, she didn't know what was fact and what was fiction anymore.

Lynette poured herself a cup of hot cocoa and threw in a splash of Baileys. Upon second thought, she poured another splash and stirred vigorously. Stomping her feet and kicking off her shoes, she slammed the cabinet doors and marched into the dining room. All these things in the house were just that. Things collecting dust. She grabbed a glass from the display case and considered transferring her drink from the hot mug to the fancy crystal. Even if the glass cracked from the heat, she wouldn't care. But then she'd have a mess to clean up. Lynette sighed and studied the intricate cuts around the base. It was too beautiful to break.

Large tears fell from her cheeks. She emptied the display case and filled a cardboard box with abandoned memories hidden amongst the knick-knacks.

She didn't stop at the glassware. Once the curio cabinet stood empty, she moved onto the hutch. Crystal, decorative teapots, Hummels, stuff. Stuff with no relevancy to Lynette, but still somehow reminded her of Mom. Like Hercules, she pulled heavy framed photos off the walls, moved tables, and overfilled boxes with candy dishes, coffee table books, and blankets. Her biceps and shoulders ached from the repetitive walk from the house to the garage. As her joints stiffened from all the bending and lifting, she embraced the pain, filling the perimeter of the garage with objects that meant nothing to her.

Every item she removed was a piece of her mother, but they weren't pieces Lynette had been invited to see.

Scanning the garage, Lynette fought back the urge to cry. She wasn't losing the memories; she was discarding the burden.

Mom kept coming to her in her dreams, but enough was enough. Lynette needed to move on. Thanksgiving was in a few weeks, and that would be the end of all the reminders Lynette needed to forget in order to move forward.

Chapter 32

R uby and Mom sat at the kitchen table the Sunday before Thanksgiving, sharing notes on any dreams that made it from their memory to the journal. Each week they shared stories and dreams, and asked questions about what it all meant. Ruby looked forward to the distraction-free hour with Mom, and each week, she felt closer to Mom and closer to Mema.

Mema's clothes had become somewhat of a competition, specifically around not just the number of times Mema came in their dreams, but what underlying theme or lesson the memory held.

"Did Mema come to you this week?" Mom asked. They had agreed that they wouldn't talk about the dreams until Sunday mornings. Holding the secrets close for days at a time, where thoughts could wander unjudged, created an authenticity that wouldn't exist if they shared the intimate memories immediately.

"I didn't have any dreams this week." At least, that's what Ruby thought. There might have been one, but she overslept and couldn't jot down the foggy haze that infiltrated her sleep without being late for work. She regretted not taking the time for Mema, but she had to get to work on time. "What about you?"

"I had one dream that I'm aware of."

Mom flipped through the same journal Ruby had, pulling up the random words scattered on the pages. Ruby had given it to Mom after their first appointment with Nora. "This is so details won't be lost," Ruby had said.

Mom stirred her coffee, her face contorted as she tried to organize her thoughts.

"Tell me about it."

Mom browsed through her fancy cursive writing. "Okay, you know Mema's checkered apron we found in the back of her closet?"

Ruby nodded.

"So, I wore that to work one day. I know, stupid, but it almost matched the parchment paper in the bread baskets, and I thought it was cute. Daniel didn't like it." Ruby watched a blush creep up Mom's neck. "He told me black and white only, so I had to tuck it into my purse."

Ruby leaned forward, trying to read Mom's upside-down cursive. "Go on," she said.

"Okay, so I thought the apron would bring me back to after my parents married. You know, when Mema was struggling with mother-hood?"

Ruby checked her watch. She had forty-five minutes before she had to leave for work. "Uh-huh."

"But it actually brought me back to the early fifties. I don't know when exactly, but Mema looked to be about five. The apron was my granny's. Now, did I ever tell you about my grandparents?"

"Not especially. All I know is that they died fairly young."

"Yes, my grandfather died of cancer. I can't remember which kind, and my grandmother died in a fire."

Ruby inhaled sharply. "Mom. Nora. Fire. That was Mema."

Mom leaned forward. "You're right! I didn't even think of that."

"Okay, so back to her parents."

"Well," Mom said. "I didn't know much about them, but based on my dreams, they were nasty. Hated my father, as evidenced by their disgust at their wedding, and based on this latest dream, were extremely strict.

Even to a young girl still learning how to behave."

A pit formed in Ruby's stomach. "What happened?"

"My dream was kind of hazy, but I think what happened was this. My mom was drawing at the kitchen table. It wasn't an especially nice table, but it was in the kitchen. My grandmother was cooking at the stove, wearing that apron. Mema, being a four- or five-year-old girl, started coloring the table. I don't think it was on purpose, but once it was done, it was done. She said, 'Look, Mama,' all proud and everything. My grandmother walked over and smacked her on the bottom with the wooden spoon she was using to stir the spaghetti. Sauce went flying, Mom started crying, and Granny sent her to the corner."

"Oh, that's awful," Ruby said. "Were her parents abusive?"

"It was the fifties. Back then, it was called discipline. But it was awful to watch. I don't think she did it to be bad. I don't even know if she realized it wasn't okay. She looked so proud, and when she got punished, her little face broke. I woke up with my cheeks wet and my heart pounding."

"Do you think that's just the way it was back then?"

"Unfortunately, yes. It was important to have manners, and it was more a 'children are to be seen, not heard,' mentality...but it got me thinking. I think Mema had big dreams, and when her curiosity got squashed at such an early age, she learned to settle. But that drive to be her own person never went away. I think that's why she was so upset about getting pregnant and marrying Papa."

"Do you think she was happy?" Ruby asked.

"I do, but I think it was a muted happiness. Her life was good. Papa loved her with all his heart, but seeing them at their wedding, I didn't get the same vibe from her. It actually seemed like she only got married to him because she was expecting. If she could do it differently, I think she would have." Mom shook her head. "I'm getting rid of that apron. I don't want to see my grandparents again. Twice is enough."

"Twice?"

"The wooden spoon and the wedding." Mom shuddered. "It couldn't have been easy."

"Yeah, I'm glad you weren't like that. I mean, you weren't supportive of my modeling, but you never forced anything on me. You raised me to be independent." Mom's eyes held Ruby's for a few moments, and Ruby sensed she wanted to say something.

Mom cleared her throat. "It's funny. I kind of understand why she was so adamant about me not leaving with your father. I think she saw herself in me and that worried her. She was the dutiful daughter and so was I. I think I scared her because it was too much of a reminder of all the dreams she had sacrificed, and it was the first time I said no to her."

"I had that dream about the pocketbook with the photo of you and Auntie getting photos taken. When you were a little girl. Remember?"

"Yeah."

"She was really unhappy then, too. It was a bit hazy, but the two of you destroyed that photography studio. Mema practically had a break down. She seemed overwhelmed by motherhood."

Mom sipped her coffee. "Yeah, and she didn't want to get married. She'd told Loretta and I over and over that she wished she'd gone to college. She sacrificed a lot of her own desires. It makes me sad."

"But don't we all sacrifice a lot? I mean, I think the important thing is finding the joy within the pain."

"We sacrifice things every day. I want to know that she didn't regret the way her life unfolded because she did the best she could to give us a beautiful life."

Ruby refilled her mug and offered Mom more coffee. "Top off?"

"No, thanks. I have to get ready for work."

"Me too, but did she ever encourage you to not be so obedient?"

Mom rubbed her chin, thinking. "You know, not that I remember, but that doesn't mean it didn't happen. I remember when I was in high school, she encouraged me to date and not settle down with one boy."

"Like Daniel?"

Mom grinned. "Oh, she loved Daniel, but Daniel was reckless. He rode a motorcycle, couldn't keep a job, and unintentionally flirted with all the girls. In my eyes, your father was a catch compared to him, but Mema saw differently. Now my dad...he did not like Daniel, especially after we broke up the first time. Anytime I wrote him a letter, Papa reminded me there were many fish in the sea."

Ruby laughed. "I don't know...Papa might have been wrong. Daniel looks at you like he misses you."

Lynette stuck out her tongue. "Speaking of, I have to get to work. But that apron is in the trash. I can't stomach anymore nightmares of my grandparents hurting Mema." She shook her head, like she was erasing the memory from her brain. She stood and kissed Ruby on the forehead. "Have a good day."

Ruby sat at the table and read Mom's recount of her dream, and flashbacks from the photographer's dream came back to her. Maybe Mema didn't handle her daughters when they were wrecking the studio because she couldn't be that kind of parent. Maybe that's what life was about. The pendulum swinging from one generation to the next, always trying to find that perfect balance where you aren't screwing up your kids the same way your parents screwed you up.

Ruby drew a heart after the last word in Mom's dream entry, and closed the book. Just like Mom, she hoped she didn't see her great-grandparents in her dreams. She'd rather believe Mema was exempt from all the hurt and pain families carried onto and through their children.

Chapter 33

Loretta showed up the Tuesday before Thanksgiving to help with the estate sale that weekend. She arrived with a suitcase larger than life and a small duffle bag across her shoulder. Her warm hug and reassuring smile put Lynette at ease.

"What's with the suitcase?" Lynette pointed to the large one. "Are you planning on taking Ruby home with you?" It was supposed to be a joke, but it fell flat, and her sister stared at her blankly. Lighter than Lynette expected, she pulled it into the corner beside the front staircase.

"It's empty. I thought maybe I'd grab some last-minute things that reminded me of Mom."

Lynette's chest constricted as she pictured Loretta grabbing the magic clothes. "Sure. If you go through Mom's closet, let me know what you take. There are some items I'd like to keep."

"Did you get a dumpster?" Loretta asked. "Mom has a lot of crap."

She winced. "Yes. It will be here tomorrow and is being picked up the following Tuesday." To lubricate her scratchy throat, Lynette guzzled a bottle of water.

"Great. When's the estate sale?"

"It's Friday to Sunday. Stay as long as you can." Lynette hadn't nearly gotten as far as she'd hoped, what with working and everything else, so she welcomed the help.

As they threw away all of Mom and Dad's treasures, Lynette could still hear Mom as they pulled furniture from the side of the road when she was a kid. *You know, that's a perfectly good table. I'm sure there's someone who could use it.*

Loretta seemed more together than the last time Lynette saw her. "You look good," she said.

"You know, it was great to get back to my life in Florida, but I missed you guys. I couldn't wait to get back and see where things stood with the house. Plus, I have another meeting with the lawyer. Where's Ruby?"

"Down in the basement, digging through Christmas boxes. Didn't Mom and Dad have a fake tree somewhere?"

Loretta looked toward the basement stairs. "I don't know. I haven't been home for Christmas since Dad died."

Another example of how fractured their family had become. "Me either. I can't believe he's been gone ten years now. Don't you feel bad about not coming home for Mom?"

"Not really. Mom had Kate."

Kate's name triggered a shudder to travel through Lynette.

Loretta continued, "We lived halfway across the country. It wasn't always easy or cheap to come home. And Mom always said she couldn't choose between us. That's why she never traveled, but I don't buy it."

"About Kate," Lynette said. "Do you think Mom loved her more than us?" Saying it out loud caused Lynette's stomach to churn, and she couldn't accept the discomfort. "Or not. Maybe my imagination is running wild."

"Our life with Mom and Dad wasn't perfect, but we all deserve someone, right? Let's be honest. You and I weren't exactly the support she needed after Dad died. I'm thankful Mom had that someone."

A tiny pebble formed in Lynette's throat. "Like you had Ruby, right?"

A flicker of regret flashed across Loretta's face. "Come on, Lynette. Again? Aren't we past this? I told you why I kept in touch with her. You should thank me. I was making sure she was still alive."

Lynette cringed and covered her face with her hands. How had she been so stupid, thinking no one in her family had been in contact with Ruby? And why hadn't Loretta come to her? "How dare you. She's my daughter. I"—Lynette pointed at herself—"should have known she was still alive. Not knowing destroyed my marriage."

"Destroyed? It was on the verge of collapse well before then. You never recognized your husband's wandering eyes, but we all saw it. Even before you were married."

Lynette felt her face drain of all blood and the room tilted. She had difficulty breathing and grabbed the edge of the table.

Loretta dropped her eyes and spoke into her chest. "I'm sorry, but it's true."

"He never cheated." Lynette said, as she pounded the table with her fist.

"Sure, that you know of. But your marriage was far from perfect. And you have no right to blame me or your daughter."

The door to the basement squeaked open, and Ruby stood holding a sloppy cardboard box. Her face drawn and her posture stooped, she said, "I found the ornaments. Hi, Auntie Lori." She walked through the kitchen, leaving Loretta and Lynette both stony-faced.

"I never blamed you or Ruby," Lynette whisper-yelled.

Loretta spun in a circle. "Yes you do. You just said that by not knowing where Ruby was, your marriage was ruined. And I was the one who kept that info from you." Her voice rose and echoed off the now-empty walls. "But it wasn't just me. Mom knew, too."

Lost for words, Lynette narrowed her eyes. "Fine. I thought I had lost her forever, and it was my fault because I was the one who pressured her to stay, which pushed her away."

"Well, I'm sorry."

It sounded half-hearted, so Lynette threw an angry glare at her sister. "Damn it!" Lynette's fist slammed into the table, spilling the drinks.

She didn't bother with a napkin, just swiped her arm across the table, sending liquid across the wall. She huffed her way to the sink and washed her hands, while staring aimlessly into the yard. "I'm Mom, aren't I?"

"What are you talking about?" Loretta said from behind, but Lynette didn't bother to turn. She stared ahead out the window, like she was searching for happy memories to prance past.

"I did to Ruby what Mom did to me. I repeated the past." She spoke more to herself than her sister, but things suddenly made sense.

"What?"

Lynette heard Loretta step closer, and she closed her eyes, feeling the hot water cascade across her hands.

A gentle shoulder rub should have put Lynette at ease, but Lynette's body jumped into flight mode.

She spun around without looking at Loretta. "I have to do something." Leaving the water running, she shoulder-checked Loretta and marched out of the kitchen to find her daughter.

Ruby sat in front of the couch, digging through a saggy box. She held up a large ornament. "Donate? Or do you want to go through this?" Her slumped shoulders and slow movements brought back a memory of when Lynette had to let her daughter leave her side for the first day of kindergarten. It was one of the hardest days Lynette experienced during early motherhood. All she wanted was for her daughter to be safe from the social repercussions of mean kids and the academic pressure from school. Tears formed in the corner of Lynette's eyes.

"I'm so sorry," Lynette said. She squatted down and her knees popped. Ignoring the pain, she wrapped her arms around Ruby. "I'm sorry I pushed you away."

After a moment of indecision, Ruby turned her body and wrapped her arms around Lynette. "I'm sorry for worrying you."

Ruby's weight shifted to Lynette, and Lynette fell back, reaching for the floor. With Ruby holding too tight, it was no use. Flat as a pancake with arms and legs sprawled amid the boxes, Ruby's laughter shook both their bodies.

"Help!" Lynette said. "I can't get up!" It was just like upstairs with the suitcase. Yet instead of loneliness and despair, Lynette felt the familiar tug of care as her daughter pulled her to safety.

Normal people hugged and laughed with one another, but Lynette hadn't laughed with her daughter in years. It was such a small sentiment, but the shared moment pulled the chasm in Lynette's heart closer together.

Chapter 34

On Thanksgiving Day, Ruby, Mom, and Auntie cooked enough food to feed a small army. Ruby's stomach pressed against the waistband of her jeans and she unbuttoned the top, allowing her belly button to breathe.

"That was delicious," she sighed.

A knock on the door sounded and Kate appeared, holding a chocolate cream pie in the doorway.

"Happy Thanksgiving!" She cheerfully set it on the counter. "It's your mom's recipe, and I just HAD to make it. I made two actually and wanted to share because I don't need that much sugar."

"Thank you, Kate. Happy Thanksgiving." Auntie Lori cut into the white, meringue topper and placed a perfect triangle on a plate.

Ruby glanced at Mom, who sulked at the table with her back to Kate. She stirred whatever food remained on her plate, fully focused on mixing the mashed potatoes and gravy.

"Do you need help with the estate sale?" Kate asked Auntie Lori, who then turned to Mom for confirmation.

"Linnie. Do we need help?"

When Mom didn't respond, Auntie Lori turned back to Kate and replied, "Actually, we already started tossing things into the dumpster. We should be all set."

Kate settled into the chair beside Mom, and Ruby offered her a plate of leftovers.

"No, no, I'm full, thanks."

She stayed for about an hour, and Ruby watched her family interact from behind her dessert plate.

"Kate," Auntie Lori said, "why don't you tell us about your friendship with Mom? We never learned the story of how your friendship developed, although it's obvious you two were tight."

Mom turned toward her but didn't encourage a story. She leaned forward, playing with the salt and pepper shakers in the center of the table.

"Well, where to start?" Kate looked around the table and Ruby recognized vulnerability hidden behind her irises. "About twenty years ago, Nick and I were living the good life. We were young, newly married, and new to the area."

"What does he do, again?" Auntie Lori asked.

"He's a real estate investor."

Mom raised her eyebrows and pursed her lips.

"In 2007, we were loving life. We had no kids—still don't—and no expenses beyond our mortgage. The economy collapsed in 2008, and so did our life. Our lifestyle of dinners out, vacations, and new cars kind of fell by the wayside. It sounds stupid, but our marriage kind of crumbled because of it."

She reached across the table and plucked a crumb of pie crust, sliding the buttery goodness into her mouth. "Our mortgage was on the brink. Nick was embarrassed and ashamed, and for the first time, I needed help...like, assistance, with food."

Ruby watched Mom's eyes soften, and she couldn't help but wonder if this was how she felt when Ruby left her for California and Dad left her for Kai. As if her life had collapsed around her, and the rubble was too sharp and heavy to recover.

"I saw your mom volunteering at the food bank, as I was filling a bag of nonperishables. I was so ashamed." Her voice rocked, and she swallowed another bite of pie. "I crouched on the floor, hiding behind a stack of boxes but she saw me. We didn't know each other well. Your dad was still alive, and she had her own life. I trusted her kind eyes and confided in her about our financial mess. She took me under her wing and showed me how to live frugally."

Auntie Lori snorted and then recovered. She quickly raised her hand when Kate shot her a look. "Sorry, I just can't imagine Mom teaching you how to save money when she bought the most ridiculous things. We have a giant rooster statue in our garage that, hopefully, someone buys."

"No, really. She taught me how to cut coupons, shop for deals, and negotiate. I loved to garden, and we canned food for the winter, made jams and jellies, and cooked in bulk, sharing the leftovers to freeze."

"She was always cooking," Mom said.

"She saved my marriage. She saved my life, and I will never forget the kindness she showed me when I was at my worst. That was how our friendship started." Ruby saw tears slowly drop from her eyes. "I'll never forget her kindness."

Mom tapped her fingers on the table and straightened the dirty placemat. "She sounds like a wonderful woman. Too bad that isn't the woman I remember."

Ruby heard the envy and disappointment in her tone and a heaviness sat between them.

"To think that she accepted you at your worst," Mom said and she shared a look with Auntie Lori.

"Imagine," Auntie said.

Ruby recognized the sarcasm in Auntie Lori's voice, and Kate's face elongated, mid bite. Kate stood from the table, pulling the edge of the tablecloth with her. Ruby grabbed her end, preventing it from sliding to the floor with all the dirty plates on it.

"I need to go," she said, grabbing for her things. "Nick is probably wondering where I am."

Auntie Lori and Mom remained at the table, and Ruby walked her to the door.

"I hope I didn't upset anyone," Kate said to Ruby.

"You're fine. They're still grieving."

When Ruby returned to the table, she noticed Auntie's cheeks were damp and streaked.

"Auntie Lori." Ruby touched her arm and squeezed. "Are you okay?"

"It's so nice she had Kate, but I wish Mema had more compassion for us. Maybe the last twenty years would have been different." She stood from the table, picked up the glassware and threw it against the wall, screeching as it hit and shattered. The glass shards clanged to the floor.

"Loretta!"

Auntie Lori slowly rose and picked up the largest chunks. "I'm okay." She cleaned up the mess and left the room, leaving Mom frozen, like her mind had moved to a different time.

The next day, Ruby and Mom bundled up in Mema's old jackets and headed into the garage. The three walled structure prevented the blustery wind from billowing against their faces. Ruby carried a box of Papa's tools and placed them on one of the banquet tables they had rented from the hardware store. The perimeter of the garage held furniture while the inside resembled a bingo hall.

"Do you think we'll have a large turnout?" Mom asked.

"Here's to hoping. I feel weird getting rid of her furniture, but it's not my style, and I'd probably replace it. If we can make some money off it, maybe we can donate it to the food pantry or something."

Lynette pointed to the curio cabinet, which once held all of Mema's collectibles. "What, you don't want this monstrosity in your house?"

Ruby ran her hand up and down the smooth mahogany. "It's beautiful, but not for me. And it's not my house. Not yet, anyway."

Mom organized the silverware and glassware. "Can you see yourself here?"

Ruby gazed outside. "I don't know. I never thought about it until now, but it's been kind of nice being away from L.A." She tightened her jacket. "Although I miss the sunshine."

Auntie Lori walked into the garage carrying old kitchen appliances from the early nineties. "Do you think anyone will want these?" She dropped a crock pot on the table.

"Nah, throw it out."

Auntie Lori grunted as she picked up the heavy metal container and tossed it into the dumpster.

They worked like that all day, filling up tables, floor space, and walls. Mema's car sat at the end of the driveway, allowing the overflow to seep beyond the garage walls.

"There is so much stuff here," Ruby said.

"An entire life. Are you sure you have everything you want?"

Ruby wanted nothing beyond candid photos and a few accessories and jewelry. A cozy blanket might be nice too. "I think so." She wrapped her arms around Mom, and Mom's breath warmed the bare space between her jacket and hat.

They walked inside where Mema's clothes flowed out of trash bags near the front door.

"What's that?" Ruby rushed over and dug through the bag, finding random dresses and jackets and pants, all folded neatly in a pile.

"Oh, I filled some bags with clothes from her bedroom," Auntie Lori said. "There's still more."

Ruby looked at Mom, wondering what was hiding in the bags. Was it something they had already worn?

Ruby pulled out the clothes, admiring each one. "Oh, Auntie, I don't know if I can let these go. From a fashion standpoint, these may be worth money one day." She couldn't help but wonder if there were memories locked in those items. So far, the dreams had shed light on why her mother was the way she was, and those clothes had helped them survive the past month together.

Auntie Lori raised her eyebrows. "Um, okay. But make sure you go through it before this weekend. Otherwise, they'll be donated."

Ruby telepathically sent Mom a message and recognition flashed behind her eyes.

"I'll help you," Mom said.

Both women sat on the floor beside the stairs with a mountain of clothes between them. Auntie Lori watched for a few minutes, and questions sparked between her eyes.

"Auntie Lori, don't you want any of this?"

"Nah, I live in Florida. Why would I need a sweater or a pair of mittens?" She turned into the kitchen and didn't return.

After a few moments of silence, Ruby assumed she was safe to speak. "Mom, did you already go through all this?"

"Yeah, but it's always good to have a second set of eyes."

Ruby separated the things they'd already experimented with, the things they still needed to try, and the things that would never fit or were so ugly, Ruby didn't want to wear them out in public.

Lynette placed them in their corresponding bags and asked Ruby to bring the KEEP bag upstairs.

In Mema's bedroom, Ruby browsed through a hope chest in the corner, which held even more clothes. Mema didn't come every night, but she came sporadically, connected to the most random items. Ruby tossed the garments into the trash bag, creating a bigger treasure trove.

Ruby bounced down the stairs. "Auntie Lori?" She found her in the kitchen, tidying up the counters. "We went through the clothes. We're all set." Ruby scribbled on two pieces of paper and held them up to

Auntie Lori. "Donate and trash. I'm putting them on the bags."

Auntie Lori glanced over. "Got it."

The stress of the day evaporated, knowing Mema's magic clothes were still safe with her.

Chapter 35

People flowed in and out of the garage like a school of fish looking to expand their territory. Hungry sharks looking for their next million dollar find low-balled Lynette, but she didn't care. She wanted it gone. Agreeing to sell the curio cabinet for fifty-bucks was fifty dollars more than she had, and it freed up precious space in the dumpster.

By the end of the day, the women sold seventy percent of the memories and counted fourteen hundred dollars in cash. Not a bad haul for one day. With two days left, Lynette hoped everything would find a new home by the end of the weekend.

"Thanks for your help," Lynette said to Ruby and Loretta. "I think Dad would be proud of our haggling."

Loretta scoffed. "I still feel bad selling his coin set. We probably handed over our millions."

Lynette handed the thick stack of money to her sister. "For the lawyer's fee."

"That'll come out of the estate."

"Put it in the savings then. We'll figure it out another day."

Loretta obliged and promised to bring it to the bank on Monday.

That night, another dream crashed into Lynette like waves after a hurricane. Heart racing, Lynette placed her hand on her chest, realizing she was safe, alive, and awake. When the mist cleared, Lynette struggled to comprehend the details.

Glancing at the sweater lying on the chair, guilt crashed upon her. She grabbed the sweater off the chair and shoved it deep within the closet. Grabbing Mom's pillow, she held it tight to her body and tried to make sense of the scene.

Lynette and Anthony happily in love. The Dave Matthews Band concert. Introducing him to her parents for the first time. Mom and Dad talking. Dad seemed fine, but Mom hated him. Her twisted face blinked at Lynette as she tried to remember. The words **NOT GOOD ENOUGH** bounced between their heads. Loretta gone. The word **FAILURE** pouring from Mom's mouth, then **PROTECT**.

There was so much that was never said, and now it was too late. Did Mom dislike Anthony from the beginning? She didn't remember that, but maybe that was another card Mom held close to her chest. Loretta was gone by then. Her parents had already pushed her away, and Lynette would do the same.

How had she allowed herself to make the same mistake with Ruby?

On Monday, Lynette and Ruby drove together to work. Loretta left early to meet with the lawyer, and the three women promised to have one last meal before Loretta's flight.

"Thanks for the ride, Mom. See you at four." Lynette watched Ruby walk into the bookstore before driving to The Last Catch. She didn't expect today to be busy, what with most people still recovering from turkey overload.

Always slow the day after a holiday weekend, Lynette spent most of her time keeping the servers busy cleaning the shelves and rolling silverware. As her shift approached its last hour, she walked a young couple to a table overlooking the water. The skies had turned pewter, and a storm was brewing. The waves rocked the boats, and they bounced up and down rhythmically.

"Lovely day for some clam chowder," she said. "Here are some food and drink specials. Your server will be right over. Enjoy."

Lynette watched Daniel move around the dining room, rearranging menus and double-checking tables. She couldn't help but appreciate his tight pants and slimming shirt.

"Lynette."

At the sound of her name on his lips, her stomach flipped, and she slowly turned. She couldn't tell if she was in trouble or did something right, but his voice drew her to him like a moth to a flame.

"Yes." She straightened her hair, fully aware that the grays had tripled since her arrival in Maine six weeks before.

"Listen, I wanted to say thank you for everything you've done." His deep voice dropped, and Lynette leaned closer to listen. She glanced at his left hand again, and still no ring. Her face burned with desire and heat traveled to her limbs from the center of her body.

"This may seem a little forward, but would you be interested in going out to dinner with me?"

Lynette had been working at the restaurant for about a month, and their interactions had been professional and platonic. Daniel was her boss. Was fraternizing with management unethical? It certainly was at the university where Lynette worked. The list of what-ifs grew, and Lynette fumbled with organizing the menus. Cautious about getting involved, she tried to brush him off, but his eyes held hers and she couldn't quite break away. "Yes. When?"

"How about tonight? I'll pick you up at seven." He winked at her and her face flushed. "I know where you live."

Giddy on the inside, she held her body in full composure. "Perfect," she mustered.

The rest of her shift flew by, and she spent any down time fantasizing about Daniel. She remembered his body like it was yesterday. His brawny arms holding her on the beach, his witty humor, and his lopsided smile, always brightening her day.

When her shift ended, she stood upright, and she struggled to swallow. Her body had changed over the last thirty years, and flabby skin had replaced her toned belly. Varicose veins decorated her thighs, and a giant scar zipped across her belly, memorializing Ruby's birth. Perhaps this was a terrible idea. Too many memories could cause confusion and then their working relationship would be ruined.

When her shift ended, she sneaked out of the restaurant without saying goodbye. Her brain listed a million things she had to do before seven tonight. She'd need Ruby's help with her makeup and clothes, and definitely needed to shower and shave her legs.

When Lynette arrived at the bookstore, energy still coursed through her veins. While waiting for Ruby to clock out, she browsed the romance section, imagining her and Daniel on the cover. She flipped through to the smutty parts, and a small flame burned through every cell of her body.

Lynette tucked the book under her arm and moved around the room, stopping at the holiday tree decorated with bookish ornaments. When Ruby appeared with her coat and purse, Lynette said, "Hey, Rubes, are we decorating a tree this year?" She held up an ornament of a book that read "Little House on the Prairie. First Christmas."

Ruby straightened the ornaments. "We can get one, I guess. It might be nice to relive some of the old traditions and build some new ones. From your childhood and mine."

Lynette pulled off an ornament with a cat curled up on a book. "Remember Pretty?"

"Yes, this looks just like her," Ruby gushed. "She was such a nasty cat. Remember that year she jumped on the tree and knocked it down?"

Lynette chuckled. "Your father was so mad."

"She was such a troublemaker, but a great snuggler."

Lynette handed her the ornament and the romance novel faced down.

"I want to get these."

Ruby raised her eyes as she turned over the book and glanced at the shirtless man decorating the cover.

"What? It's for our not-yet-purchased tree...and that's for research."

Stella grinned and dropped the items into a small bag. "Merry Christmas."

"Merry Christmas to you too," Lynette said.

When they got to the car, Lynette blurted, "Hey, I have a date tonight."

Ruby's eyes shot to the left, and a smile erupted. "With Daniel?"

"Yep, and I need you to help me get ready. I want to look and feel irresistible."

Instead of a mom and daughter battling for control, Ruby felt like a friend and Lynette felt a connection to her daughter that she hadn't felt in years.

Chapter 36

When Mom pulled into the driveway, Auntie Lori's rental was gone. "Oh no, did we miss her? I thought she said she had a night flight," Ruby said.

The sun had just settled on the horizon, tempting the night with its speedy descent.

"No, she wouldn't leave without saying goodbye." Lynette pulled out her phone. "No messages." She called Auntie Lori and put the phone on speaker.

"Hi." Auntie Lori's breathy voice traveled through the phone.

"Auntie Lori," Ruby interrupted. "Where are you?"

"Oh, I just dropped some last items off at the donation place. I'll be home in two minutes to say goodbye, and then I have to go."

"No dinner?" Ruby asked.

"No sweetie, I'm worried about traffic."

"No problem. Mom has a date anyway."

Auntie Lori whooped when she heard it was Daniel.

"Bye Loretta, I'll see you soon. I have to get ready for my date!" She disconnected the call and grinned at Ruby.

"I'm going to miss her," Ruby said.

"Me too."

When they walked into the house, Ruby felt like she was home. Not home like L.A., but home in her heart. Comfortable, warm, and full of love. Mema's presence sat on the wallpaper and on the old kitchen counter. Her love decorated the fridge with the local business magnets holding up Christmas cards from last year. "I actually like it here," Ruby said.

Auntie Lori barreled through the door. "I'm back, but only for a few minutes. My bags are in the car." She pulled her arms around Mom and hugged her tight. "Happy holidays."

"Oh, sis. Thank you for all your help with the house and everything."

"Of course. We're family." She hugged Ruby and squeezed her tight. "Bye sweetie. Keep in touch."

Ruby's eyes filled with tears. "When will I see you again?"

"My door is open whenever you need to escape from the cold." She tightened her hat over her head.

"Hey." Mom squinted her eyes and her forehead created waves and rivers. "Where'd you get that hat?"

"Oh, I dumped those bags you guys filled with clothes. I found some near the door and some in Mom's room. I kept the one that said keep, but got rid of the rest."

Mom's face drained. "Wait, what?"

"Those bags."

Mom turned toward Ruby, and her eyes flashed with fear.

"Where did you take them?" Her thin voice barely carried over the steam heater hissing in the dining room.

"Good Donations. Why?"

Ruby raced upstairs and scanned Mema's bedroom. All the bags were gone. Even the ones that hadn't been labeled. A strangled laugh erupted at the absurdity of the situation, and she fumbled with the door handle to get out of the bedroom. Tripping down the stairs and sliding along the final third, she exclaimed, "They're gone!"

Auntie Lori gripped the doorknob. It seemed she knew something was wrong, but didn't know what. "What has gotten into you? I was only trying to help."

Mom ran around the house and Ruby paced the kitchen.

"Auntie Lori, those were Mema's magic clothes."

Auntie Lori burst out laughing. "What? You're not making any sense."

"Her clothes. You won't get it because you don't believe in ghosts or spirits, but those things allow Mema to come to us in our dreams."

"Ridiculous." Auntie Lori checked her watch. "I have to go. I'll call you later."

The door slammed shut and Ruby held Mom's shaking hands as they leaned over the counter. "What do we do? Is that it? Is it over?"

"Good Donations," Mom replied. "Maybe we can get the bags back before they're separated."

Ruby picked up Mema's keys. "Let's go."

Ruby drove like a crazed maniac through the narrow downtown roads until the long rectangular building came into view. She slowed down and gently pulled into the parking lot. Before the car was parked and the ignition was off, Mom was halfway through the parking lot to the donation door.

Ruby chased after her, her pocketbook flapping in the evening sky. When she got inside, Mom spoke quickly to an employee who didn't seem to care. He leaned against the wall with his hands jammed in his pockets, gazing over Mom's shoulder as she spewed out her story like a magician pulling a never-ending ribbon from her mouth.

"You see, my sister just dropped a few bags of clothes, not knowing they weren't meant to be donated."

The man shrugged his shoulders, complacent to her agitation. "The truck just came and picked up a load. What'd it look like?"

Ruby rubbed her forehead massaging a growing tension headache. "There were probably five bags. White trash bags. They might have had a piece of paper attached to them."

"Let me check. Follow me." He motioned for the women to follow, and they raced around the counter to the back room.

Ruby and Mom scanned the garbage bags and boxes like a tiger hunting its next meal. In a sense, they were, because these memories nourished their souls.

"He may have picked up a load of furniture, I don't know. This is where we keep the clothing and textiles." In the corner stood a crate overflowing with sealed trash bags. White, black, and gray dotted the container.

Ruby peered over the top. "Can I look?"

"No, employees only." He crossed his arms as if to say, 'too bad'.

"Can you look?" Ruby fluttered her eyelashes at him and watched his face soften. She placed her hand on his arm and stroked his skin. "Please?"

"Uh." He rubbed his neck with his other hand and Ruby squeezed. She felt his muscles tense, and she knew she had him.

"Sure. I'll look." He opened the metal door and pulled out the first bag he could reach. Black and extra-large, Ruby shook her head. Mom walked over to the edge, pointing at bags that may hold their secrets.

"It's white," Ruby called. "Try that one." She pointed to a bag at the top of the container. He reached up, grabbed, and ripped open the top slightly. A lime green bedspread oozed out, and Ruby shook her head.

They did this for at least a dozen bags, and Ruby's heart dropped to her toes. Maybe it was too late, and the key to Mema was lost. She glanced at Mom and recognized the defeat that pressed into her lips and eyes.

"Ruby, I think we're too late." Mom's voice carried through the back room and the young man digging through the trash bags stood.

"One more," he said. He pulled open the top and pulled out a beaded necklace. "Does this look familiar?"

Ruby squinted and Lynette pressed her face against the metal grate.

"Yes!" Lynette yelled. "Ruby, that necklace was in her jewelry box. Yes, that's it."

He dragged out the bag and Lynette hugged it close to her body.

The young man closed the metal gate and leaned against the wall again. His red face carried tiny beads of sweat, despite the frosty November air. "I hope you found what you need." A shy grin crept up his face.

Overcome by relief, Ruby stepped closer and hugged him. "Thank you," she breathed into his ear. "You don't know how much this means to us."

"You, uh, you're welcome."

Before the moment could get any more awkward, Ruby and Mom ran to their car, tossing the bag into Mema's backseat.

"It's not much, but it's something," Ruby said.

Mom nodded. "Better than nothing." She looked at her watch. "Crap!"

Ruby slammed on the brakes, and the car skidded to a stop. "What?!?"

"I have a date in thirty minutes."

Ruby glanced at Mom.

"Drive!"

Ruby stepped on the gas and the old car lurched forward.

Chapter 37

Lynette peeked through the sheer curtains, her toe tapping and her fingers shaking. One minute before seven, Daniel's fancy sports car pulled up in front of Mom and Dad's house and he climbed out, causing her heart to stutter.

She scrambled from the window and dropped on the couch, not wanting to seem too eager when the bell rang. *Ding!*

"Ruby, can you grab that?" Lynette called. Ruby was upstairs, and certainly couldn't hear her request. Lynette counted to five, heaved herself up from the soft cushion, and straightened her shirt. Staring at her reflection in the hall mirror, she unbuttoned the top button, tilted her head and rebuttoned it, flipped her hair, and opened the door. Daniel greeted her with a flirty smile, and she couldn't help but reciprocate.

"Wow." He appeared at a loss for words. "You look great."

Lynette's eyes traveled from his messy hair to full lips and she felt her face flush. "You do, too." To prevent him from seeing her turn magenta, she bent down and grabbed her purse. "Bye, Ruby!"

She paused at the stairs until a muffled voice responded. "Bye! Have fun!"

"This is a fancy car," Lynette said as she shimmied into the leather seats.

"Yeah, it was a birthday present to myself when I turned fifty. Half a century. That's nothing to sneeze at."

Lynette gave a shy smile. "When I look at you, I still see the fun, crazy, lovable eighteen-year-old," *that I fell in love with.*

He responded with a sideways smile as the car climbed to sixty.

"Where are we going?" Lynette asked.

"There's a new place that just opened up outside of Portsmouth. Right along the river. I thought we could try it out?"

"Sure, that sounds beautiful." The cloudy night sky created an ominous haze, and Lynette wondered if snow wanted to fall. She hoped it would snow because the white, rugged beaches took her breath away. "Sounds great." Lynette pulled her shoulders back, feeling the leather seats mold against her frame.

Seven in the evening in November was dark. The narrow back roads took them to the city, and Lynette couldn't help but feel like she was on an adventure. The date itself was magical.

Daniel took her to a steakhouse right on Portsmouth Harbor, and because it was off season, they were the only table in the room. Forgetting what it was like to be wooed by a man, she leaned closer, soaking up every compliment and seductive look Daniel gave her.

Instead of sitting across from him, they sat side by side, her thigh rubbing against his. She wanted to kiss him. She hadn't felt a man's lips on hers in over two years, and the desire burned deep. The rhythmic sounds of the ocean waves in the not-so-far distance, and the glass of wine that went straight to her head distorted all sense of reasoning. She touched his thigh with her hand, and when he turned, she pressed her lips into his. Like a series of butterflies emerging from their chrysalis, a sense of rebirth and beauty erupted within her. She pulled back slightly, but the feeling of his lips on hers felt familiar and secure, and she kissed him again.

"I've been wanting to do that for a while," she said.

Like a gentleman, he was back in his seat, smiling like a teenage boy in love. He picked up his fork and took another bite of broccoli.

"Let's talk," she said. "Because we have many years to catch up on."

"You go first," Daniel said.

Lynette thought for a moment, considering where to start. Their break up? Her marriage? Her baggage? It was all too much. "Let's go back to my senior year of high school and your freshman year of college."

"That was a long time ago."

"Yes, but we have some unfinished business. Why'd you stop calling me?"

"I didn't."

"You did. After you left for college, I called all the time. Your roommate answered, told me he gave you the messages, yet I never heard from you."

"I called you back and left messages with your mom and dad. Don't you remember? Eventually, you stopped calling."

Lynette let his excuse roll around her brain. Finally, she said, "I went to UM with some friends to find you. I think it was the weekend of homecoming. I remember it like it was yesterday. I hadn't heard from you in about six weeks. You were in the parking lot at the game and you had your arm around a girl."

He shook his head, refuting her memory. "I don't remember that. Could it have been someone else?"

"You were probably drunk. Wasn't that the year you almost failed because you were partying too much? At least, that's the rumor I heard." Lynette's harsh voice cut through the restaurant and the server approaching them slinked away.

"Maybe I was. But I didn't have a girlfriend, I promise. I tried to contact you, but we played phone tag and eventually you stopped returning my calls. Scout's honor."

Searching his face, Lynette recognized the truth behind his round eyes. His truth didn't match up with her truth, but it was a long time ago. "Okay," she said. "I guess it happens to everyone. One person goes to college, the other stays in high school, and you grow apart."

Trying to lighten the mood, Daniel reached for her hand and Lynette let him hold it. "What happened after high school?"

"I met Anthony. We fell in love, moved to Chicago, and had a baby." She ticked off her timeline like a grocery list. She wanted to share that he later broke her heart by being too friendly with the ladies, but she had no explicit proof. To Lynette, emotional infidelity was just as real as physical adultery. She shook her head, forcing her ex-husband out of her mind, and focused on Daniel's strong hands resting on the table. "You?"

"I turned thirty, realized my life was traveling at the speed of light, got scared, proposed to my girlfriend even though she wasn't right for me, and got divorced less than two years later. I moved back home, bought the restaurant to distract myself, and here I am."

"Kids?"

"No kids. I barely had a wife."

"How are your parents and brother? They still around?"

Daniel shook his head. "My parents are in North Carolina, loving life where it's warm, and my brother is out in Denver, loving where it's cold."

Lynette giggled. "He always loved the outdoors. I can picture him skiing every day."

Daniel grinned. "He does. I came back here because I felt like something in my life was missing and I needed to get back to my roots. When the restaurant came up for sale, I knew I needed to jump on it."

They fell into a straightforward conversation, reminiscing about high school shenanigans and family. His velvety voice hadn't changed in the more than thirty years Lynette had last seen him.

After Daniel paid the bill, they drove back to her parent's house.

Sitting in the driveway, they watched the snowflakes splatter the windshield. "I love how each flake is so different," Lynette said. "Yet, they come together and create this powerful force. It's really quite amazing."

She looked over at him and his lips pressed against hers. All the memories came rushing back, and she felt seventeen again. It had been ages since her body had responded in this way, a tugging in her abdomen, pulling her towards him. She shifted and ran her hand down the side of his face. His beard bristles poked at her hand, reminding her they both had lived many years apart.

"Thank you, Daniel. I had an amazing night."

He gave her a brief kiss and the magnetic hold between them grew. "Can I see you again?"

"Of course." She pushed open the door and climbed out. Leaning into the car, she said, "I'll see you at work tomorrow," and winked.

Walking into the house, she felt like a million dollars. Something inside re-ignited, and she wasn't sure she could put the flame out before it turned into an inferno. Like a teenager, she slinked into the house late for curfew. Instead of Dad sitting on the couch with his legs crossed waiting, she saw Ruby curled up on the couch with a book in her hand.

A sly smile spread across her face as she analyzed Lynette's movements.

"What?" Lynette asked, narrowing her eyes at her daughter. She dropped eye contact and sat beside Ruby's outstretched legs.

"You look good," she smirked. Her eyes sparkled with eagerness, but instead of waiting for a response, she picked up her book and watched Lynette from the top of the pages.

Lynette threw her head against the top cushion and grinned at the ceiling. She leaned across and kissed Ruby on the forehead. "Good night. I'm going to bed."

Walking up the stairs felt like cotton candy against her feet, and Lynette pirouetted at the second-floor landing. She was over fifty, but in her mind, she was a teenager in love for the first time. Her heart hadn't fluttered in years. Too many years. And it felt tremendous.

Lynette changed out of her clothes and climbed into bed. She stretched her tired legs until they hit the foot board and her nerves shot from her core to her legs to her feet. Squealing in delight and pulling her arms to her chest, every neuron fired. The dopamine hit her limbs, and she fell asleep in a haze of bliss.

By the time Lynette's eyes opened, she found herself back in Mom's old bed. Her heart beat against her chest like a rabid fox desperate to escape. "That was a nightmare," Lynette said.

She slowly rose and poured herself a cup of coffee before jotting down keywords on the blank pages of her dream journal: **DANIEL, BREAKUP, SABOTAGE.** Lynette stared at the giant doodle, unable to make heads or tails out of the dream.

"Hey, Mom. Did you have another dream?" Ruby sat beside her, staring at the journal. "Sabotage, huh? That's intense."

"Yeah, I think my dad sabotaged my relationship with Daniel."

"How so?"

"Well, in my dream, Mema and Papa were talking and Papa admitted to not giving me Daniel's messages. A big word bounced between them and it said 'SABOTAGE.'" Lynette moved her hand across her forehead as she said the word. "Does that happen to you? In the dreams? Like, random words are spelled out and bouncing or floating around?"

Ruby nodded. "Yeah, I never thought about that, but yes, I think so. So what was the piece of clothing that brought you back?"

Lynette rolled through the images like a View Master. "Gosh, I think it was those clip-on earrings I found in her jewelry box. I can't remember. I was too wrapped up in Papa's betrayal. Why would he do that?"

"I don't know. Maybe you should ask Nora. You sabotaged my friendship with Jennifer, didn't you?"

Lynette had completely forgotten about Jennifer. "She was bad news, Ruby. She was smoking in middle school. I couldn't have you hanging out with her."

"So you made me quit cheerleading to avoid being around her...seems a little harsh, don't you think? I mean, I could have been the next NFL cheerleader and I would never know."

Lynette took a sip and refilled her cup. "Okay, I get it. So, you think it is true?"

"Do you believe all the other dreams are true?"

"I do."

"So yeah, probably. Have you seen my gloves? I put them in the basket, but now I can't find them."

"In here." Fully clothed with her long, blonde hair brushed and curled at the ends, Ruby looked stunning. "You look nice. Where are you off to?"

"Work. I told Stella I'd go in early today." Ruby kissed Lynette on the cheek and grabbed her purse. "I gotta go. Can you drive me? I don't want to keep the car if you need it," she said.

Lynette's phone dinged. Daniel's name lit up the screen and Lynette's mood lifted like a romantic hot-air balloon ride. **Good morning** followed by a happy face emoji decorated her screen.

She wanted to write back, she really did, but she didn't want to seem too eager. Instead, she placed her phone in her bag, threw on her shoes, and walked outside with Ruby. The picturesque ride to and from Portland kept Lynette quiet as she thought about her dream and her history with Daniel.

She had been living in her old home for almost two months now, and surprisingly, she had given little thought to her old life in Chicago. Martha checked in now and then, but beyond that, Lynette hadn't kept in touch with anyone. She hadn't checked her email in ages, and when she did, her eyes glazed over a screen full of correspondence from her department head asking if she was prepared for her next round of students.

January first was coming up quick, and Lynette dreaded the return to her humdrum, boring life. Knowing she only had a few weeks before she had to say goodbye, she made the best of it. Engaging Daniel didn't need to be for forever. It could be for a brief season in her life, just like last time, and she'd be grateful for the memories of how her body responded to his touch.

After getting dressed, Lynette picked up her phone to message Daniel. Social niceties, like **how are you?** and **how'd you sleep?** occurred first and then he offered to cook her dinner. Lynette threw her hand against her chest, begging it to stop drumming at supersonic speed. Her fingers froze, unable to move around the digital keyboard. Smiling too hard, her rosy cheeks ached, as her imagination ran wild with the romance smut she read earlier.

Curious about where he lived and what his home looked like, Lynette said yes. She needed to apologize to him, still uncertain if what she witnessed the night before was truth or fiction. He needed to know it wasn't her who had ignored him all those years ago.

Yes, that would be wonderful.

Completely taken aback by how her life had shifted, she went shopping for a low-cut top that would tease Daniel with memories of them in his car, in his teenage bedroom, and at the beach. Lynette recalled all the places they got hot and heavy during her most formative years. She needed to remind him she still had it in her and was most desirable despite the saggy breasts, soft thighs, and round belly.

On the way home from the mall, Lynette stopped at Nora's. Drawn to the medium, Lynette suspected Nora knew why Mom was coming to her in her dreams. But why Ruby? The lesson or message remained unclear, and until Lynette knew for sure, she would continue to anticipate Mom's stories with jittery limbs and a rapid heartbeat.

The bell above the door jingled as Lynette stepped into the dim room. Nora sat at the table, organizing her cards and crystals.

"Hello, Lynette. Nice seeing you again."

"Yes, hi." Lynette straightened her hair and slid off her purse, putting it beside Nora. "I was wondering if you had room for a quick walk-in?"

"Ah, we've been waiting for you. Or so I've been told."

Goosebumps erupted on Lynette's arm and she shook her shoulders. "We?"

"Yes, the same person who was here before came through the door with you."

Lynette's head whipped toward the door, almost expecting her mother to be standing there. She looked back at Nora, searching for humor behind her eyes, but the only thing she saw was intrigue. "Um, great."

"Is there anything specific you'd like to know? Think specific, yes-no questions. Those are easiest, so her messages to you through me don't get mixed up."

Lynette's sweaty palms rubbed against her pants. She needed to know. "Okay, great. Did she and my dad sabotage my relationship with Daniel?"

A distant look erupted across Nora's face, and she quickly returned her eyes to Lynette. "No."

Relief rushed through Lynette.

"Okay. Did my dad sabotage my relationship with Daniel?"

Nora's hands fingered the crystals in the small bowl, and Lynette's heart thudded in her ears. "Yes."

A small but audible gasp escaped. "But why?"

Nora squinted her eyes and pressed her eyebrows together. "I'm not getting an obvious message, but what I see is an image of a car. A fast car." Her eyes moved to Lynette. "Does that mean anything to you?"

Lynette shook her head. Maybe the connection would come later. She'd have to ask Daniel about it.

"I need to know why Mom is coming to me."

Folding her bony fingers into a clasp, Nora redirected Lynette. "I need a specific question to get an accurate answer."

"Is Mom trying to teach me a lesson through these dreams?"

"Yes."

"Will she eventually stop coming?"

"Yes."

"Will she stop coming when I learn the lesson?"

"Yes."

"Is she communicating with us for my benefit or Ruby's?" Lynette found it strange that Mom would come to both of them, and she needed to know the purpose behind these memories.

Nora closed her eyes and rubbed her temples. "I'm getting a fickle response. Can you rephrase the question?"

Lynette pondered, and after a few seconds leaned forward. "Is she teaching Ruby a lesson?"

"No."

Another audible gasp escaped Lynette's lips. *Mom is coming for me.* Lynette reached into her purse and pulled out a fifty-dollar bill. "Thank you, Nora. I don't want to or need to know any more. Bye, Mom," she said to the surrounding space.

She got up from the table and scooted out the door before Nora could request a follow-up appointment.

Even though it wasn't time for dinner, she drove to Daniel's in a hurry, racing through the narrow streets until she stopped at a small Cape Cod-style house on a dead-end street surrounded by woods. This neighborhood brought back fond memories, when she and her girlfriends swam in the lake just beyond the trees.

Lynette sat in front of Daniel's house, admiring the quaint home perfect for a family of two or three. Her heart thumped against her chest and her fingers struggled to remove the keys from the ignition. This was it.

Standing in front of his door, she knocked gently at first and then louder. He wasn't expecting her, but his car sat in the driveway and she saw the lights on through the opaque glass in his front door. She rang the bell and pounded on the decorative glass.

Just when she was about to return to the car, the door swung open and Daniel stood before her in his blue jeans and loose-fitting t-shirt. He looked so comfortable and inviting.

"Hi," she breathed. "Sorry to just show up like this. Can we talk?" Without waiting for a response, she pushed past him and entered his home.

He closed the door behind her and followed her inside. "Are you okay? Do you want to sit?"

Lynette did as he said and crossed her ankles under the glass covered coffee table. She quickly uncrossed them, looked back at the door and noticed a pile of shoes in the corner. She kicked off her shoes and pulled her feet up and under her on the couch. "I'm okay." Her jittery feet shook under the weight of her body and she shifted to silence them.

"What's going on?" His body leaned closer to hers and she smelled his cologne on his shirt collar.

"Um, okay. I know I sound crazy, so I'm going to just say it. My dead mother has been communicating with me from the other side."

He leaned back, pushing against the arm of the couch. He arched his eyebrows and grinned.

"No, really. Every few nights she comes to me in my dreams, and I, uh, you were right. My dad knew you called all those years ago, and he never gave me any of the messages. I don't know why. I've been going to a medium to help me decipher why she can't just leave me alone, and the medium told me, 'fast car,' when I asked why my dad would do that." She pressed her lips shut, considering her next move. Finally, she leaned forward. "Do you know why she would say that? Fast car. Does that mean anything to you?"

Daniel rubbed his forehead and bit his lip. "Fast car," he repeated. "That's why he wanted us to break up?" His face drained from all color. "I know."

Lynette leaned forward. "You do?"

"Yes. When I first got to school, I met this guy who was commuting from home. He was obsessed with classic cars. He had cars in his garage in various states of repair. I went for a ride with him one day. I can't remember why. Maybe a joyride? He knew the roads, I didn't, and he was driving. He took a turn too fast, and the car slid off the road into an embankment. We weren't hurt, but the cops came and he got ticketed. The cop knew my grandfather, and somehow my dad found out what happened. I got in trouble, but not so much trouble that I didn't go for another joyride with him. I knew the risks." His eyes met hers. "I bet my dad told your dad."

Lynette leaned forward, waiting for more. "That's it?"

"That's all I got. That was the only time I was in a fast car, and we got into a minor accident. I can see your dad not wanting you near me after that, right? Especially if my dad told him."

Daniel stood and Lynette followed him into the kitchen. "What are you doing?" she asked.

He reached for his phone. "Calling my dad."

She stood in the corner, biting her fingernail and tapping her foot, watching Daniel's body language and facial expressions as he asked his hard-of-hearing father to recall a conversation from thirty years before. A big smile spread across his face, and Lynette waited. He placed the phone down and wrapped her in a hug.

"He said he bumped into your dad at the grocery store and your dad asked how I was. He told him about the car escapade. See? I was right. Fast car."

Lynette inhaled his cologne, and her heart fluttered. "I'm so sorry I blamed you for not calling me back."

"Old news. Don't beat yourself up over it."

Lynette stared into his eyes, searching for the what-if's. "It could have been different, though. What if we had stayed together?"

Daniel grinned and pulled her close. "Who knows? Maybe we needed to have some heartache and pain before it would make sense for us to be together. Maybe it was supposed to be like this."

Feeling at ease, Lynette leaned into his chest and inhaled. "I'm sorry."

"Me too."

He led her back to the couch, and she placed her feet across his lap and pulled a blanket over the two of them. "Want to watch a movie?"

"Do you want to watch an oldie?" His eyes sparkled.

"Like what?"

"Roxanne?"

Every time Lynette watched that movie, she thought of Daniel. They would watch that movie under blankets in his basement during all of junior year.

Lynette snuggled up against the couch and watched C.D. Bales and Roxanne fall in love despite his attempt to help Chris win her heart. Maybe life wasn't how she had imagined, all those years ago, but maybe C.D. Bales was right. Maybe you needed to love without limits.

Chapter 38

Standing behind the counter with nothing to do caused Ruby's mind to wander. Her brain always found its way to Shayla and her apartment three thousand miles away, causing her sweaty hands and feet to tremble. She felt like such a jerk for bailing, but Ruby had a history of running away from uncomfortable conversations. No matter how many times she ignored the ping of missed calls, voicemails, and text messages, Shayla never stopped.

According to the messages, management towed Ruby's car because someone smashed the windows and the other tenants had complained of the broken glass. A giant pit at the base of her stomach and a growing bubble in her throat made it difficult to breathe. The worst-case scenario emerged in her mind. Her car was a goner because she didn't have the money to get it fixed. She made a note to call the police station and the insurance company to get the mess sorted.

Being three thousand miles away from the life she had built suddenly felt like a foolish decision Ruby made after Mema died.

A few minutes later, Ruby's phone dinged again, and she debated looking. After the second reminder ding, Ruby glanced down and saw Shayla's name across the screen. Her hands flew to her opened mouth, and she inhaled quick bursts of air. The message read, 'I got a new roommate.' Her eyes widened like saucers and her shoulders slumped in despair.

So much for friends turned family. In Ruby's deepest core, she wasn't surprised. She knew she'd been avoiding her sisterly best friend, but it still stung.

Things had seemed to have gone from bad to worse. No job, no car, and no apartment. Ruby needed to get home. Her mind raced on a speed track, as the domino-effect of poor choices and irresponsibility fell around her. And not to mention, Mema's dreams had become less and less frequent.

The bell above the door jangled, and Ruby snapped her head up. Stella walked in carrying a box of books and three oversized tote bags hanging off her narrow shoulders. Ruby raced to her side, happy for a distraction.

Stella ripped off her coat and tossed it on the stool behind the counter. "I just waited thirty minutes in line at the post office to mail gifts. Why does everyone wait until the days before Christmas to do their shopping? Don't they know their packages won't get there in time?"

Ruby's lips pulled into a small smile at Stella's disheveled hair, crushed from her winter hat on top and frizzy on the bottom from the blustery wind. "Aren't you part of that group?"

"Yes, but I was sending a birthday gift to my cousin, and her birthday isn't until January tenth. I have plenty of time. All those other people? Poor planning and I end up wasting thirty minutes of my life for their inability to manage their time." Stella pointed. "That box has to go out today. Put them in the system and arrange them in the stacks and the front table. You may have to rearrange some books."

Ruby nodded and pulled the top book from the box. "Living in a Hygge Home," she read.

"Yeah, if you are alone this holiday season but want to create a cozy environment to forget about your loneliness, this is the book for you."

Ruby flipped through the slim book, paying attention to the bolded tips. "What if you don't know where your home is?"

"It'll help you create the sense of home no matter where you are."

Ruby grinned. "Got it. I think I need this for myself." She placed it beside the register for further skimming.

Stella rummaged through the register, pulling out cash and change. "Why's that?"

Ruby settled on her stool. "Oh, I don't know. I'm from California, you know. It's a totally different world over here." She hadn't told Stella she was leaving in a few weeks, which was the definition of irresponsibility, but now that her apartment was gone, she didn't know if she needed to.

"Do you like it here?"

Ruby hesitated and weighed the pros and cons of life in Maine. "I miss the glamor attached to my life in Cali, but I don't miss the constant stress and the unknown. Not knowing when or where your next job is, if you'll have enough money to pay your bills, or if the starving artist is something to admire or fear. Let's just say I've had more panic attacks than I'd care to admit."

"That's L.A. I would never live there, but what about here?"

"Here is weird, right? I never imagined myself here, yet here I am. There aren't any modeling opportunities, and without that, I don't know who I am. My grandmother left me her house, so I could live here rent free and start over. The problem is, I don't know what my life would look like. I also never realized how much I'd like to be part of a community, like working here. I have so many fond memories, but they happened with my grandmother, and now she's gone. It's different, and it hurts." Ruby thought about how much she'd learned from Mema, even in her death. "It still hurts."

"Well, I enjoy having you here. You're an outstanding employee, you're good with customers, and you're a reader, which is unheard of these days. I know I can count on you to make recommendations to customers as they come in. Here, I have something for you." Stella reached into her purse and removed a white envelope. "It's not much, but it might help with Christmas shopping."

Ruby took the envelope and inside sat a single hundred-dollar bill. Her body warmed and her vision blurred. "Oh, Stella." Throwing her arms around Stella's neck, she pulled her close. "This is so sweet, thank you."

Stella blushed. "Just a small token of my appreciation. You've earned it. With your marketing skills, our sales have doubled as compared to this time last year. I see how much you do for this little shop, and I'm grateful."

Looking into Stella's warm, brown eyes, Ruby knew what she needed to do.

"Stella," she said, holding the envelope close to her chest. "I'm going back to L.A. December thirty-first, but I promise I'll be back. I need a few weeks. A few things need to be addressed before I start my new life here."

After work, she drove through the quiet streets of Maine, admiring the newly fallen snow draping the trees like donut glaze. Evergreen branches poked through the coating, reminding Ruby that winter was here.

She compared the rugged landscape to the brightly lit streets of Los Angeles, and couldn't quite fathom how vastly different the two locations were. Sometimes she felt like she was living on another planet.

She drove by the lake Mema and Papa took her to when she was in elementary school and recalled the encouragement they had yelled as she kicked her legs and fanned her arms, believing in her superpower to fly through the waves.

The narrow roads led to the wooded area outside their street, and Ruby remembered the first time she saw a moose in real life. Mema drove the same road Ruby was driving, and the car skidded to a halt as a monster emerged from the foliage. Tall, strong, and beautiful, its head seemed larger than Ruby's body. The moose stopped directly in front of the car and craned his neck toward the windshield. Ruby screamed, and Mema placed her hand on Ruby's leg. Frozen with fear and admiration, Ruby watched the animal bustle across the street.

Those experiences brought back simple memories of life before her parents split and her relationships deteriorated.

When she got back to the house, she curled up on the coach wearing the oversized sweatshirt she had given Mema during a surprise visit. Ruby had visited Mema to announce her acceptance into her first-choice university and Mema threw her arms around Ruby and danced with her in the living room. Ruby tripped over Mema's clunky shoes and tossed her head back in laughter.

They were so happy then. Mema immediately pulled the sweatshirt over her body and said she'd never take it off. Mema always had a way of making Ruby feel special.

Her heart pounding, she pulled out her phone and stared at Shalya's name at the top of her Favorites list. Shayla was listed first, and before Mema died, they texted nonstop. All the funny, boring, and exciting things that happened when they weren't together read like disjointed dialogue in their phones. Since Mema died, the correspondence between her and Shayla had been minimal.

Ruby's pointer finger pressed her name, and she pressed the speakerphone, hoping Shayla wouldn't answer. When she did, Ruby's body stiffened. "Hi," she said.

"Hi." Shayla's clipped voice stopped Ruby in her tracks and she questioned if she was making the right choice.

"Hi, Shayla." Ruby cleared her throat, assessing Shayla's reaction to hearing Ruby's voice. "How are you?" Her enthusiastic voice sounded forced, even to her.

"Good, busy. I'm on my lunch. What's up?"

Ruby pulled back at the curtness behind Shayla's response. "Oh, well,

I wanted to talk. I saw you got a new roommate?"

"Yeah, you're not here, and I need someone to help with the bills."

"But I am helping. I'm still covering my rent." Her shrilly voice echoed off the walls.

"Yeah, but what about everything else? Electricity, water, food. We split all that."

Ruby shook her head, not understanding. "But if I'm not there, those bills should be less."

"Yeah, but not by much. I hate living alone. I'm lonely and scared. It's not safe being a young, single woman living here. I can't sleep at night because every noise puts me on edge. You're not here, and there was a robbery three doors down." Her voice rose. "What if it was our apartment? I could be dead."

Although Shayla hadn't said it aloud, Ruby sensed her next sentence. *And it would be all your fault.* "I'm sorry, I had no idea."

"Of course you didn't. You haven't returned my calls in weeks."

"I'm sorry, I've been a little busy here," Ruby said.

"And when I heard someone needed a place, I jumped on it."

"Ugh." Ruby exhaled. "Is my car still impounded?"

"Yeah."

Biting her lip, Ruby quickly considered when she could get it back. "Okay, I'm flying home next month. I'll take care of my car." A quiet silence hung between them on the line, so Ruby continued. "Um, did I tell you that my grandmother left me her house?"

"Yeaaa." She dragged the word out, not sounding at all interested.

Hurt by Shayla's indifference, Ruby asked, "When is she moving in?"

"Who?"

"Your new roommate."

"As soon as she can."

Ruby's stomach twisted. "Well, if you need her to move in sooner, she can stay in my room." Ruby bit her lip, not wanting a stranger to be near her stuff unsupervised, but she felt bad, leaving Shayla afraid and alone. "Since my life out there has turned to shit, I'm starting over. I'll be home for the month of January. I'll pack up as much shit as I can, sell or donate the rest, and then say goodbye."

"Okay, keep me posted. I gotta run."

Before Ruby could respond, the phone clicked. "Well," Ruby said to herself. "That solves that problem." The conversation only lasted five minutes, but the content of what they discussed left her in a haze, unable to focus. *No car, no job, no apartment. Could life get any better?*

Ruby pulled up her internet browser and searched for advertising jobs in the area. If anything, Mom was right about saying she needed a back-up plan. Portland was a tiny city, but they still had businesses. And thanks to Mema, she was living rent free.

She applied to three jobs, using her grandmother's address as her own, and prayed to Mema. If it was meant to be, it would happen.

Feeling brave, Ruby pulled out her computer and searched for a flight from Boston to Los Angeles. Her heart churned as she scrolled through the list of flights, gazing at their times and prices. *Why is it so much?* Even with Ruby's airline credit, and six weeks of savings, she hoped she had enough to fly across the country and back. Pulling out her credit card, she bit her lip, input the numbers, and hit purchase. An error message popped up, requesting she use another form of payment. *Damn.* Her card had been declined.

Ruby scrolled through her phone, needing to talk to someone, but all the people in her contact list were fellow models or random friends of Shayla's. She pushed Auntie Lori's name, and the phone rang.

"Hey, sweetie, how are you?"

"I'm okay, I just wanted to hear your voice. How are you?" Ruby wasn't okay. Her life, no matter where she lived, was crumbling.

"Oh, I'm good. How's your new job?"

Settling back against the chair, Ruby stretched her legs. "It's great, actually. I have time to catch up on reading, and I still use my skills to market the store online. It's been fun. I created a booktok and bookstagram account, and we have a combined ten-thousand followers so far. Stella, my boss, is pleased."

"That's wonderful. How's everything on the home front? How's your mom?"

"She's fine. We work opposite shifts, so we have our space. It's good."

"You seem kind of down. Are you sure you're okay?"

Like a slow leak, the protective bubble Ruby built slowly deflated. "Not really. I was going to go back to L.A., but my roommate gave my room away. My car was broken into and towed, and I don't have any cash to fly home. It's actually a mess." Sharing the burden of her bad day released some of her dissatisfaction with the current state of her life. "But I'm fine. It's fine. Everything is fine."

Ruby grinned at Auntie Lori's husky laugh. "One thing I know about us Waller women is that we are survivors. I wish I could do more to help you, but I'm strapped for cash."

"Oh no, Auntie! I wasn't asking for money, I just needed a friendly voice to talk to. I miss you and I can't wait to see you. I'll be fine. I promise."

She hung up the phone and snuggled on the couch under Mema's hand-knit blanket. It was already six p.m. and Mom hadn't returned from work yet. She had agreed to cover a dinner shift, and probably wouldn't be home until after eleven. Ruby smiled as she imagined Mom, with her strands of gray and fine lines decorating her face, hanging out with the twenty-something bartender as they closed for the night. Ruby imagined the young adults working at the restaurant looking up to Mom like a mother figure, someone who could help solve problems, give words of encouragement, and also gently advise them with their life choices. Just like how Mema was to Kate.

Ruby leaned against the couch and threw on a movie. The lullaby of laugh tracks common in the nineties pulled her to sleep, and her eyes became heavy. She straightened her sweatshirt and pulled the blanket up to her chin. Mema's couch was more comfortable than it looked, especially when she didn't have to share it with anyone. Her eyes closed like dead weight, and Ruby welcomed the cloudy fog that invited her in.

When she opened them again, she was on Mema's couch, still wearing the sweatshirt. The movie still played on the flatscreen tv and Ruby was alone. She checked her watch and saw that only an hour had passed.

In one hour, she'd fallen asleep and dreamed, but this dream felt different. It felt like goodbye. Ruby pulled her legs up to her waist and hugged them. The blanket rubbed against her face, catching the tears that created small puddles from her grief.

By the time Mom got home, Ruby was fast asleep in her bed, hoping to dream another memory, but the memories never came.

On Sunday, Ruby and Mom sat at the kitchen table for their weekly pow-wow.

"I don't know, Ruby. I feel like I've worn everything of hers, and the dreams just aren't coming. Have you had any?"

She took a deep breath. "I had a dream a few nights ago. I kind of had this weird feeling she was saying goodbye to me. It was one of the last times I had visited her before moving to L.A. It wasn't a dream, like the other ones. It was like I relived that visit with Mema. I totally forgot about this conversation, probably because I was a naïve eighteen-year-old who didn't care about anyone except myself. I'm glad I relived it, although it made me sad."

"What'd she say?" Mom leaned forward.

"She said she was a better grandmother than mother, and that one day I would understand."

Mom snorted.

"And she told me to live life with no regrets. I think that's why I moved to L.A. I needed to see for myself if modeling was right for me."

"And? Now that you've had some time to reflect, what do you think?" Mom asked.

"I'm glad I went, and I know I'm still young, but I won't have my looks to carry me through my long life. Hopefully, my very long life." A small smile rose from the corners of her mouth.

Mom's face matched Ruby's. "What's that mean?"

"It means, Mom, that I'm going to L.A. for a little while to tie up loose ends, but the next chapter of my life is here."

Mom pumped her fist in the air and whooped at the ceiling. "Wonderful!"

Surprised by her excitement, Ruby continued. "Mema told me she regrets letting you walk away. I don't know if you knew this, but Papa pressured her to say sorry to you and Auntie Lori, but she couldn't. At that time, she was relying on Kate for all the daughterly stuff, especially when Papa died."

Mom's eyes dropped to her hands. "Yeah, well, that was a hard time."

"I don't know why," Ruby continued, "but I don't think she's coming back to me."

They sat in silence, sipping their coffees and gazing through the sliding glass doors. A red cardinal perched on the deck rail.

"Mom, look!" Ruby pointed and Mom rose.

"Do you think that's her?" Ruby moved to the door and pressed her face against the translucent glass. "A cardinal showed up when I found out she died. Maybe she was saying hi then, and goodbye now." She pressed her palm on the glass and wiggled her fingers. "Hi, Mema."

Mom draped her arm around Ruby and kissed her forehead. "Hi, Mom. Thanks for the help, but I think I have it from here."

The cardinal hopped away, leaving tiny footprints on the white dusting coating the rail.

"I don't want to make the same mistake she did, Ruby. You're my only daughter, and I can't risk losing you for the rest of our lives. You have so much life before you, and I would be ecstatic if you allowed me to be a part of it. Sometimes, I wonder if I secretly blamed you for my marriage failing, but now I know how childish and selfish that was. It was bad timing is all, and I apologize for not being there."

Ruby's heart thundered, and she swallowed the ball in her throat. "Oh, Mom. As terrible as it is that Mema's gone, I almost wonder if her death was a blessing in disguise. I haven't felt this at home since elementary school when Santa was still real and my favorite thing to do was read bedtime stories with you."

Lynette walked to the kitchen and refilled their mugs with hot water. "You know, I saw Nora one more time a few weeks ago. She told me that Mema would stop coming when I learned the lesson she was teaching. I haven't seen her in my dreams since she revealed that my dad purposefully prevented me from keeping in touch with Daniel."

Ruby raised her eyes.

"That's right. None of us are perfect. At first, I was really upset, because I loved Daniel and I wonder now what life would have been like if we had stayed together. Would we have gotten married?" She blinked a few times. "But then I realized, if Daniel and I worked out, there would be no you, and that would rip my heart out. Maybe I needed the pain from your father to make me appreciate what Daniel could give me." Mom shook her head. "It's silly, but it's the only way I can rationalize it."

"I'm sorry, Mom. I really like Daniel. Ever since you started dating, you're so much happier."

"I have been, haven't I? The thing is, Nora said Mema would stop coming once I learned my lesson, and maybe the lesson was to give people the benefit of the doubt. To forgive. I had assumed Daniel had avoided me, Mom loved Loretta more than me, and you purposefully defied me. All those assumptions were wrong, and if I had only been strong enough to ask, it would have prevented a lot of heartache."

The hot water burned Ruby's throat, and she added more milk to lower the temperature.

"Would you be sad if that was the last dream?" Ruby asked.

"Yes, but I know she's still here."

"What are you going to do? Aren't you supposed to go back to work next semester?"

Mom buried her head in her hands. "Yes," she groaned. "But you're staying here, Daniel's here, and I'm tired of being alone. How about I stay here until you get back from California? I'll put the Chicago house on the market in the spring and reassess then. Work doesn't need to know the details."

"But won't you miss it? Won't you miss Martha?" Ruby asked.

"Of course, but I think I'm ready to start over, too. Your father certainly has, and that house only brings sad memories. Let me start here, with you. What do you say?" Her smile brightened the room.

"I would love that. I don't know what I'm doing with my life."

"Neither do I."

"But it's never too late to try again, right?"

Mom kissed Ruby on the forehead. "Life is too short to be stuck. You gotta keep moving forward."

Chapter 39

L ynette curled under the blankets with her nose buried in the smutty romance, a gleeful smile pressed against her face. When she turned the last page, she closed her eyes and inhaled the moments she and Daniel had shared on their date.

A peace settled over her as her problems in Chicago vanished.

A gentle buzz vibrated on the bed beside her, pulling her out of her fantasy.

"Hey, Martha!"

"Hi, how's it going?"

"Oh good," Lynette said. She wasn't yet ready to share Daniel with Martha. "How are you?"

"Oh, I'm good. I wanted to tell you I got another envelope from the Illinois Post."

Suddenly interested, Lynette sat up straight. "Oh yeah? Open it, will you?" She heard paper ripping through the earpiece.

"It says..."

Lynette waited, imagining Martha scanning the document.

"Your picture won! Lynette, in here are two vouchers for round trip airfare from Chicago to L.A. and a five night hotel stay!"

"Unbelievable!" She had sent that photo on a whim, hoping it would lead her to Ruby.

"Congratulations!"

Lynette hopped out of bed, an extra bounce in her step, forgetting that Ruby was at work. "Oh, Martha, thank you! I have to call Ruby. She's working until ten tonight, but maybe I can catch her. I'll call you later." Lynette quickly hung up the phone.

Ruby didn't answer her phone, and this news was too monumental to leave on a voicemail, so Lynette hung up and researched her trip to L.A. She couldn't wait to go out there and see what kind of life her daughter was living.

A few hours later, Lynette rested on the coach, waiting for Ruby to return from work. Her eyes closed and the warm bliss from Martha's announcement turned to a muddy haze.

Lynette recognized the freefall into Mom's past. When she woke up, it was morning but still dark. Lynette climbed the stairs and checked on Ruby, just as she had when Ruby was a child and sick with a fever. Ruby's head snuck out from under the blankets and Lynette watched her chest rise and fall. She wrote a quick note and taped it to Ruby's door before getting dressed.

More questions emerged and she needed to find the answers. Lynette needed to talk to Nora. She pulled Mom's parka over her body, slid her winter boots over her chilly feet, and climbed into Mom's old car.

The drive to Nora's was beautiful, with the sun rising just beyond the ocean, and Lynette watched the sky transition from a deep purple to a pink haze. Knowing Nora wouldn't be there this early, Lynette pulled into the public beach parking lot and walked down to the water.

The beach was empty except for a few birds digging their beaks in the sand. Beyond the waves crashing against the rocks, Lynette didn't hear a sound. She walked the beach, thinking about her dream from last night.

It was Mom and Kate. Divorce and Ruby were referenced, but Lynette couldn't remember the context. She focused hard, like remembering or not would determine life or death. A birthday card drifted past her with Mom's fancy writing spelling out California. California. On the fridge were the words California-Anthony-Ruby-College. No matter how hard Lynette tried, it made little sense. *Did Kate know about Ruby in California?* A jealousy burned within her. *Did Mom and Anthony stay in touch?* The betrayal made it difficult to see.

Lynette leaned against the large rock separating the beach from the parking lot until she lost feeling in her fingers and toes. She moved back to the car, cranked the heat and drove to Nora's.

The sign said Closed, but the light was on. Lynette pounded on the door, hoping someone was inside. Her heart raced with a strange sense that this was it. That cardinal yesterday must have meant something.

She banged on the door again and peered through the window. Nora's frizzy hair bounced in the distance and Lynette knocked louder, and waved her arms like an air traffic controller.

The door opened. "Lynette, good morning." Nora's face lacked the makeup Lynette expected, and she wore sweatpants and a t-shirt. "We aren't open."

Lynette shimmied her body between the door's opening and the door frame. "Yes, I'm sorry, but I need to talk to you." She eyed her attire. "Do you live here?"

"I do. I was actually sleeping. I thought it was an emergency with all that banging."

"I'm sorry, but I must speak with you. One last time. Please, Nora, please. I have just a few more questions that I need answered."

Nora sighed and opened the door. "Come in."

Lynette thanked her and walked into the waiting room she had frequented many times before. She sat in the chair. "I'll wait here until you're ready."

Nora chuckled. "No need to wait. I don't need to be dressed to communicate with spirits. Come with me." She waved Lynette to the back room and Lynette hurried behind. "Take a seat."

She had Lynette pick a tarot card and proceeded to channel Mom.

"Is she here?" Lynette asked.

"There is someone here with us, yes."

"Did she come to us as a cardinal?"

Nora's dark eyes connected with Lynette's. "Spirits come to us in many forms."

"Was she saying goodbye?"

"Lynette, they may not make their presence known, but they are always nearby."

Visions from her dream the night before passed behind her eyes. The words on the fridge stood out, and she needed to ask. "Nora, did Mom keep in touch with Anthony after our divorce?"

Nora leaned forward, her eyes darting around the room. "I am seeing a college. A young woman at a college. In class. Learning. Does that mean anything to you?"

Lynette shook her head, her blonde hair swishing. "No, that doesn't. Did she send Ruby to college?"

Nora closed her eyes. "I see a diploma, yes."

Shocked and confused by Mom's generosity and secret, Lynette stared ahead, refusing to blink. She crossed her arms over her chest. "She did. And they never told me. And did Anthony know?" The truth of the past three years crushed her. "I'm such a fool."

"No."

"No what?" Lynette asked.

"No to Anthony—Wait," Nora whispered. "I see a mother and child bonded by unconditional love."

Maybe it should have comforted Lynette, but all it did was remind her of how she had failed Ruby. Lynette smiled glumly and thanked Nora. "Sorry for waking you," she said. Placing a stack of bills on the table, Lynette gathered her belongings and left.

Chapter 40

"Hey Ruby? I need to talk to you," Mom said.

Ruby recognized the seriousness in her voice and she put down her phone to fully attend to Mom's words.

"I never told you, but Mema came to me one last time. I learned a few things from that memory. I hadn't realized how badly I had fallen into a depression after you left, or how my misinterpretation of the people I loved contributed to the fall-out. I mean, I'm not taking all the blame, but maybe if I had gone to a therapist sooner or hadn't ignored calls, letters, or texts, things would have played out differently. And I'm sorry for making you feel like your choices weren't valid. That wasn't my intention, but I didn't want you to make the same mistakes I did."

"It's okay. I'm sorry I never contacted you. At first, I was angry at how everything fell apart, and then once I got settled and back in school and working, I just didn't have the time."

Mom's face pulled back like she had been stung by a bee. "Well, I will always make time for you."

"That's not what I meant," Ruby said.

"The other thing is that I never knew you finished school."

Ruby dropped her eyes and played with the blanket. "Yeah, I, uh, felt weird about it because Mema paid for my tuition."

Lynette smiled sadly. "Yeah, you're very fortunate. I'm thankful she did that for you."

A lopsided grin rose on Ruby's lips. "Do you forgive me?"

"Yes. Do you forgive me?"

"Of course. Do you forgive Mema?"

Mom stared at the snowy yard out the front window. "I do. I know she tried and did the best she could. Her and Papa, but life happens, and sometimes it causes us to stumble. I think the most important thing is to get back up and forgive the past. Even though I didn't learn the lesson until she was gone, that's what she taught me."

Ruby snuggled into Mom's shoulder and rubbed her arm. It had been an interesting few months, but with Mom beside her and Mema in her heart, she knew they were home.

"Oh!" Mom's face lit up like a Christmas tree. "I never told you!" Her voice sped up and her hands danced in front of her. "I never told you, but I submitted a photo to the Illinois Post, and I won!"

"What'd you win? It looks like it's something good." Based upon her jumpy body, it was a million dollars.

"A trip for two to L.A."

"Congrats!"

"I have a plan. It's good, I promise. You fly out there, as planned. I'll meet you out there. I'll get a hotel and you can be my tour guide, showing me where all the famous people live. We'll get facials and massages, and go shopping, and the beach. It'll be great. You'll take my other ticket home to Chicago and we'll drive back here in my car."

Ruby cleared her throat. "Uh, actually, I uh. My card was declined. I wasn't able to book a new flight or reschedule my ticket."

"Oh no, really?"

"Yeah, I screwed up, so I wasn't going to ask you to bail me out. Again."

"But now you don't have to. How about you come with me to Chicago and we fly out together? Like a mother-daughter road trip."

"But aren't you going back to work next semester? That's in a few weeks."

Lynette leaned against the counter with her palms pressed against the side. "No. I'm not."

Ruby squinted at her. "Huh?"

"I'm staying here. You're here and life is too short. I can't be half a country away from you again."

Ruby clapped her hands, bounced on her toes and hugged Mom, like she hadn't hugged her since she was a child. All the pain that had transpired between them was gone.

Ruby and Mom spent Christmas Day together in front of the small, fake tree they found in the basement. Auntie Lori wanted to sell it during the estate sale, but Mom hid the box under her bed, knowing they would still be here for Christmas.

There were no more dreams or past demons to be discussed, and Ruby and Mom's road trip from Portland to Chicago started next week. The nerves built inside her, knowing she'd have to face yet another mountain with Shayla. Having Mom nearby made her racing mind slow down, knowing it would be okay.

In the late afternoon, a gentle knock sounded on the door. Ruby and Mom had just eaten a monster meal of orange chicken, pork fried rice, and a variety of appetizers you'd find in a pu pu platter.

"Who's that?" Ruby asked, wrapping her brand-new scarf around her neck. She opened the door to find Kate holding a deep-dish chocolate cream pie.

"Merry Christmas," she announced. "May I come in?"

Ruby opened the door wider, and a gust of cool air rushed behind them. Kate made her way to the kitchen and set the pie plate on the counter. "Merry Christmas, Lynette."

Mom smiled and gave her a polite hug. "Merry Christmas. Kate, I wanted to thank you for being there for my mom when she needed someone. Really, from the bottom of my heart. I'm happy to know she wasn't alone, especially after my dad died."

"Of course." Her voice, all choked up, wavered. "It's Christmas." Kate didn't remove her coat, but stood awkwardly in the kitchen. "You know, I made this pie in honor of your mother."

Mom pulled out a few plates, a knife and forks, slicing and serving. "Would you like a cup of tea?"

"That would be great," Kate said. She pulled off her jacket and Lynette dropped it on the empty chair. "That's where your mom used to sit." Her eyes moved to the chair, now holding the jackets, and Ruby rushed to move them to the couch.

They sat down as an unusual family, and ate Mema's favorite pie. Soon, stories about the feisty woman who left them too soon erupted, and laughter and appreciation filled the room. An element of familiarity had replaced the tension between Kate and Mom, and the feeling of home had cemented itself into Ruby's heart.

After Kate left, Ruby and Mom sat on the couch, watching old Christmas movies. Nostalgia from when life was easy had erased the pain Ruby and Mom had endured over the years, as well as the hurt that had healed with the help of Mema.

The phone rang, and Mom heaved herself up from the couch to answer. "Merry Christmas, Lori!"

Ruby smiled, realizing Mom had finally called Auntie Lori by her nickname. It seemed a quiet growth between them had occurred.

Lynette activated the speakerphone, and Ruby hollered, "Merry Christmas, Auntie!"

"Merry Christmas, Ruby," the distant voice said. "Linnie, I have to tell you something." Her voice sped up, and Ruby and Mom leaned forward to listen. "Remember when you said Mom was coming to you in your dreams? And I laughed at you?"

"Yeah."

"Well, guess what? She came to me! I took that winter hat and wore it home, and a few days later, she came to me in a dream. Linnie, it was amazing. It felt so real, and it was when we were kids. We used to be close, weren't we?"

"Yeah."

"What happened?" Auntie Lori's voice quieted.

"I don't know. Life. Hurts. Sadness. Betrayal. So many things happened."

"Well, I miss you, Linnie. I miss your laugh, your crazy ideas, and the trouble we used to get into."

Mom turned away from Ruby, but Ruby saw a tiny smile sneak through.

"What I'm trying to say," Auntie Lori said, "is that I miss you, and I want that sister back. Can we do it, Linnie? Can we?"

Tears slowly fell down Mom's cheeks, yet she looked happy.

"Yes. And I'm sorry for allowing us to grow so far apart. I was in an awful place, Lori, and I couldn't dig myself out. I cut so many people out because of my pain."

"It's okay, Linnie. I wanted to call and say I love you and I love Ruby. Ruby, I'm coming home this summer to meet with the lawyers, so expect a visitor in a few months."

Ruby clapped her hands in glee.

"You know what, Lori? I'm staying here," Lynette announced. "I'm not going back to Chicago, so I'll see you, too."

A series of whoops and hollers sounded through the phone.

"Love you, and Merry Christmas."

"Merry Christmas!" Ruby and Mom yelled.

She hung up the phone and the two women settled on the couch. A shared blanket spread over their legs. Ruby leaned against Mom's shoulder and sighed, breathing in the moment of togetherness.

Epilogue

T he warm sun and cool breeze invigorated Lynette as she walked the ocean shore barefoot with Daniel beside her.

"I'm so happy it's summer," she said.

"It's a crazy time of year. Are you up for the challenge, Ms. Front-of-the-House Manager?"

Lynette blushed at how her new role guaranteed time with Daniel. "I'm always up for the challenge. If it means seeing you every day, I'm up for it."

Their working relationship had strengthened as their romantic relationship redeveloped. It forced them to relearn how best to communicate, whether it was through negotiating schedules and menu items, hiking, or cooking dinner together. Lynette and Daniel had found their rhythm.

Lynette wanted to take it slow, and she found that dating in her fifties differed completely from her teens and twenties. Yes, the attraction was still strong, but there were other priorities in each of their lives. Like family, and making a decent living.

When Lynette told work she was extending her leave of absence, they threatened to end her teaching contract for not following procedure related to time off, but Lynette didn't care. After her trip to L.A., she knew there was nothing better than being near family. Putting the house on the market was the final nail in her old life, and she couldn't wait to discard the painful memories.

"Did the house sell yet?" Daniel asked.

"No, not yet. It's hard to look at it so bare. I mean, I'm ready to move on, but it still hurts. I think the hardest thing was getting rid of my library collection. Most of those books came from Martha's bookshop, so it made sense that they made their way home. If Martha looked carefully at what I donated back, she might have enough to retire. Some of those original copies are worth something."

"Maybe Stella can help you start a new library here."

"Maybe. You know, I spent half my life in that house. It's hard to disassociate the memories that made me who I am today from the memories I'd like to forget."

"I'm sure it'll sell quickly."

"That's what they say." Lynette was worried though, because her salary at the university paid considerably higher than the hourly rate at the restaurant. It was nothing against Daniel, but Lynette had gone through her savings quicker than she expected and her mind wandered as she traveled down the never-ending road of what-ifs.

"How's Ruby?" Daniel asked, and Lynette's mind immediately turned back to the present.

"She's coming along. I think she's enjoying her new life here."

"How's her new job?" Daniel squeezed her hand and pulled Lynette away from the rising tide.

"She loves it. She officially started on Monday. It's a start-up advertising agency focusing on Maine commerce. I think it will give her a great opportunity to explore the area and get to know other young people. Her official title is Social Media Marketing Manager. She's so good at that stuff, and she gets to manage all their accounts. I think it'll keep her busy and will satisfy her."

They walked further down the beach and Lynette watched a handful of birds circle above the ocean water.

"Do you want to come over for dinner?" Lynette asked. "Lori will be there. I think Ruby went to pick her up, and they were meeting Kate at the lawyers. Why Lori scheduled the meeting the same day as her flight is beyond me."

As she rambled, she leaned down to pick up a rock and, when she rose, Daniel's lips met hers. "I'd love to."

They'd been doing that often. Dinner dates, stolen kisses, and quiet moments. It was exactly what she needed.

When they returned to the house a few hours later, Lynette and Daniel found Ruby, Kate, and Lori waiting. They each wore wide smiles and jubilantly moved around the kitchen. Kate's arms danced as she talked, and Lori hopped from one side of the room to the other. Ruby sat back in the kitchen chair with her legs extending to the seat beside her.

"Hello!" Lynette called, embracing her sister in a hard, deep hug. "You look amazing." She grabbed Lori's hair, admiring the length, cut, and color.

"Yeah, new season, new me."

Lori scanned up and down Lynette's body. "You look great, too. Happy."

Lynette gave her another hug and whispered, "So happy." A blush traveled up her face and her eyes darted to Daniel, explaining that he was the reason for her happiness.

Lynette greeted Kate and Ruby, who both seemed giddy with exhilaration. "What's up?"

Kate waved a large manilla envelope. "Well, the estate is ready to be finalized."

Her heart thudded at the prospect of money and her stomach twisted at new beginnings and final goodbyes. "Oh, yeah?"

"Yep," Lori said. "All we have to do is sign, and the estate is done."

"Wait, I thought it would take a year to finalize. Maybe more," Lynette argued.

"That's what we thought too, but it turns out that with nothing being contested, things move quickly," Lori said.

"Not contested?" Lynette scrunched her eyebrows and glanced at Kate.

"I convinced Kate to take the inheritance," Lori said. "It's what Mom wanted. If she really feels bad, she can always donate the money to a cause Mom supported. Here." She pushed the paper to Lynette. "Sign."

Lynette quickly scanned and scribbled her signature across the page. Goosebumps erupted on her arm, and she rubbed them away. She couldn't believe this was really happening. She no longer had to worry.

The four women passed around the pen, accepting their fate.

Ruby dragged a chair over to the fridge and opened the small cabinet above the old appliance. She pulled out a bottle of wine and poured five glasses.

"These glasses were from Mom and Dad's fortieth wedding anniversary," Lynette said. "I found them in the basement mixed in with the Christmas boxes."

They each held their glass and Lynette began. "Thank you, Mom, for teaching me about forgiveness."

"And acceptance," Lori said.

"And unconditional love," Ruby added.

"And friendship," Kate said.

Mom may have left this world, but she left a legacy. Although it took years to teach her girls the essence of sisterhood, the strength of family, and the importance of acceptance, she did it through her secrets and untold memories.

Lynette sipped the sweet drink and smiled.

That night, Loretta, Ruby, and Lynette picked up a dozen red roses at the florist shop.

"You used to do this?" Loretta asked.

"Yeah, when I was in my deepest depression. I felt alone and needed to connect with someone, just to feel human. I'd walk the cemetery, dropping flowers on gravestones that looked as neglected and lonely as I felt."

"That's kind of creepy, Mom," Ruby said.

"I like to look at it as beautiful. We all live these complicated lives, right? No matter how minuscule it was, we impacted others, and we should be remembered."

They walked up and down the cemetery, talking about Mom and Dad's life together. Lynette knew their marriage wasn't as cracked up as they made it appear, but she was grateful they held it together for her and Lori. They may not have been perfect parents, but they taught her many valuable lessons.

"See this grave? It has moss growing around the edges and the lettering is faded. This man needs some love." She dropped one rose along the base of the stone. "Mr. Michael Porter, we remember you."

They did this until one rose was left.

"Can we leave this one for Mema and Papa?" Ruby asked.

Lori led them to the gravestone. Flowers lined the front and sides and an American flag flapped in the breeze. "Linnie, this looks great. Did you do this?"

"Yeah, Ruby and I. We come here often to visit Mom and Dad."

Ruby placed the rose along the blooms and said, "Mema and Papa, you lived a wonderful life. You influenced us, you taught us love, understanding, and compassion, and to this day you're still teaching us things." She kissed her fingers and pressed them into the gravestone. "We miss you."

Lynette and Lori did the same. All three hands touched the top of the tombstone and a spark traveled through Lynette's body. She dropped her hand and rubbed her fingers along her jean shorts. "Did you feel that?" Lynette asked with wide eyes.

Ruby and Lori nodded, both rubbing their hands.

"Hi Mema," Ruby said with a laugh.

Lynette hooked her arms through Ruby's and Lori's and they nervously chuckled and shook their heads as they walked back to the car. With her two favorite people beside her, Lynette was finally home.

The End.

For more information about upcoming novels that investigates family, friendship, and love, please join E.D. Hackett's newsletter at https://www.edhackettauthor.com

A Note from the Author

Mending Broken Threads started with a spark and evolved into this beautiful yet complicated story about family. I had always wondered what life was like for my grandparents and wished more stories had been shared about their lives before me. Their successes, their failures, and their secrets as they navigated life could have shed light onto the dynamics within my own family. Life is messy and there is no shame in the rocky road we all travel to get to the beautiful parts.

This novel was perfected with the help of my author friends, especially Annie M. Ballard and Heidi McIntyre, my critique partner Caitlin Avery, my beta readers, and my proofreader. Nicky, at Granite Editorial, goes above and beyond when editing, and my newest cover designer, Shelby Haraldsen, made my cover dreams come true.

I hope this novel sparks intrigue around your own history and leads to conversations with your loved ones about the stories from the past that helped shape you.

Thank you for reading.

Edy.

Also By E.D. Hackett

All novels are available across all retailers or in my shop. All links can be found at https://www.linktr.ee/edhackett

A Trip Down Memory Lane-winter novella, second chance romance, forced proximity, best friend's wedding

The Havoc in My Head-medical fiction, family saga, and a strong protagonist

Reinventing Amara Leventis-new adult, best friend's wedding, Greek family and traditions, and a Greek bakery

A Match Made in Ireland-new adult, new found family, American in Ireland, college romance, and forced proximity

Farm Cove Bliss- single parent romance, unexpected inheritance, later in life love, and miscommunication trope

The Block Island Series-island life, friendship fiction, new found family, bed and breakfast life, and parent-child drama
  An Unfinished Story
  Hope Hanna Murphy

About the Author

You can connect with me on:

🌐 https://www.edhackettauthor.com

📘 https://www.facebook.com/edhackettwrites

🔗 https://www.instagram.com/e.d_hackettwrites

🔗 https://www.linktr.ee/edhackett

www.ingramcontent.com/pod-product-compliance
Lightning Source LLC
Chambersburg PA
CBHW020825260626
47169CB00003B/830